———————— ★ ————————

I hadn't driven more than a quarter of a mile before I noticed the big black 4x4 pickup coming up fast in my rear view mirror. Too fast for the winding road. There was no place to pull over, not even a wide shoulder. Holding as far to the right as I dared, I sucked in my breath as the truck rushed closer, the driver invisible behind the tinted windshield. Would he slam on his brakes at the last second? Or take a chance and pass on the upcoming blind curve?

As the truck loomed in my mirror, it lined up squarely behind my car.

I gripped the steering wheel and took my foot off the brake. The impact was deafening. Metal crunched. Glass shattered. Then the damned air bag blew up. I had an iron grip on the steering wheel and tried to hold my upper body back and my head forward to protect myself against whiplash. I slammed into the air bag with enough force to take my breath away. The car's momentum took me left, across the oncoming lane and toward a rocky hill.

———————— ★ ————————

Previously published Worldwide Mystery title by
PATRICIA STOLTEY

THE PRAIRIE GRASS MURDERS

THE
DESERT HEDGE
MURDERS

Patricia Stoltey

W🌐RLDWIDE®

TORONTO • NEW YORK • LONDON
AMSTERDAM • PARIS • SYDNEY • HAMBURG
STOCKHOLM • ATHENS • TOKYO • MILAN
MADRID • WARSAW • BUDAPEST • AUCKLAND

This one is for Bill
My husband and very best friend

Recycling programs
for this product may
not exist in your area.

THE DESERT HEDGE MURDERS

A Worldwide Mystery/September 2010

First published by Five Star.

ISBN-13: 978-0-373-26721-7

Copyright © 2009 by Patricia Stoltey.
All rights reserved. No part of this book may be reproduced
or transmitted in any form or by any means, electronic or
mechanical, including photocopying, recording or by any
information storage and retrieval system, without permission
in writing from the publisher. For information, contact:
Five Star Publishing, 295 Kennedy Memorial Drive,
Waterville, Maine 04901 U.S.A.

This is a work of fiction. Names, characters, places and incidents are
either the product of the author's imagination or are used fictitiously,
and any resemblance to actual persons, living or dead, business
establishments, events or locales is entirely coincidental.

® and TM are trademarks of Harlequin Enterprises Limited.
Trademarks indicated with ® are registered in the United States
Patent and Trademark Office, the Canadian Trade Marks Office
and in other countries.

Printed in U.S.A.

Acknowledgments

To all whose names or titles I borrowed, thank you, and please remember that only those names are true. The story and its characters are fiction.

No experts or officers of the law were consulted to make the story more credible. If you find mistakes, they're all mine. Stories just happen when I rely on my imagination, my powers of observation, my life experience (flawed though it may be), and the occasional truths I pick up from reading or surfing the web. If you find a true thing in this story, it is either used fictitiously, or it's an accident for which I sincerely apologize, or it's a wonderful piece of good fortune bestowed upon me by the muse who occasionally allows my brain to connect with my fingers while I'm typing.

Laughlin and Oatman are real places, and great fun to visit. There is a wonderful gold mine near Oatman that offers tours, although it's not called the Lone Cactus Mine. However, all of these places are used fictitiously in this story. You'll find burros in Oatman. Mock gunfights in front of the Oatman Hotel. Even some ghosts. But you must not go expecting murder and mayhem.

To all who have read chapters and critiqued, and the many who continue to help me along the way, I am so grateful. Special thanks to Diane Cheatwood, April Joitel, Bev Marquart, Melissa Pattison, Sidna Rachid, and Carolyn Yalin.

I'd like to express my appreciation to John Helfers, Denise Dietz, and Tiffany Schofield, three of the many folks associated with Tekno and Five Star who make books happen. I also can't say enough good things about the Five Star authors with whom I've signed, or talked, or just exchanged e-mails. Thanks to all of you for your friendship and your support.

CAST OF CHARACTERS

Sylvia Thorn—ex-FBI employee and retired circuit court judge of Palm Beach County, Florida

Willie Grisseljon—Sylvia's brother, retired accountant, age sixty-five, never married; Vietnam veteran with post-traumatic stress syndrome and an ability to sense when his sister is in jeopardy

Kristina Grisseljon—Sylvia and Willie's mother, age eighty-five

Peter Grisseljon—Sylvia and Willie's father, age eighty-six

The Florida Flippers:
Marianne Gruber—age seventy-five, widowed; lets her inner cowgirl come out to play

Gail Heblonsky—age eighty, married; volunteer park ranger, cantankerous when forced to deal with Marianne

Diane Chacon—age sixty-seven, married; author who thinks everything her friends say and do is fair game for her novels

Linda Swayble—claims she's seventy-seven, married; a worrier, talented actress in little theater

Sandra Pringle—age sixty-five, married; no occupation

Velma Rasher—age seventy-eight, single; no occupation, breaks hip and cannot go on trip

The Rest of the Story:
Damon Falls—FBI agent, age a mystery but he's much younger than Sylvia

Patsy Strump—age fifty-five; acquaintance of Sandra Pringle, takes Velma's place on the trip

Frieda Schneider—old friend of Peter Grisseljon's from World War II

Barry Pringle—Sandra's husband; travels a lot but doesn't tell Sandra where he's staying

ONE

I BARELY HAD time to slide my hotel key card into the slot before a loud crash, thud, and clatter set my heart racing. My elder travel companions, two at each door, cocked their heads toward the sound. I froze, unsure whether to rush toward the room down the hall or usher my eighty-five-year-old mother through our door and slam it shut.

"Sylvia, don't just stand there! That noise came from Sandra's room. Go see what's happened."

That order came from my mom, Kristina Grisseljon—always eager to hear about my adventures, always egging me on, but not always so anxious to join me. She talked me into getting a butterfly tattoo on my hip a few years ago, and then beat a fast retreat when I suggested she do the same.

"Sylvia!"

I grudgingly pulled my key card from the slot and took a tentative step toward the room at the end of the corridor. Its door stood open, as though inviting us inside. Marianne Gruber and Linda Swayble lurked in the doorway to their own room, watching me expectantly. A scuffling noise came from behind me. I stopped in my tracks and turned to face my mother and two more of her friends, Diane Chacon and Gail Heblonsky, who formed a triangle with Mom at the apex. They were so close to me we could have touched noses.

Before I could suggest they go to their rooms, a hand clamped down on my shoulder. I sucked in my breath. Why had I turned my back on that open door at the end of the hall when I had no idea what had happened inside?

"Sylvia, come quick," said Patsy Strump.

Patsy, Sandra's friend and roommate and a last-minute

addition to the trip, had a sharp, authoritative voice. She urged me to follow her down the hall.

I took a deep breath. *Why me?*

Why did I, Sylvia Thorn, former circuit court judge of Palm Beach County, Florida, ever agree to accompany the Florida Flippers, my mother's travel club, on a gambling and sight-seeing trip to Laughlin, Nevada, and surrounding attractions? Here's why: I was forced to retire from the bench to avoid embarrassing myself and the judicial community after a retired mob boss arranged to have my picture taken with him at a party—a small matter of revenge on his part because I'd meddled in his family affairs and was partly responsible for the incarceration of his niece. Unemployed for four months now, I was, frankly, bored stiff.

"Hurry." Patsy tugged at my arm. "Sandra found a body in our room and she fainted. I can't revive her."

Body?

Through their open door, a call for help wailed down the hallway like a banshee's warning. Apparently Sandra had regained consciousness on her own. Patsy grabbed my wrist and dragged me down the hall while I threw questions at her, one after another.

"Body? In your room? Who is it?" I pulled my wrist free and did a quick head count to assure myself our group was accounted for.

"Sylvia. Hurry!"

I followed Patsy, nearly running into her when she made a sudden stop at the door into the bathroom. She pointed inside where Sandra Pringle lay sprawled on the floor, her bleached-blonde hair soaked in blood.

"She smacked her head on the floor when she fell. The scalp wound is superficial but she might have a concussion." Patsy stepped over Sandra to reach the sink and turned on the cold water with one hand while grabbing one of the snowy white hand towels with the other. She thoroughly soaked the towel, wrung it out, and knelt by Sandra's side. Patsy tucked the folded towel under Sandra's head. Sandra's eyes popped open.

"Patsy, you said there was a body?" I still wasn't sure I'd heard her correctly.

Sandra whimpered and closed her eyes.

Instead of answering, Patsy reached out and grasped the blue plastic shower curtain that now lay draped across the tub with the curtain rod on top. She yanked it aside.

Yep. There was a body.

"Are you sure he's dead?" My question was ridiculously inane since the smell of death, though fainter than I would have expected, made it unpleasant to breathe in the tiny room.

Patsy gave me one of those incredulous looks that convey the giver's total superiority and the receiver's complete stupidity. "Hell, yes, I'm sure. He's been dead at least twenty-four hours."

The man was neatly laid out, his eyes closed and his arms tucked down at his sides. His khaki slacks and light blue, short-sleeved polo shirt were clean and unwrinkled, with no sign of blood anywhere on his body. His feet, shod in white crew socks and running shoes, were propped against the end wall since he was at least six inches longer than the tub. From a distance, it was only the pale gray hue of his skin that supported Patsy's hypothesis.

"Did you check for a pulse?" I asked.

Busy applying pressure to the back of Sandra's head, Patsy didn't bother to give me another one of those looks. "I checked him. Made sure CPR wouldn't help. He's cold and very dead, honest." She stood up and rinsed the blood-stained towel with more cold water.

Sandra moved her legs and raised one hand to her forehead. "Oooh, my head hurts."

Patsy replaced the shower curtain over the body. "You'd

better call the manager, Sylvia—tell him to call the cops. An ambulance, too."

I turned away to do as I was told and ran smack into the rest of the Flippers, who were standing in a tight semicircle outside the bathroom door.

"Is Sandra okay?" Linda said. She stood on her tiptoes to see over my shoulder, and the other four followed suit. Once again I was nearly nose-to-nose with the whole pack.

"She's fine," Gail answered, although she'd not yet seen Sandra close up nor spotted the blood on the floor. "She'll be downstairs playing the slots in an hour."

"Where's the body?" my mom whispered. "I thought there was a body."

I whispered back, but since all five now had their heads together, waiting for my answer, they had no trouble hearing me describe the body in the tub. "Now I'm on my way to use the phone," I added as I made my way through the group. I looked over my shoulder and saw that each one was jockeying for the best position, presumably hoping to be the first to see the corpse. There were a few sighs and a lot of whispering. My best guess told me they were acutely disappointed that the shower curtain blocked their view and Patsy knelt near the bathroom doorway so no one could sidle past.

It took less than five minutes for the hotel manager to march in, his lips pursed and his eyebrows raised to show his displeasure, if not skepticism. By now, the ladies were scattered throughout the room, perched on the edges of the beds and chairs in spite of my attempts to herd them out the door. The manager surveyed the room full of elderly women, and me—I'm only sixty—as though we'd conjured up a tasteless prank to annoy him.

"What's going on here?" His voice was considerably higher than one would expect from a manly six-footer with broad shoulders and a Rhett Butler mustache. Out of the corner of my eye I saw Linda slap one hand over her mouth. Mom bent over and fiddled with her shoes, and Marianne stared into her huge purse and frantically dug around in its cavernous depths. Gail and Diane made eye contact, a fatal error. Diane, her gold hoop earrings jiggling, failed in her attempts to suppress a giggle. It escaped through her nose with a violent snort. She bent forward and rubbed her nose with both hands while she moaned, "Ow, ow, ow."

"My gawd," said Gail. She clomped up to the manager in her orthopedic hiking boots and peered at his brass nametag. "Mr. Looper?"

"Yes," he squeaked. His face flushed a mottled pink and white.

"My gawd," Gail repeated.

"Did you phone the police?" I felt it was time to change the subject.

"Of course not. I can't call them until I've verified there's a good reason."

"The good reason is in the tub." I pointed Looper toward the bathroom door, and we both watched while Patsy helped Sandra struggle into a seated position, her back leaning against the wall. She stepped in between Sandra and the tub before lifting the shower curtain so the manager could see the body while Sandra could not.

Looper audibly sucked in his breath and clamped his hand over his mouth as though to contain a surge of gastric reflux.

Patsy dropped the shower curtain and stepped closer to the wall in self-defense.

Sandra, who'd been staring at the manager from her position on the floor, drew her legs up against her chest. Her reflexes were good. I figured she was going to be okay.

Looper lurched out of the room and into the hallway.

Gail followed to the doorway and leaned out to watch. "He didn't puke. Now he's pushing the elevator button. Whoops. My gawd, he did it—right into the elevator."

"He'll call the police now, won't he?" Linda was the worrier of the group, having already spent hours agonizing over the chances of a terrorist hijacking, airplane malfunction, lost luggage, or a mix-up with the hotel reservations.

"We'll wait a few minutes and then call the front desk to make sure," I said. "In the meantime, why don't you all go to your rooms and try to calm down. Unpack or whatever—"

"Sylvia," Diane said, "the police will want to talk to us. When I researched police procedure for my second novel, I—"

"I don't think that's necessary. Sandra and Patsy, yes, because they found the body. There's nothing the rest of you can do, and if the police want to talk to you, they'll find you."

"Fine," Marianne said. She flung the straps of her bag over her shoulder, ran her fingers through her garishly red curls, and strode toward the door. "If anybody needs me, I'll be at the blackjack tables."

"Swilling bourbon and flirting with the dealers, more than likely," Gail mumbled.

"Gail, that's not nice." Linda frowned at the gibe aimed at her roommate.

Diane came to Gail's defense. "Maybe, but it's the truth."

"Yeah," Gail added. "Get a couple of drinks in that old broad and she thinks she's thirty instead of seventy-five."

"Seventy-five does not qualify one to be an old broad." My mother straightened her back and squared her chin, signs she was ready to do battle.

Linda stuck one foot out and admired her own slim ankle and the two-inch chartreuse, backless sandals that caused her to walk with a strange mincing gait. "That's right. I'm seventy-seven and I've never felt younger."

"Okay," Gail said. "I'm sorry." Then she ruined it all by delivering her next line to me in a stage whisper. "She's actually eighty-three and a half."

The whole exchange was making me nervous. It was time to intervene. "Okay, ladies, move it. You can finish this discussion later."

Preferably when I'm nowhere around.

Mom gave me a disgusted look that said she knew exactly

what I was doing and she didn't appreciate me spoiling her fun. Feisty old broad!

I wandered out to the hallway to make sure the retreat was peaceful. Marianne was missing; apparently she had already headed to the casino. The other four stood in front of Marianne and Linda's door, chatting and giggling as though nothing had happened.

Willie set me up.

As soon as the thought popped into my head, I knew it was true. My older brother, Willie Grisseljon, had traveled extensively with our parents, especially in the months since he sold his accounting firm. He also took at least two trips with the Flippers. Not one complaint. Not one snide remark. After he escorted them to Key West, he told me he'd never had so much fun in his life.

When Willie told me about the trip to Laughlin and said I could go in his place, he made it sound as though he had so many heavy responsibilities at the homeless shelter where he volunteered that he simply could not get away this time. And I fell for it.

I leaned against the doorjamb and waited, hoping the Flippers would finish their conversation and go to their rooms. If they took off in four different directions, there wouldn't be a thing I could do about it. I shrugged my shoulders. These women were intelligent, well-traveled, and totally self-sufficient. Willie had not instructed me to keep the flock together or to control their activities. I had to believe they could take care of themselves.

One of the elevator doors opened, and Looper emerged with two uniformed policemen and a burly man who had a badge clipped to his belt. The second elevator door opened and three emergency medical technicians rushed out, two carrying bags and the third pushing a stretcher on wheels. By this time, Patsy was at the door to direct the EMTs inside. I stepped aside to give them room.

Gail, Diane, Linda, and my mother abandoned the pretense

of returning to their rooms and followed the stretcher down the hall.

That was enough excitement for the day, I decided.

I should have known by their squared shoulders and determined pace that I was fighting a losing battle. My hands in the air signaled stop as I hurried toward them. My authoritative tone said I was in charge. "Don't go in. Give them some room. Let's wait—"

They paired off and walked right around me.

"Can't go to our rooms until the cops have been inside to check them." Mom had a satisfied expression on her face that I chose to ignore. "There might be another body. Or the killer."

I went across the hall and leaned against the wall where I could see into the room without getting in the way. There were five people crammed into the bathroom, not counting the corpse, and eight more in the small area right in front of the bathroom door. They were all on the move within that small space, resulting in a dense mass with a constantly changing shape.

"Everyone back away from the door and sit down." That came through loud and clear. I suspected the plainclothes detective was the one asserting his authority. The mass bulged on the side farthest from the bathroom. The bulge then popped free and scurried into the room, away from my line of sight.

After another moment, more pieces of the mass struggled to break loose. First Patsy, gasping as though deprived of oxygen. She moved across the room where I could no longer see her. One of the EMTs exchanged a few words with someone inside the bathroom then rushed into the hallway, pushing the still-unoccupied stretcher. He trotted toward the elevator, glancing over his shoulder with alarm.

Mr. Looper squeaked a few words that I couldn't hear. No one that I could see paid any attention to him. He pursed his lips, clutched his arms to his chest, and shuffled backward, away from the bathroom and into the hall.

"Can't you do something with those women?" he said when he saw me.

I grimaced and shook my head.

"The detective told me to give these two ladies another room. Can you at least come down to pick up their key cards?"

"No problem," I said. "Do I need to rescue my friends before we go?"

"Detective said they should stay right where they are until he tells them they can leave."

"Maybe I should stay—"

"You'll be back in three minutes. Come now."

I repressed the desire to bonk Looper on the head for his haughty tone and followed him down the hall. Inside the elevator, the powerful fumes of a strong ammonia-based cleaner had replaced breathable air. I tried to inhale through a wad of tissues I pulled from my bag. Looper pretended he didn't notice.

TWO

LOOPER AND I stepped out of the elevator into the lobby and I had a clear view of the bar. Patsy was there, knocking back an amber-colored liquid from a shot glass. I did a double-take, wondering how on earth she'd escaped from the Flippers and made it downstairs so fast. She must have raced out of the room, done a record-breaking sprint down the hall, and thrown herself down the stairs instead of waiting for the elevator.

I stared at her as I walked past the bar. Several times during the day I had been struck by the feeling that I knew Patsy Strump from somewhere. If I'd met her before, you'd think I'd remember, especially with her distinctive last name. But after years in legal practice, followed by the judgeship, there was a very long list of oddball characters with weird names who had paraded through my life. I couldn't remember them all.

Patsy thumped her empty shot glass down on the bar and walked away. She saw me and waved, motioning toward the elevator. I nodded and followed Looper to the front desk, still thinking about Patsy. For one thing, she was much younger than the rest of the Flippers, even younger than Sandra, who was the baby of the group at sixty-five. I'd peg Patsy at fifty, maybe fifty-five at the most. Also, she wasn't like the others. Not only was she cool and reserved, but she was extremely uncommunicative. The Flippers were excitable, silly, voluble, and tended toward the extreme, if not bizarre, behavior many elders claim to be their right. Patsy, on the other hand, was… well, street tough.

So where have I seen her before?

I took the elevator up, fretting about the annoying condition that eats away at our memories as we age. Like failing vision and aching joints, short-term memory lapses were one more reminder that the body was wearing out, even if the psyche still considered itself to be thirty or forty years younger than that unfamiliar face reflected in the mirror.

Thoughts of aging didn't help my mood one bit, so I let my thoughts return to Patsy. No one in my mother's circle of friends had met Patsy before except Sandra. I wanted to have a chat with Sandra after she had recovered from her fright.

By the time I returned to Patsy and Sandra's room, where the body still rested in the tub, all of the other ladies were gone. The police detective stood guard at the bathroom door. Sandra sat on the edge of the closest bed, still pressing the wet towel to the back of her head. Patsy leaned against the doorjamb, waiting.

"How's Sandra?" I asked.

"She's fine. Has a bit of a headache, but the EMTs don't think she has a concussion. They wanted to take her to the hospital but she wouldn't go. I'll watch her tonight, keep her out of the casino—maybe we'll order room service for dinner."

"I'll help you get Sandra moved." I handed over the new key cards. "Did Mom go to our room?"

Patsy frowned. "Not sure. They scattered like dandelion fluff when the detective yelled at them. He called Looper to have security check all their rooms so they didn't have an excuse to hang around."

I got the picture, although I'd bet the Flippers weren't cowering behind their respective closed doors. More likely they were all together, conspiring to get a look at the body.

"So what's happening?" I motioned toward the bathroom. "Is he waiting for somebody?"

"The crime scene crew. They're on their way."

"Did Looper know the guy in the tub?"

"Nope. Says he never saw him before."

Patsy had a distinct accent, definitely not Florida. I was thinking Chicago.

"What's the matter?"

I'd been caught staring. "Just thinking," I said. "This dead guy didn't have anything to do with us. Best to forget it and get on with the fun. Right?" I walked over to Sandra and offered her my right elbow for support.

"Absolutely right," said Patsy. She grabbed Sandra under her right arm, trying not to dislodge the hand that held the towel. Sandra was a little wobbly at first, but grew steadier as we moved down the hall.

Patsy helped Sandra to the bed nearest the bathroom, where she curled up on her side. I soaked a clean towel in cold water and wrung it out. I exchanged it for the bloody towel Sandra was using, then noticed the key card on the other bed.

"You won't forget to take that with you when you leave the room, will you?"

Patsy glanced at the card. "That's the old one. The new one is already in my pocket." She took the soiled towel from my hand and went into the bathroom. I heard the clunk of the drain cover closing, then a rush of water.

"I'm going to get your bags before they tape up the room," I said.

A few minutes after delivering the two suitcases, I collapsed onto one of the beds in my own room and wondered idly where my mother was, since her purse and cell phone were on the other bed. I considered going downstairs to search for her but immediately gave up the idea. I needed a rest. I was sure Mom would fetch me before going to dinner.

Mom's travel club was formed seven years ago when all of the ladies and their husbands lived in the same retirement community in Deerfield Beach. At the time, they had one fanatical interest in common: the Miami Dolphins. They bought season tickets, wore team shirts and caps, collected anything with a Dolphins logo on it, traveled to out-of-town games, and regularly bet on their team in Las Vegas, even during the disastrous 2004 season. That's why they called themselves Florida Flippers. Made sense at the time.

Gradually things changed, however, as they have a way of doing. Marianne's husband, Bobby, was attacked and killed by a three-legged alligator at Ding Darling Nature Preserve on Sanibel Island. The old fool had stepped in close to take a picture, apparently unaware how fast a three-legged alligator can lunge in one short burst. Marianne grieved for a while, but then she got her ears pierced and had her hair cut short, permed in wild curls, and dyed red. She bought tight blue jeans and hand-tooled leather cowboy boots, and took lessons in line dancing and the Texas two-step. Every Friday night she went down to the First Rodeo Saloon and Dance Hall in Davie to boogie with the tropical cowboys. Young or old, she didn't care, as long as they could dance.

Linda's husband, Tony, was now a NASCAR fan and wouldn't leave his big-screen TV if there was a race on. Unable to fathom why anyone would sit for hours and watch a bunch of cars speeding around a track, Linda hooked up with a Boca Raton theater group, landed a part in a feminist version of *The Odd Couple* the first time she auditioned, and received rave reviews for her comedic talent. She said applause "rocked her socks," and she played her part full-time. Her dangly earrings, sunglasses, and chartreuse floppy hat and high heels attracted plenty of attention. I'd seen it firsthand at the Bullhead City airport.

Diane and her husband, Ramon, won the Florida lottery and moved to the Sanctuary, an exclusive Boca Raton gated community full of multi-million-dollar mansions. He played golf every day, but Diane wasn't content with golf widow-hood and didn't bond with her rich and famous neighbors. She enrolled in Florida Atlantic University to study creative writing. Her first novel caught the interest of a literary agent, who in turn convinced a big publishing house that an audience of active seniors would soon send the demand for lively elder novels through the roof. She'd confided in me during the flight that her new book was called *Sex in the Seventies* and was autobiographical. She said her two sons, who lived in Denver, thought she was cool.

Sandra's husband, Barry, was involved in a business venture that required him to travel quite a lot, leaving Sandra free to take up a new hobby. However, she preferred worrying about what he was up to, calling him frequently while he was out of town. Mom was worried about Sandra—thought that she was acting odd, even paranoid, and that her obsession with her husband's whereabouts and activities was unhealthy.

Gail and her husband, Shark, which he was now called at his request, kept their season tickets for the Dolphins, but his new love was deep-sea fishing and his second favorite activity was drinking beer. Less tolerant of the rolling waves than her spouse, and a staunch environmentalist, Gail volunteered to lead tour groups on trails in the Everglades National Park. She didn't drink beer, but she was hell on wheels after a couple of frozen peach margaritas.

In addition to football, my mother loved shopping, traveling, piña coladas, and dispensing advice, mostly to me. My dad loved being retired and making my mother happy. It was an easy relationship. Mom decided what she wanted to do and where she wanted to go, and Dad followed her around the country, serving as her escort and driver. I think Dad had more fun than Mom did, simply because he never had to make a plan or a decision.

Every couple of months those six women—plus Velma Rasher, who was now out of commission with a broken hip and therefore replaced temporarily by Patsy, and Willie, replaced just this once by me—flew off to a new destination somewhere in the continental United States. And that is how I came to be in Laughlin, Nevada, with the Florida Flippers.

I rolled over to look at the clock. It was only three, plenty of time for a nap.

The next time I opened my eyes it was nearly five, which was eight o'clock Florida time. Still no sign of my mother. Most of the ladies were accustomed to early bird specials at their favorite restaurants. Had they eaten without me? Surely not. I hoped they weren't drinking their dinner in the casino.

I forced myself off the bed and into the bathroom to freshen up. Examining my face in the mirror was a mistake—my skin was dotted with red spots from the chenille pillow cover. I patted my face with cold water and applied a tiny bit of liquid foundation to my cheeks. It didn't help much.

With a quick swipe of the brush, I smoothed the bunched-up sections of my short gray hair, grabbed my purse, and opened the door just as Mom inserted her key card in the door's slot. She jumped, let out a yelp, and dropped her card. I gasped and dropped my purse. We leaned forward at the same time, and for once my reflexes didn't fail me. I stopped before we bumped heads and took a step backward into the room.

Mom came up with her card and my purse. "C'mon," she said. "We're starved. While you were napping like an old woman, Gail, Diane, Linda, and I power-walked to the south end of the strip and then all the way to the north end and then back here." She hurried inside and grabbed her purse and phone.

"You were walking all the time I was sleeping?"

"Well, not all the time. We sat on the deck by the river and had cocktails while we recovered."

"How many cocktails?" I tried to sound nonchalant. I could see Mom was fine, but I'd known the rest of the gals to over-indulge from time to time.

She slipped her purse strap over her shoulder and turned on her phone as she airily waved me off. "Sylvia, you worry too much."

I probably do. I'd had plenty to worry about over the years and worrying was a hard habit to break. I'd spent a few years with the FBI, rescued Willie from homelessness after his medical discharge from the Marines toward the end of the Vietnam War, lost the love of my life—an FBI agent—in an automobile accident, went to law school, practiced law, made a disastrous second marriage to another lawyer, then divorced him, and finally accepted an appointment to the bench. Nothing I'd done or experienced since high school was conducive to a stress-free existence.

On top of all that, I had recently been involved in an Illinois murder case. That whole mess had led to the professional limbo in which I was now languishing.

"I know I worry too much, Mom. Where was Marianne while the rest of you were out walking?"

"At the blackjack table with a huge pile of chips in front of her. She was ready to quit, though. We're eating at the Hickory Pit in the Edgewater," Mom said. "They have a filet mignon with gorgonzola—"

"Enough said. I'm ready." The Flippers, except for Sandra and Patsy, were waiting for us by the door onto the deck overlooking the Colorado River. We took the scenic stroll south to the Edgewater and then rode the escalator down to the restaurant level.

It was obvious from their calm demeanor that the group was tired...or so I thought.

As soon as drinks and appetizers were served, however, Mom and her friends got their second wind. I listened to a slightly different version of their afternoon activities than I'd received from my mother.

"I talked to the maid for our floor," said Gail. "No new guests were assigned to the room yesterday afternoon. She cleaned the room at ten yesterday morning and her supervisor did a walk-in inspection at two. She checked the bathroom, including the tub. The same maid also took extra towels to a room down the hall at three. She didn't see anyone in the hall or elevator."

"One of the waiters delivered room service across the hall at seven," added Diane. "He didn't hear or see anything unusual. And two different waiters brought breakfast to our floor this morning—one at six and the other at seven."

The others looked at Linda as if waiting for her report. "It seemed unlikely that anyone could bring a body in here in broad daylight," she said, "so I asked the maintenance guys if they expected any deliveries yesterday, like new carpet or furniture. They didn't think so, so I tried to ask the same questions at the front desk, but Looper caught me and ordered the desk clerks not to talk to anyone except the police."

I looked at my mother, who sat on my right, staring innocently into the distance. She made a point of turning to her right to speak to Marianne. "What did you find out?"

"Well, I talked to every single one of the dealers on the floor. They're a bunch of gossips but they don't know much. There's a rumor that the dead man was a small-time loan shark on the lookout for losers in need of a stake. Another rumor says he was a loser who missed a payment. I'll ask again tomorrow and see what they've learned."

"If Looper doesn't get to them first," said Linda.

"He won't," Marianne said. "The casino is totally separate from the hotel, so the dealers don't report to him."

I cleared my throat to get their attention. "Mom, I thought you said you went power-walking this afternoon."

"Oh, we did," insisted Gail. "That's when we made up our minds to investigate the crime."

"We can't investigate this crime," I said. "We wouldn't have a clue where to start. We don't know the people here, we don't know the victim, and we don't have a sympathetic cop who'd be willing to talk to us."

Oh, for Pete's sake, listen to me. I sounded like I was taking their silliness seriously.

"Sylvia," my mother said. "*We* were investigating. *You* were napping."

"And what was your assignment, Mom?"

"I talked to the police detective."

"The one who yelled at you and sent you to your room?"

Mom lifted her chin and pursed her lips. "He was very polite and he said he'd be happy to answer all my questions."

There was an implied "You are not being very polite, Sylvia" in her tone.

"What else did he say, Kristina?" Marianne and the others leaned closer.

"He said," she announced just as the waitress appeared, "that he'd be glad to have me—oh, it's my cell phone. Let me—Hello? Peter? Oh, Willie. It's Willie, everyone. Where are you, dear? Where's your father?"

THREE

"DAD'S WITH ME," Willie reported to his mother. He hunched over his father's cell phone, trying to shut out the noise of the Marlins fans at Dolphin Stadium. "It's the bottom of the ninth, no runs, Marlins up. We could be here a while."

"My word. You poor thing. You don't like baseball."

"That's okay. Dad's having a great time. That makes it fun. But I found out he had his phone turned off, and I was afraid you might be trying to call us." Willie glanced at his father as the older man jumped to his feet then sat down again after Cabrera's swing failed to connect with the ball.

"You didn't let your father stuff himself with junk food, did you?"

"Mom, do I try to control what you eat or drink when I'm with you?"

"Well, of course not, dear. That would be a foolish waste of your time and energy. Wait a minute, the waitress is asking us something."

Willie turned to his father. "They're in a restaurant."

"Don't tell her I ate three hot dogs. Or that I drank a beer."

"I'm back," his mother said. "Tell your father I heard everything. He knows what hot dogs will do to his stomach. Did he take his pill before he ate?"

"He did. Right before he took the first bite. So what's going on, Mom? I tried to call you a couple of times this afternoon but got your voice mail. Did you check your messages?"

"Not yet, dear. We had a little excitement, and then I was walking with the girls. I left my phone in the room."

"I knew something was going on. I felt it."

"You must mean the body. We only got a tiny peek at it but it had nothing to do with us."

"Body? Where?"

"In the tub in Sandra's room."

"Mom, is Sylvia there? Let me talk to her."

He heard a clunk as his mother's phone was passed to his sister.

"Hello, Willie? Is something wrong?"

"Funny, Syl."

"Okay, so what set off your alarm?" His sister knew he'd come home from Vietnam with a heightened awareness of impending disasters and that his sensitivity was most keen if she was threatened in some way. She accepted, though she'd resisted the notion for a long time, that Willie was a sensitive, possibly clairvoyant. Thankfully, his visions usually occurred during meditation or intense concentration, as though he had to stop and open the right door in his mind or the visions could not gain entrance. Willie's ability to function had teetered on the edge of destruction for a time after the war. He didn't want to end up in that place again, so he avoided the visions, fearing some otherworldly being might gain entry to his psyche.

Willie wasn't sure he could explain the vague feeling he'd had all day that something was out of kilter. There had been no visions, no images, even when he sat in his apartment and focused on his mother and Sylvia.

How could he explain it? A crawly sensation on his arms? A tingling down his spine?

"Not sure," he answered.

"It has nothing to do with us. Some poor guy got knocked off and dumped in a hotel room. Sandra and Patsy happened to be the ones assigned to that room. It could have been anybody."

Willie didn't always trust his sister's ability to recognize trouble even when she stumbled over it. "Are you sure neither one of them knew the guy?"

"Sandra or Patsy? Oh, I'm sure they didn't. Sandra found the body and fainted. Hit the tile floor hard enough to make her head bleed. Patsy called me down to help—to call the manager—and then she tended to Sandra. Although…"

"What?"

There was silence for a moment and then Sylvia cleared her throat. "Nothing. It was nothing."

"Are you still in the restaurant?"

"Yes."

"They're all listening?"

"You got it."

"Okay, Syl. If tomorrow I go see how Velma Rasher is doing and ask a lot of questions about Sandra and Patsy, would I be on the right track?"

"You are amazing, Willie. That's exactly what I would have suggested, although I'd concentrate on number two."

A roar from the stadium crowd interrupted their conversation. "What's all the noise, Willie? Where are you?"

"Marlins game. Home run with bases loaded."

"Marlins home run, I hope?"

"What? Can't hear a thing. Gotta go. Tell Mom that Dad will talk to her tomorrow."

Willie handed the phone to his father and, as soon as the stadium noise died down, told him about the body that had been discovered in Sandra and Patsy's room.

"Wow. A body, huh?"

"I'm going to see Velma and ask her about Patsy Strump," Willie said.

"Why?"

"I asked Syl if anyone knew who the dead man was. She started to say something but stopped mid-sentence like she didn't want to talk in front of the others. She wants to know more about Patsy and Sandra, mostly Patsy, and Velma is one person who might be able to answer our questions."

"Fine. I'm in."

Willie looked at his father, surprised at his interest.

"Hey, son, that's my wife and daughter out there. If there's a problem, I need to know."

Willie nodded. "You're right. Do you want to drive then? I was going to ride my bike over."

"Happy to. What time do you want to go?"

"Ten, ten-thirty?"

"Sounds good. We'll go to Boston's after. I want one of those crabmeat salad sandwiches you guys like so much."

AT ELEVEN O'CLOCK the next morning, Willie and his father knocked at the door of Velma Rasher's room in the Oceanside Rehabilitation Center.

"Peter, Willie, what the devil are you doing here?" Velma grabbed her control and jabbed at the buttons until she found the one that raised the head of her bed. She winced, then poked at the control again until she'd lowered the bed to a more comfortable angle.

Willie exchanged an amused glance with his dad. Velma's blue hair looked as though she'd just come from the beauty parlor, her face was powdered, her eyelashes darkened, and her lips—which matched her nails—were the color of tangerines. Velma Rasher wasn't letting a little thing like a broken hip interfere with her appearance.

"We wanted to check on you since the rest of your friends are out flitting around the country," Willie's dad said. "Figured you might be feeling neglected."

"You lying bag of…oh, I know better than that, you old goat. You never go visit anyone who's laid up unless Kristina makes you do it. Did she order you to come?"

"Absolutely not. She didn't say a word." Willie's dad appeared to bristle at the "old goat" designation, since Velma was closer to ninety than he was. He looked at Willie. "You tell her."

"I knew it," Velma shouted. "If she didn't send you, then something's wrong. What's this all about? I know the plane didn't crash. Watched the news. Somebody get hurt? It's not Kristina, is it? Sandra maybe. She's the one who's accident prone. Why it was me who fell down the library steps when she was standing right there, I'll never know. So tell me. What happened?"

"It's not that bad," said Willie. "It's just that Sandra and Patsy are roommates and when they walked into their room, Sandra pulled open the shower curtain and found a body in the bathtub—"

"A body," Velma yelled.

The volume of Velma's voice tended to increase as her excitement level rose. Willie patted her hand and told her that none of her friends were in danger.

"Nobody got hurt?"

"Sandra fainted and banged her head on the floor," his dad said. "That's what you told me," he added when he heard Willie's exasperated sigh.

Velma relaxed. "That was to be expected. But if everyone else is okay...Peter, are you sure?"

"They're fine. Apparently this murder has nothing to do with our girls. They're going on with the vacation as though nothing happened."

Velma sat straight up in bed, grimaced with pain, and gently repositioned herself against the pillows. "That's a crock of... baloney if I ever heard one. You think those girls are going to pretend nothing has happened? They'll return with stories about the great dead body adventure and how I missed all the excitement. Darn it. I should be there."

She glanced at Willie, squinting her eyes as if that would help her read his mind. "And that's all? You came to tell me they'd found a body and make me jealous?"

"Not exactly," said his dad. "Actually, Willie wants to ask you some questions."

Velma's face brightened. "About what? Something that will help solve the case?"

"We're not trying to solve the case," Willie told her.

"Then what are you asking questions about?"

"Mostly Patsy. Who is she and why was she invited?"

"You think she has something to do with this?" Velma's eyes sparkled and she lowered her voice so that Willie had to lean forward to hear. "The rest of them didn't want to take Patsy, you know." Velma raised her eyebrows, her gaze shifting from Willie to his dad and back again. She did not elaborate.

Willie sighed, realizing how long Velma could keep them there if she doled out bits and pieces of information and then waited for their reaction before continuing.

His father didn't hesitate to step in. "Why not?"

"They wanted Sylvia to take my place, and then still have Willie along because he always takes such good care of us and helps with the luggage and he has such nice manners—"

Willie scooted his chair a little closer to her bed, a wasted motion since Velma's next words were loud and clear. "And because it was Sandra who railroaded us into going to Laughlin. The rest of us wanted to go to New Orleans and pour a little tourist money into their economy."

"If the majority wanted to go to New Orleans, how did Sandra convince the rest of you to change your minds?"

Velma snorted. "That old…girl started twisting arms and throwing out scary stories about murders and muggings in the French Quarter, and she tried to convince us that the beignets were so full of cholesterol a person could have a heart attack on the spot."

"That's probably true," Willie said.

"Really! How do you think I got to be this old if eating a little thing like that could be fatal? I'm a walking advertisement for the beneficial effects of consuming at least three doughnuts a week. And I'm talking about those fried kinds where the grease soaks through a paper bag in three seconds flat."

Willie cringed at the thought. That sounded like something his sister might eat, but nothing he'd touch, even if his life depended on it.

"All that aside," said Willie's dad, "Sandra apparently convinced the rest of the Flippers to change their votes."

"Yeah, she got Linda on her side first, and then the rest of us caved, one by one. Of course, then I broke my hip and the

next battle was under way before my morphine kicked in."
Velma leaned forward conspiratorially. "Sandra suggested
Patsy. The rest of the group protested, so Sandra started to
cry. Well, she's pulled that kind of maneuver before and we're
long past falling for her tricks. The Flippers dug in their heels
and said they didn't want to take a stranger."

"What happened to change their minds?"

"I don't know."

"What?" Willie said. He stared at her in surprise.

"Seriously, they didn't tell me. We didn't get a chance to
talk before I had the surgery on my hip. With all that pain
and being drugged up like a doper, I probably wouldn't have
understood what the heck they were talking about anyway.
By the time I was thinking straight, the plans were all set. I
decided to keep my nose out of it." Velma crossed her arms
over her chest and pursed her lips.

"What else?" Willie asked, convinced that Velma was
feeling more miffed at being left out of the loop than self-
righteous that she'd chosen to mind her own business.

Velma looked startled and glanced away from Willie's
direct gaze. "Nothing else."

Willie waited for a moment but Velma didn't say anything
more. It was his dad who stirred first, uncrossed his legs,
leaned forward, and planted his hands on his knees.

"Velma, you said something earlier about Sandra being
right there with you when you fell. Did Sandra bump into
you?"

"No way of knowing."

"Are you sure? There couldn't have been that many people
rushing out of the library at the same time. And why weren't
you using the handrail? You know at your age…"

His voice trailed off when Willie poked him in the ribs
with his elbow. The indignant expression on Velma's face
faded as Willie said, "At our age, Velma, Dad's and mine,
we've become a bit timid about things like stairs and curbs,
so we assume everyone else is the same." He hurried on. "Was

Sandra next to you on the stairs? Or beside you? Who else was there?"

Velma leaned against her pillow and frowned. Then she sat up a little straighter and seemed to brush away her aggravation with a tiny wave of her hand.

Willie nodded encouragingly.

"Actually, there *was* a rush of people. The thing is," Velma confided, "someone had set off the fire alarm in the library and we had to evacuate. It was after school, there were kids all about, a whole group of ladies from the book club, the library staff—probably thirty or forty people trying to hurry down those steps. It was hard to get anywhere near the handrail." She glared as though remembering something unpleasant. "It wasn't like someone lost her balance or nudged me accidentally, you know, it was more than that."

"I hadn't heard about the alarm," Willie said. "Maybe folks panicked."

"What do you think happened, Velma?" his dad said.

"I hate to say it. It sounds crazy. With all those people, and so many kids, it would have been easy to lose my footing if someone bumped against me..."

"But..."

"As I lay there on that blistering hot sidewalk, sweating from the heat and the pain, all I could think about was whether there was a damp handprint on the back of my blouse. I wasn't thinking clearly enough to understand why there might be a print there. Now it keeps popping into my mind. Was it my imagination, foggy brain-rambling, resulting from the fall? Or did someone plant her hand against my back and give me a big shove? I honestly don't know."

"Do you know where Sandra was when you were coming down the steps?" Willie asked.

"She was on my left. After the alarm sounded she tried to grab my book bag to help me but I didn't let go. Then she dropped back a step and I couldn't see her. I thought maybe she was angry that I'd refused her help, but I figured I'd straighten things out once we got down to the sidewalk.

The next thing I knew, I was sprawled at the bottom of the steps, hollering like hell because I thought people were going to run over me.

"I know what you're thinking," Velma continued, "but I've thought it over and decided it's not something Sandra would do. Why would she?"

"I don't know," Willie's dad said. "But if Sandra didn't do it, and she was a step behind you, then she must have seen who bumped you."

"She might have glanced away right at the wrong time," Willie said. "Wouldn't she have said something otherwise? Did she tell you anything after the accident, Velma?"

"Actually...I haven't seen her since I was carted off to the hospital."

FOUR

I SNAPPED MOM'S CELL phone closed and handed it to her with a smug little smile.

"What?" she asked.

"Nothing." I would tell her later, of course, but not while the others were listening. Willie had picked up on my curiosity about Patsy, and I knew he would dig in and do a little sleuthing. Velma would have to suffer through the interrogation while she was still bedridden, but perhaps she'd enjoy the company enough that she'd overlook Willie's ulterior motives.

The Flippers' chatter had continued while I was on the phone, but they'd completely changed the subject. All I heard was "sexy as all get out" from Linda and "could listen to *Should've Been a Cowboy* all night long" from Marianne. I knew they were talking about Toby Keith, their favorite country singer.

"He's not performing in Laughlin, is he?" I asked.

"No such luck. He's in Vegas," Marianne said.

"We couldn't get tickets this late anyway," Mom added.

The other three reluctantly agreed.

Less than a minute later our meals arrived. No one uttered more than an "Mmm" or "Yummy" between bites until it was time for dessert. One lonely but delicious slice of plain cheesecake made its way around the table for a community sampling.

I was stuffed way past comfort and teetering on a fine line between sober and tipsy from two glasses of wine. We walked out of the restaurant and straight into a trio of Laughlin's finest—one uniformed officer and two plainclothes detectives with their badges displayed on their belts. I recognized the husky detective from earlier that afternoon and greeted him with a smile, all the while wondering if the cops were following us.

He did not return my smile. And this was the guy my mom said was so polite and willing to answer all her questions? I had my doubts.

Out of the corner of my eye I saw my dinner companions, including my mother, back away and take off, each in a different direction. I grinned at the cops, hoping to divert their attention from the fleeing Flippers. "Did you want to talk to me?"

The uniformed officer, a tall young man with a blond buzz cut, a square jaw, and ramrod-straight posture, stared off toward the Hickory Pit's doorway, squinting as though trying to read the fine print on the posted menu.

The second detective, the one I hadn't seen before, was shorter than the other cops, maybe five feet, nine inches, and looked in excellent physical condition in spite of his age, which I guessed at about sixty. Short gray hair, receding a bit. Weathered skin as if he spent a lot of time outdoors. Warm brown eyes. He had a tiny lift to the left side of his mouth, which could have been aimed at me. I suspected there was a big and very attractive smile lurking there.

The first detective didn't respond to my question. He was staring into the distance and I had the distinct impression he was counting to ten.

His silence gave me time to take a closer look. He was possibly forty, forty-five, brawny without being fat, his weight not out of line for his six-foot height. His hair was dark, not a hint of gray that I could see, and his eyes were also brown, cold brown, like a frozen fudge bar.

He looked down at me and caught me staring at him.

"You're in charge of that group?" he asked.

"No."

"Who's in charge?" He spoke as though looking for the teacher who'd lost control over her unruly students during a field trip.

I shrugged. Who could I point to as being the "go to" person in the club? "They go their own way," I said. "But I know them pretty well…most of them. Maybe I could answer your questions. I'm Sylvia Thorn."

The detective with the suppressed smile cleared his throat and stuck his hand out. "Name's Trilby. Uniform here is Officer Snyder." Detective Trilby tipped his head toward his partner who was still glaring at me. "This is Detective Dunbar."

I nodded at each of them in turn, then crossed my arms across my chest and waited until Detective Dunbar spoke.

"Any chance we can get your group together in one place, preferably at your hotel?" He looked at his watch.

"Sure. But it might take a while to track them all down."

"Then how about rounding them up first thing in the morning? We'll come there—meet you in the lobby at eight."

I nodded. "Our bus leaves for Oatman at ten. Will we be done by then?"

"We'll do our best," Trilby said. That remark earned him a dirty look from Detective Dunbar.

"Depends on whether they cooperate or go wandering off again," Dunbar said. "I need their names." He pointed at Detective Trilby who pulled a notepad and pen from his inside pocket, flipped to a blank page, and stood poised to write.

I spelled the Flippers' names as I listed them, and noted their ages in an effort to remind the detectives that a gentle approach would be appropriate. All three men raised their eyebrows when I told them Patsy was about fifty-five.

"Lots younger than the others. She somebody's daughter?" Trilby asked.

"No. She's a friend of Sandra's. Patsy was added to the trip at the last minute because one of the other ladies couldn't come."

"Ah. And this Patsy…?" Trilby glanced at his notes. "Strump? And Sandra…she's the one who banged her head, right?"

I nodded.

Dunbar spoke up. "So they just happened to be along on

this trip, and there just happened to be a dead man, which just happened to get dumped in the hotel room that this Sandra and her new friend Patsy were booked into?"

"I don't know much about it, Detective, but I think Sandra and Patsy already knew each other before the trip was planned."

"Why here? Why did you come to Laughlin? Here to play the slots?" He snickered like the thought of little old ladies doing any real gambling was out of the question.

"We booked a couple of side trips. Some of us are going to Oatman tomorrow—eat lunch at the hotel, do the gold mine tour. Then Saturday there's a trip to Hoover Dam."

"All of you going?"

"No. I think Sandra has other plans tomorrow. And I'm not going to Hoover Dam—been there before."

Detective Dunbar said, "I need to talk to this Patsy again, and Sandra Pringle, too. You'll tell them?"

I nodded.

"Anything else I ought to know?"

I shook my head. "Can't think of anything offhand."

"You'll all be at the hotel if you're not on one of those bus tours?"

"I can't say for sure, Detective. Sandra rented a car at the airport. She took Patsy with her and the rest of us came over on the shuttle."

"She say why?" Trilby asked.

"Why she rented the car?"

He nodded.

"She said she had tentative plans to meet an old friend who'd moved down to Needles to be closer to his kids. She said he had a real nice pontoon boat and he was going to bring it up to Lake Mohave so they could cruise around, maybe have a picnic."

"He?" Dunbar's eyebrows jumped up to meet his hairline.

"That's what she said."

Trilby glanced at his notes again. "Sandra Pringle. She married?"

"Yes."

Detective Dunbar let a loud snort escape through his nose. Trilby's face pinked up a bit but he didn't say anything.

"Really!" I said in an effort to show my indignation—which didn't accurately represent what I'd been thinking at the time. I kept wondering what Sandra's husband would think.

The difference between me and the Flippers was that I had said nothing and tried not to let my thoughts show on my face. Gail had held nothing back, belting out her fourth "My gawd!" of the day. Diane had bounced her eyebrows up and down as she asked if Sandra's old friend was sexy. Marianne wanted to know if Sandra's friend could bring a friend for her. And Linda had giggled all the time she was trying to hush the others up and assure them that Sandra and her friend had a purely platonic relationship.

I chose not to tell any of this to the detectives. It was obvious they were going to waste way too much time on us without me adding fuel to the fire.

"We don't have anything to do with the dead man, Detective. You should focus your investigation on finding out who the guy was and what he was doing in Laughlin."

That piece of advice didn't earn me any points with Dunbar.

"Eight o'clock sharp," he snapped. "In the lobby. Make sure everyone's there." He strode toward the escalator without checking to make sure his posse followed.

Trilby winked and grinned before he also walked away.

Officer Snyder gave me a soulful look and said, "Ms. Thorn," nodded, and then glanced once more at the Hickory Pit's menu before hurrying to catch up to the detectives.

I hadn't told the cops that I was a lawyer and a former Palm Beach County circuit court judge because that might have triggered a background check, which might point to my recent close encounter with the retired mob boss and certain mem-

bers of his family. I didn't want to invite any more attention
from Detective Dunbar than I already had.

It took an hour and a half to track down Mom and most
of her friends to tell them about meeting the detectives at
eight the next morning. They'd already experienced Dunbar's
brusque approach in Sandra's room after the body was first
discovered, so they weren't particularly happy about spending any more time with, as Gail put it, Detective Sourpuss.
Hopefully, they would curb their natural inclination to ask a
thousand questions or offer their expert opinions.

The last ladies on my list were Patsy and Sandra. I tapped
at their door. There was no answer. I knocked a little harder.
Still no answer.

If they were sleeping, I hated to wake them up, but I had my
orders. I called from my room but no one answered. Maybe
Sandra was feeling so much better they'd gone out to eat. Or
maybe down to the casino. I scribbled a quick note, walked
down the hallway, and slid the note under Patsy and Sandra's
door.

The elevator door opened. I straightened up and looked
around but saw no one in the hall. The doors slid shut and
the light over the door went out. I hurried to my room and
with one last peek through the crack, I closed the door and
flipped the safety switch. Leaning my forehead against the
door, I peeked out the little peephole.

"What's wrong?"

While my mother's voice registered on my brain, my body
reacted as though it had heard gunfire. I staggered over to
the bed with one hand pressed against my chest, thinking
that if I exaggerated my response I'd have a better chance of
getting Mom to laugh it off. "When did you come back to the
room?"

"Just now. Where were you?" She grabbed my hands. "Cold
as ice. Did I scare you?"

"I left the room long enough to slide a note under Sandra's
door. I didn't see you get off the elevator. The door opened
and closed but no one was there."

"Oh, for Pete's sake, Sylvia." Mom cocked her head and frowned. "It's not like you to be skittish, dear."

"I know. Did you happen to see Patsy or Sandra downstairs? They didn't answer their door or the phone either. I left the note about meeting the detectives in the morning."

"Haven't seen them since they moved to their new room. Should we look for them?"

I didn't answer right away. On the one hand, Mom and I could not be held responsible for everyone in the group. But on the other hand, Detective Dunbar could ruin the ladies' weekend by restricting their activities until he'd talked to all of us.

"No, I'll go," I said. "Would you please call them again? If they don't answer, leave a message."

It took me less than twenty minutes to cover the lobby, bar, casino, restaurant, and gift shop, but there was no sign of Patsy or Sandra. Marianne was at the blackjack tables, and Diane had just fed a hundred-dollar bill to one of the newfangled five-dollar slots. I asked them to watch for the two missing ladies, but that was probably a foolish request since neither one seemed interested in anything but the cards and spinning wheels of their respective games.

Linda and Gail had already retired for the evening, so I called them from the lobby. They were watching television and had not seen Patsy or Sandra since before dinner. I couldn't think of anything else to do.

Mom was cozily propped up in bed, a book perched on the pillow in her lap. "Any luck?"

"Nope."

"I'm sure they're fine."

"It's odd, though. Patsy said she would order room service and keep Sandra in. If they changed their minds, why wouldn't they leave us a message so we wouldn't worry?"

"You're the only one who's worrying, Sylvia. Patsy and Sandra are grown-ups. They can take care of themselves. You don't have to make a mystery out of every little thing that happens."

Ah. The perfect distraction. Without saying another word, I changed into my pajamas and got ready for bed, grabbed my new book, and snuggled into the pile of pillows. Long after my mother had fallen sleep, I finally put the book aside and turned out my light.

FIVE

I STRUGGLED AWAKE and grabbed for the phone at the same time my mom reached out. She won, mumbled "Hello?" and then listened briefly before flipping on the lamp over her bed. "Where were you?" she asked. Then she listened some more.

Must be the missing ladies, I thought. I rolled over with my back to the light, hoping to catch a few more minutes of sleep, but only a few seconds later my mother said, "Is her car gone?" and I regained consciousness, alerted by her tone more than her words.

Well, crap. It's not going to be that easy, is it?

I rolled over again, swung my feet out from under the covers, and sat up on the edge of the bed. Mom gave me the "I don't know what the heck's going on" gesture. "Do you want Sylvia to go with you?"

"No, no," I whispered, after glancing at the clock. "It's three in the morning." I pinched my pajamas between my fingers and jiggled the fabric up and down to remind her I'd have to get dressed if I went anywhere with anyone.

This time she gave me the "I can't help it" shrug.

"Is it Patsy?"

She nodded yes. "Wait, Patsy. You better talk to Sylvia." Mom held the receiver out. "Sandra's missing."

"Patsy? What's up?"

"Sandra's gone," she said.

Wow, what a load of information to get all at once.

"What happened? Were you sleeping? Did you go out for dinner? I tried to find you earlier and couldn't."

"What time was that?"

"After dinner and my little chat with the detectives. Did you see my note about meeting with them tomorrow morning?"

"Yes. I'll be there. But Sandra—"

"I don't understand, Patsy. Did the two of you go out?"

"Just me. At least that's what I thought. I had room service bring dinner, and Sandra seemed to feel better after she ate. She said she was fine but wanted to stay in and watch television, maybe go to bed early so she'd feel like going to Oatman tomorr—today. She practically shooed my butt out the door because she knew I wanted to play a little poker down in the Hold 'Em Up Room."

Hold 'Em Up Room?

"I took her at her word," Patsy continued. "Came back a few minutes ago and she was gone."

"Did she take anything with her? Her purse? What about her luggage?"

"Her purse is gone. But her suitcase is sitting here unzipped, just like it was. And her stuff is still in the bathroom, her toothbrush and everything."

"Could she have gone to look for you? Maybe you passed each other in the elevators."

"Maybe, but I wondered...your mother asked a good question, about whether Sandra's car was gone. I'll check out the parking garage, but would you come down here while I'm gone in case Sandra tries to call the room?"

I sighed. "Sure. I'll be right there."

Mom watched sympathetically as I slipped my raincoat over my pajamas and jammed my feet into my running shoes, not bothering to put on socks. The lamp over her bed switched off before I'd pulled the door closed behind me, so I guessed she wasn't too concerned.

Patsy had her door open, ready to take off as soon as I slid inside.

I grabbed her arm. "Are you sure it's safe for you to go down there alone?"

She tipped her head back and looked out at me from under

the hood of her black sweatshirt. "Do I look like someone you'd want to mess with?"

"No," I conceded. She really didn't. The hood did nothing to hide her squinty eyes, the sharp lines around her mouth, and the angry set of her jaw. In her black sweats, black Nikes, no makeup, and with her hands thrust into her pockets, Patsy resembled a street hood looking for a score. I meekly stepped away. Patsy strode toward the elevator, and I let the door swoosh shut.

One side of the room was tidy, the bed rumpled as though someone had taken a short nap. The other bed was strewn with clothes...and papers, none of which were any of my business. But I made a beeline toward those papers as if lured by a bed of wildflowers.

Which was a wasted effort—nothing but a bunch of print-outs from websites touting local attractions. Most of those attractions were rumored to be haunted—the Oatman Hotel, the Pioneer Saloon in Goodsprings, places said to be visited by the late Clark Gable and Carole Lombard, among others. I replaced the papers the way I'd found them, then slowly surveyed the rest of the room, concerned enough about Sandra to set aside any guilt I might have felt over being so blatantly nosy.

The unzipped suitcase caught my eye. I hurried over to lift the top and take a peek inside. Nothing visible but neatly folded underwear and knit tops. I drew the line at rummaging any further and closed the case.

The mirrored door of the closet slid open with a touch of my finger. Clothes were neatly hung at both ends. Patsy's suitcase was tucked into one corner, sitting up on its wheels. The suitcase was locked, and it had two sweaters folded on top. Patsy apparently wasn't as blasé as Sandra about leaving the contents of her luggage accessible. She'd even refused to check her bag for the flight, saying she traveled light to avoid delays and lost luggage.

After sliding the closet door closed, I checked the bath-room. One hand towel had been wadded up and tossed on the toilet tank lid, and another one, wet and showing the faint residue of Sandra's blood, was draped over the shower curtain rod. Two zipped toiletry kits perched on separate sides of the sink. A lavender toothbrush was propped partially out of its red plastic holder and sat next to one of the kits. Nothing to be seen there without further intruding on Patsy and Sandra's privacy.

Outside, the streetlights were still aglow. A couple of lights moved slowly along the Colorado River. It was too early to stand at the window and wait for the sun to rise. I sat down in a nearby easy chair and would have dozed off if Patsy hadn't returned seconds after I got comfortable.

"Car's gone," she said as she walked in the door.

I frowned. "Could she have gone to see her friend? The one with the boat?"

"Why wouldn't she tell me, or leave a note? Or take her stuff? No, she explicitly said she would stay here."

"What do you think? Should we call the police and report her missing? Have them put out an APB on her car? But I suppose that's a bit premature. You know, it's possible she's still in the hotel. Maybe she moved the car for some reason. Or maybe it was stolen."

"You're right, I guess." Patsy chewed on her lip and paced back and forth. "I'm not calling the cops yet. I'll go downstairs and look for her some more. Do you mind staying a little longer? And while you're here, could you look in her suitcase and see if you can find her calendar? That's where she had the address and phone number of her friend. I'll call and see if he's heard from her."

Ah. Permission to snoop.

"Sure," I said, perhaps a little too quickly. Patsy didn't seem to notice. She was gone before I pushed myself out of the chair.

With Sandra's suitcase lid propped against the wall, I poked my fingers around the contents and into corners and crevices. I felt something hard, marked its location with my left hand and lifted clothing with my right to take a look. Curious. It was a five-by-seven brown envelope that Sandra had addressed to herself in Florida. I lifted it up to see if it was empty. It was not. Something small and hard, like a purse-sized notebook, was inside. The envelope was sealed shut. I put it back and resumed my search.

Finally locating the daily calendar, I pulled it out and opened it to the current week. There were no entries for the weekend, except the numbers and departure times for the Thursday flight to and the Sunday flight from Bullhead City.

In the address section, each of the club ladies and their phone numbers were listed, as well as Patsy's name and number, and five or six other names or initials I didn't recognize. I also noted that the unknown folks did not have Florida area codes. Some of the area codes were the same as Laughlin's.

Who does Sandra know in Laughlin?

In the *P*s I saw Barry, Sandra's husband, listed along with two phone numbers, one marked "cell." Until then, I hadn't given Sandra's husband a thought. He should be notified if Sandra was missing, especially if the police became involved.

Among the remaining unidentified entries, one was marked Needles, which was where Sandra's friend lived. I tossed the book on the bed and dropped the suitcase lid into place.

I dozed off in the easy chair and didn't wake up until Patsy tapped me on the shoulder. "Didn't find her," she said, "but she was in the casino for a while. Apparently she wandered around a bit and then sat down at one of the quarter slots for maybe a half hour. The cocktail waitress remembered her because Sandra won fifty bucks just as the waitress brought her a cup of coffee. Sandra gave her a five-dollar tip, cashed out, and took off toward the payout booth with her receipt and her coffee."

"Did the waitress remember what time Sandra quit playing?"

"Three, maybe three-fifteen. About the time I called and woke you up."

"Did anyone else see her?"

"Only the gal at the payout booth. She remembered because Sandra tried to put her money away with one hand while juggling the cup of coffee with the other, and she ended up spilling coffee into her purse."

"Did the cashier see where Sandra went after that?"

"Yep. Straight to the ladies' room. But the cashier got busy and didn't notice when Sandra came out so I have no clue where Sandra went after that."

"Maybe she hit her head harder than we thought. She could have been sick, or felt faint. Did you check the restroom?"

"You bet. Opened every stall door. Even checked the men's room. Tried the other doors in that corner of the casino, all marked 'employees only,' but they were locked. I knocked but no one answered."

I took a deep breath and let it out. It was already four thirty. Only three and a half hours until we'd have no choice but to tell Detective Dunbar we'd misplaced a member of our party.

"Look," Patsy said, "there's no sense calling the cops this soon. There's not a force in the country that will start looking for a person who has been missing for one hour.

"When it gets light out," she continued, "I'll scout the grounds, the river walk, around the boat ramps, in case she wandered out there and passed out. If I see no sign of her and she hasn't returned to the room, I'll call all the numbers in that book."

"We need to touch base with the rest of the Flippers, too. For all we know, Sandra's with some of them."

"Good point. Would you call?" She glanced at her watch. "If they're early risers…"

I said I would and returned to my room, switching on the bathroom light so I could see to dial the phone. I was going to be extremely annoyed at Sandra if she turned up and had no good excuse for her disappearance. Sleep deprivation makes me cranky. I dialed Diane and Gail's room, hoping they weren't going to be mad at the early call.

My concern was wasted. There was no answer.

Hurriedly I called Marianne and Linda's room. By the third ring I was getting very nervous, so I nearly jumped out of my skin when the fourth ring was followed by a loud clunk and a shrieked, "Oh dear, I'm sorry, it's…hello?"

"Linda?"

"Yes?"

"Thank goodness you're there. It's Sylvia. Sorry to wake you up so early, but have you seen or heard from Sandra since dinner last night?"

"No. Is something wrong?"

"We're not sure. Could you wake Marianne up and ask her?"

"Just a minute." Then louder, "Marianne?" A clunking sound as if Linda had dropped the receiver on the table. Shuffling. A tap on a door, probably the bathroom door. "Marianne, are you in there?" More shuffling. "She's not here."

"She's not there? Where did she go?"

"She doesn't need much sleep. Unlike some of us."

I ignored the unspoken accusation.

Linda said, "I told her last night that my alarm was set for seven and that if she got up earlier than that, she was not to wake me. We agreed to meet at eight to talk to that horrible detective."

"What about Gail and Diane? Do they get up early, too?"

"Yes. They said something about taking a walk at sunrise. Maybe Sandra went with them." Linda hung up the phone.

A tremendous sense of relief took immediate possession of my body, relaxing my jaw and easing the tension in my shoulders. Finally, a logical explanation for Sandra's absence.

Except, where is her car?

SIX

"Damn it," I muttered.

"Sylvia Lucille," Mom said, using the same admonishment I'd been hearing ever since I'd uttered my first mild profanity.

"I thought you were asleep, Mom."

"I was, until you got back on the phone." She rolled over to face me. "What time is it?"

The bedside clock said ten after five. I glanced at my watch. "Quarter after five. Did you see or talk to Sandra after dinner last night?"

"No, but Marianne said she was going to call her."

"Marianne's not in her room. Linda thinks she went walking early with Diane and Gail and that maybe Sandra went along."

"You don't sound so sure."

"Patsy checked out the parking garage. Couldn't find Sandra's rental car."

Mom blew out a puff of air and pushed herself into a sitting position. I knew better than to hop up to help her so I watched as she moved and stretched to work the kinks out. While she put her body into functioning mode, I called Patsy to report what little I'd learned. She said she was heading downstairs to search outside the building.

"We'd better find the others," Mom said when I got off the phone. She eased herself out of bed and stretched some more, bent and touched her toes a couple of times, walked back and forth the width of the room twice, then grabbed her suitcase and swung it onto the bed.

While Mom rummaged through her clothes, I slipped into

the bathroom and brushed my teeth. Mom took her turn to do whatever, then I hurried in to take a quick shower. By a quarter 'til six we were dressed and ready to go.

I'm ornery if I don't get enough sleep, if I don't get my coffee first thing in the morning, and if I don't have breakfast soon after that first cup of coffee. Stopping by the hotel's coffee bar, conveniently placed next to a bakery counter, was a priority and solved two out of three problems. If the coffee and sugar masked my fatigue through the next couple of hours, I could grab a catnap on the bus to Oatman.

It was hard to juggle my coffee and pecan roll while matching my mother's brisk pace on the river walk, but Mom was determined to help Patsy look for Sandra. Somehow, I kept up without sloshing hot coffee on myself. I was licking gooey caramel stuff off my fingers when Mom stopped, dug around in her purse, and pulled out two little packets of antiseptic hand wipes.

"For heaven's sake, Sylvia," she said as she ripped one open and handed it to me.

"What?" Trying to look innocent, I obediently wiped my mouth and hands and tossed the wipes in a trashcan along with my cup.

"Should we be walking closer to the water?" Mom asked.

"Maybe."

"Or searching in between the hotels?"

I looked toward the landscaped lawn with its trees and bushes and nodded. "Let's do both. We'll walk a half mile along the river and then work our way back by checking all the nooks and crannies along the buildings." I looked over my shoulder to see where Patsy was concentrating her efforts, as she searched in the other direction. "Patsy's down by the river. She must be doing the same thing."

We met Patsy at the hotel shortly before eight. We had found nothing and had not seen Marianne, Gail, or Diane. No one else waited for us in the lobby. Who was going to tell

Detective Dunbar that five of the Flippers had blown off the meeting? I didn't want it to be me.

Judging from Mom's crossed arms and the set of her jaw, she had no intention of explaining her inconsiderate friends to the detective either. Patsy jumped up and announced that she was going to the ladies' room and would stop for coffee on the way back; did anyone else want a cup? She took our orders and disappeared.

It was all on me. I watched the lobby entrance, hoping to catch a glimpse of Dunbar as he came in the door so I could prepare myself. It was wasted anxiety. The only policeman who walked through the revolving door and into the lobby was Detective Trilby.

Marianne, Gail, and Diane rushed into the lobby from the direction of the restaurant. As soon as they saw Trilby, they visibly relaxed. After the three huddled briefly, Marianne scooted off toward the coffee bar and the other two met Trilby halfway. By the time they joined Mom and me, they were chatting like old friends.

Trilby thrust out his hand. "Detective Trilby. We met last evening."

I shook his hand and nodded. "Sylvia Thorn."

"Yes. Judge Thorn, I believe."

"I'm retired." The cops must have checked up on me but hadn't done a thorough job. "Will Detective Dunbar be joining us?"

"No. He had something else to take care of."

I nodded again and tried to keep a straight face, but I was thinking happy thoughts.

Trilby looked around. "Who's missing?" He counted heads. "Four of you?"

"No, Patsy will be right back. Marianne should, too. Linda may need a wake-up call. No, here she comes."

"And the other one?"

"That would be Sandra," I said. "We don't know where she is."

"Who did she share a room with?"

"Patsy. But she doesn't know where Sandra is, either. We've looked everywhere. And Patsy says Sandra's car is gone. If Sandra hasn't shown up by the end of our meeting, Patsy said she'd call all the numbers in Sandra's address book."

Patsy and Marianne sauntered into the lobby, each carrying a cardboard tray loaded down with coffee cups and doughnuts.

"Plenty for everyone," Marianne said. "Help yourself, Detective."

He obligingly plucked a cup of coffee from Marianne's tray with his right hand and a chocolate-frosted cake doughnut with his left. After everyone else was seated, Trilby sat down and took a sip of his coffee and a bite of his doughnut. "I'm going to be quick so you can make the tour bus to Oatman. Does anyone have firsthand information about the body we found in the tub? I mean, anything you saw or heard or know to be true, not picked up from someone else?"

Trilby had worded his question well. I suspected the ladies' efforts to question hotel and casino employees had been reported and most likely received with amusement.

None of the Flippers spoke up.

Trilby looked at me. "How about you, Judge Thorn?"

"No, I don't know anything."

"Okay. The member of your party who's missing, Mrs. Pringle? Anyone have information about her?"

Marianne, Gail, Diane, and Linda all talked at once, trying to out-shout each other to get their questions answered.

Trilby held up his hand for silence. "You four didn't know she was missing?"

All except Linda shook their heads and shot accusing looks at Patsy and me.

"I tried to call you," I protested. "Linda, tell them."

"She did. But I didn't think—"

Marianne, Gail, and Diane now aimed their glares at Linda, effectively shutting down her attempts to explain.

"You three were out before I called your rooms," I said.

"And you showed up here at the last second. There's been no chance to tell you."

"How long has she been missing?" Marianne asked.

Detective Trilby held up his hand again. "Wait. Let me get the information I need so you can leave." He addressed Patsy. "Do you have the license number for Mrs. Pringle's car?"

Patsy nodded.

"What's the number? Maybe the car is in the parking lot at the mall or one of the other casinos."

Patsy took one of the napkins from the coffee shop tray and a pen from her purse, jotted a number down, and handed it to the detective.

Trilby looked at the number. "What kind of a car is it?"

"Little silver thing, some kind of Ford. Gray interior with black trim."

Trilby pulled a pen from his pocket and scribbled on the napkin. Then he said, "Has anyone called Mr. Pringle?"

"Not yet," Patsy said. "I'll do it."

"Okay, that's it then." Trilby folded the napkin, tucked it in his pocket, then stood up. "Ladies, you are now free to go." And with that, Detective Trilby left before any of the Flippers could grab him and ask more questions.

"Sylvia, I need to talk to you."

"Sure, Mom. What's up?"

"Not where the others can hear," she said under her breath. Mom turned to the group. "Everyone, I forgot something in my room. Don't let the bus leave without me."

"You have plenty of time, Mom. I'll go with you."

Mom beamed at me approvingly for falling in step with her wily deception.

"Wait," Marianne said. "What about Sandra?"

"Patsy, fill them in, would you?" Mom called as she and I scurried away. As soon as we were out of earshot, Mom leaned toward me and whispered, "Willie called early this morning and left a message on my cell phone. He said that he and your father visited Velma yesterday, and that Velma might have been pushed down the steps at the library."

"Pushed? Who would have pushed her? Who was with her?"

Mom's eyebrows lifted and she pursed her lips. "Sandra."

I shook my head. "I don't believe it."

"I don't think Velma accused Sandra directly of doing it. She told Willie there was a rush of people and several were close enough to bump into her, but that she has this lingering feeling it wasn't an accident. It's not that she knows Sandra did it, it's just that Sandra was there and could have done it."

"You know Sandra better than I do. Is this possible?"

Mom shrugged. "Sandra's been acting so strange lately that I've worried about her. But…" Her voice trailed off and she shook her head as though she couldn't imagine Sandra hurting anyone.

"What else did Willie say?"

"Not much. Just to be alert, and if we had a chance to talk to Sandra that we should see if she'll tell us about Velma's fall, but if she acts the least bit suspicious, we should drop the subject."

"And that's all?"

"No. He said Velma didn't know anything about Patsy so he was going to see what he could find out."

The elevator door opened; we stepped inside and pushed the button for our floor.

"I'll pop in and use the bathroom," Mom said. "Then we can go chat with the girls while Patsy makes those calls." She grinned and nudged me with her elbow. "How do you feel about our trip now? Exciting, isn't it?"

"Mom—"

"I know, I know. But you've been fretting about what to do with the rest of your life instead of enjoying the life you have right now. We've found a body and one of us has disappeared. Two mysteries to solve. You should be ecstatic."

"Well, yes, I love mysteries to read, but not be stuck in the middle of. I need something more practical and constructive to do with my time—like starting my own law practice."

"Oh, practical, shmactical. Sylvia, you weren't happy doing

that. You know you weren't. You don't need to work at all unless you want to. You have plenty of money. You've invested well."

Mom was referring to the huge insurance settlement awarded after my husband Andy's fatal accident. Add that to the savings I'd accumulated over the years and I was indeed a well-to-do woman with absolutely nothing to fill my time except my family, a large collection of unread mystery and suspense novels, and whatever busywork Mom or Willie dumped on me.

"Sylvia! Are you listening? What about that coastal Norwegian cruise? Are you going?"

The elevator doors slid open.

"Yes, absolutely."

"Will you go alone?"

"Why? Would you and Dad be willing to come along?"

"Perhaps, but I was thinking more of your friend Tequila. She's self-employed; she might be able to get away. I know she travels and I'll bet she's never been to Norway."

I laughed at the thought of Tequila Picon on a coastal cruise amongst the fjords, bundled against the cold north winds, refusing to step one foot on anything that might be frozen. Her father was Puerto Rican and her mother Mexican. As far as I knew, her travels have never taken her to a climate that didn't qualify as tropical.

Mom believes that Tequila, known to all of the rest of us as Tak, has an adventurous spirit that knows no bounds, and that I would do well to emulate her free-spirited ways. In the last few months I've advanced as far as mastering a couple of Latin dances so I'll be able to hold my own at the upcoming Cinco de Mayo celebration. And I've come mighty close to scheduling a ride in a hot air balloon. Mighty close. My spirit of adventure is holding its own.

The more I thought about it, though, the whole family and Tak joining me on a cruise seemed like a spectacular idea. Mom and Dad loved to travel. Willie tolerated trips that didn't involve loud noises or flashing lights that might trigger a stress reaction. Tak might take some convincing, but she loved my family. If we ganged up on her, she might give in.

"I don't know how we got on this subject anyway," Mom said. "I was talking about Willie's phone call. Did you ask him to find out more about Patsy?"

"Not exactly. I was curious about her. He picked up on it and thought he'd get some answers from Velma. Apparently that didn't happen."

After we'd stopped in our room and then returned to the lobby, it was nearly time for the tour to leave. We hurried out of the elevator and strode past the coffee shop and bakery without stopping, although I was briefly tempted by a tray of blueberry scones sitting on top of the counter.

The Flippers, minus Sandra, were clustered at the entrance, waiting for us. A ten-passenger tour bus pulled into the circle drive. We spilled through the revolving door one by one and formed a line behind a man and two women, all much younger than our group. Mom chatted them up right away, then came back to report their hometown—Memphis—and their marital status—husband, wife, and wife's sister. The Flippers quickly lost interest, however, when the Memphis folks admitted they'd never met Elvis or visited Graceland. The discussion returned to Sandra's whereabouts, a discussion that concentrated mostly on Sandra's relationship with her friend from Needles and whether Sandra's husband knew about him.

Patsy had been on her cell phone ever since Mom and I had come downstairs, but she finally snapped it shut and dropped it into her purse. She frowned and made no effort to communicate what most of us had hoped would be good news. There were several surreptitious glances thrown Patsy's way, but none of the Flippers asked the obvious question.

"You're awfully quiet," I whispered, slipping into the seat next to her on the bus.

She shook her head. "Just concerned. No one knows where she is. And I had to leave a message on her husband's phone. Maybe I should stay here and search some more."

"You'd have to rent another car to cover all of Laughlin."

"Bullhead City, too."

"And if she went for a longer drive—"

"I know." Patsy sounded resigned. "She could have gone any distance in any direction. I'd never find her."

"Listen, if she hasn't turned up by the time we get back to the hotel, I'll help you look. Mom and her friends are going to Hoover Dam tomorrow on that guided tour. You and I can stay here, pick up a rental at the airport, and spend the whole day trying to find Sandra."

Patsy nodded, which I took as acceptance of my offer to help. I could think of ways I'd rather spend a vacation day, but on the other hand, I'd probably find out everything I wanted to know about Patsy, straight from the horse's mouth.

Although, if Willie came through like the trooper he is, he'd call and I'd have the whole scoop without asking Patsy one single question.

"There were some phone numbers in Sandra's book with a local area code," I said. "Who were they?"

"One was the hotel. One was the car rental place, but there was only a recorded message so I'll have to call them later. The one with initials D.H. had an answering machine. It was for Desert Hedge Investors."

"That's odd," I said. "Why would Sandra be in contact with an investment company way out here?"

Patsy didn't answer.

SEVEN

"I'M GOING HOME to take a nap," Willie's dad said as he dropped Willie off in front of his apartment building. "Too much excitement for an old man, asking Velma all those questions, especially for an old man who was up all night with indigestion."

Willie thought about his dad's hot dogs, beer, and caramel popcorn at the ballgame the day before. Add the crabmeat salad sandwiches at Boston's on the Beach, and his dad had the makings of another bad night. Especially since he'd also had a beer, claiming that Sylvia always did it that way, so why shouldn't he?

Which one of the two, his sister or his dad, had the unhealthiest eating habits? If Willie was a gambling man, he would put his money on Sylvia. His dad, at least, had to answer to Willie's mom when she wasn't gallivanting around the country with the girls. Sylvia had an iron gut, was in perfect health, and had no problem with her weight, so she respectfully refused to take nutritional advice from anyone.

"You're okay to drive home?" Willie asked his dad.

"Oh, sure. I'm fine now. Just need a little shut-eye."

"You could take your nap here."

"Nope. I like my own bed. You doing anything more this afternoon?"

"Yeah. I'll see what I can find out about Patsy Strump. That whole thing with Velma's fall and Sandra insisting on going to Laughlin and taking a stranger along sounds funny."

"Yes, it does." His dad nodded thoughtfully. "Maybe I'll get some inspiring ideas if I think about it. I'll call you later."

"Thanks for the ride, Dad."

In his apartment, Willie grabbed a bottle of water and a bunch of grapes before sitting down at his table with the telephone book. There were no Strumps listed in the residential section.

Turning to the business section, Willie tried again. There was one entry—"Strump Investigations." He looked up "Investigations" and found a boxed entry for Strump's firm. There was still no confirmation that this Strump and Patsy Strump were one and the same. Willie jotted down the address and phone number on a piece of scrap paper, then dialed the phone number. The call went to an answering machine, and a female voice instructed him to leave a message. Willie hung up, studied the address he'd written down, and stuffed the note in his shirt pocket.

Ten minutes later he was on his bicycle, his bottle of water tucked in one of the saddlebags mounted over his rear tire. It took him twenty minutes of hard riding in the South Florida heat and humidity to reach the Federal Highway address. Sweat dripped from his nose and soaked his shirt. He rested a moment before locking his bike to the steel post of a handicapped parking sign and entering the one-story office building that anchored one end of a small rundown strip mall. At least a third of the retail sites in the center sported huge "For Lease" signs in their windows. Invasive greenery had pushed through cracks in the parking lot and sent crawlers searching for more openings in which to root.

The office building appeared to be fully rented. Considering the worn brown carpet in the halls and the dingy green walls, however, the businesses were not wildly successful.

Willie perused the list of tenants by the front door and followed the signs to the rear of the building. The frosted glass door with "Strump Investigations" painted in black letters was locked. On either side were offices for "Hall Insurance Company" and "Favor and Kane, C.P.A.s," suggesting Strump's space was a one-room cubbyhole.

There was a light on inside the accountants' office, so Willie walked in. Two desks were arranged back to back, and four file cabinets lined one wall. A pale balding man with a noticeable paunch sat at one of the desks, a newspaper spread open to the sports page. He looked up when Willie opened the door, but didn't bother closing his paper. The CPA firm apparently had little business even though the end of tax season was just around the corner.

"I was looking for Strump," Willie said. "Do you happen to know where—"

"Haven't seen her since Wednesday."

"Her?"

"Yeah. Strump's a broad." The man looked at Willie and raised his eyebrows, inviting more questions.

"You don't happen to know where—"

"Nope."

"Or when—"

"Nope. She and I don't talk much."

"Do you think the insurance guy next door—"

"Hall's a broad, too. She's been gone all week. You're about the twentieth person who's stopped in here looking for one or the other."

"Twentieth? They must be doing well."

"I don't know. Maybe not twenty. I know a couple of 'em were asking about flood insurance. Busy hurricane season coming up, if you believe that forecaster out in Colorado."

"Do you happen to know Ms. Strump's first name?" Willie asked.

"Sure. Patsy. And that's what I am for letting those two broads walk all over me like this."

"How is it they walk all over you?"

"Times like this," he said. "They leave, and I get the interruptions. I hear both phones ring—three rings before a call goes to the answering machine."

"The PI doesn't have a secretary?"

"Not that I know of. Probably can't afford it."

"Why do you say that?"

"Would you have an office in this dump if you could afford

hired help? Nope, you'd have a nice setup near one of the fancy malls."

"She hasn't been in business long?"

"I don't know. She's only been in this building about a year." The accountant looked Willie over. "Why? You looking to hire her?"

"Maybe."

"She does mostly domestic cases. Takes pictures, looks for dirt on people. You looking for that kind of PI?" The accountant leaned forward, seemingly eager to hear Willie's story.

"Domestic cases. Like divorce?"

"Yeah, like divorce from a rich husband maybe. Or folks contesting a will. You know, the kind of stuff you'd expect in Boca Raton."

"You said you two didn't talk much. How do you know about her cases?"

The accountant leaned back. "Don't know for sure. I'm judging by the people who come around here asking questions." He looked Willie up and down. "Like you."

Convinced he'd learned all he was going to, Willie gave up. "Hey, thanks for your help."

The accountant nodded and returned to his newspaper.

Willie backed through the doorway, wondering what fictional story the accountant would create to describe Willie's visit. But he was pleased with the information he'd obtained. Patsy Strump was a private investigator and her business did not seem to be thriving.

When he got home, Willie called his mother.

Her voice mail answered.

"Mom," Willie began. "Tell Sylvia…oh, never mind. Have Sylvia call me."

It was only four o'clock Florida time, which, he calculated, was two o'clock Arizona time and one o'clock Nevada time. Sylvia and the Flippers were probably still in Oatman if they went on their scheduled tour. They wouldn't return to the hotel until late afternoon, maybe seven or eight his time.

He glanced around his apartment and spied the pile of library books by the door. He divided the books into two canvas bags and lugged them to the Boca Raton Public Library less than a quarter mile away.

He trudged along happily, sweat dripping from his nose. He swung one book-laden arm up to wipe his brow on his sleeve.

Today's a good day. At least, so far.

A superstitious man would knock on wood, but Willie was not superstitious. He was somewhat intuitive, especially where his sister was concerned, but superstitious? Definitely not.

Sylvia's firm conviction that the dead man in Patsy and Sandra's room was an unfortunate coincidence had set his mind at ease. The curiosity they had about Velma's fall, the trip destination, and Patsy Strump's identity were just that— curiosity. If there was danger, he would know, would feel it. He entered the library with complete confidence that all was well with his world.

EIGHT

I COULD HAVE HAD THAT quick nap on the bus if all the passengers had been like Patsy—withdrawn, staring out the window as though every shop, restaurant, gas station, or motel was worthy of intense scrutiny.

Unfortunately, the other ladies were full of energy and excitement as they planned their day. They drowned out all other conversation as well as my hoped-for peace and quiet.

I moved to an empty seat across the aisle from Patsy so I could have my own window. The main drag along casino row in Laughlin was busy, but traffic looked worse on the Bullhead City side of the river. The bus, however, did not turn south to tangle with the town's busy streets. The Bullhead Parkway took us past the airport and around the city, circling toward the main drag on the south side. It wasn't until we reached Boundary Cone Road that the bus headed toward the rocky hills and desert scrubland surrounding Oatman, more than thirteen miles to the east.

As signs of civilization dropped away, we were surrounded by the illusion of isolation. The hills and rocky bluffs blocked all noise except that from our bus…and the wind. We fell silent and stared thoughtfully at the tan and sage countryside. This strange land had a mood of its own.

But that sure as hell didn't last long. In Oatman, the Flippers excitedly pointed out the burros roaming the streets. Where one would expect to see saddled horses tied to a hitching post in front of the Oatman Hotel, motorcycles lined up instead. Weathered signs hung askew on old storefronts. Kids wandered out of the hotel, their ice cream cones dripping brown or pink trails down their shirts and onto the toes of their dusty sneakers. The bus driver was trying to explain the history of old Route 66 and something about *Easy Rider,* but his words were drowned out by Marianne, who seemed to know more about the movie than he did.

As I gazed through my window toward the little houses perched on a nearby hill and wondered where Mom and her friends found their unending enthusiasm for all things bizarre, I caught movement out of the corner of my eye. A cowboy wearing a black hat, black vest, and black boots crept along the side of the bus under my window. He pulled up a black bandanna tied around his neck to cover his nose and mouth. He raised his arm. I knew what was coming. Knowing didn't stop me from jumping a foot when the man fired his pistol.

The ladies got downright silly at that point. Marianne flirted with the robber when he boarded the bus and demanded our valuables. She seemed ready to give up her money and her jewelry and Lord knows what else, but the sheriff showed up in the nick of time and hauled the robber off to the pokey.

Or so they said.

By the time we stepped off the bus, the same fellow in black showed up again, only to be killed in a gunfight with that same sheriff. The theme to *High Noon* kept running through my mind as the two faced each other on a street ringed with gaping tourists.

All this time I stood in the sun, trying to keep an eye on the Flippers, who were accustomed to heat but not the extremely low humidity. I'd already made sure they carried bottled water, but were they actually drinking the stuff? After the gunfight scene ran its course, I watched the crowd disperse. Mom disappeared into the Oatman Hotel, Marianne ducked into the Blue Buffalo Saloon across the street, and what might have been Gail's orthopedic boots paced back and forth below a rack of T-shirts on the wooden sidewalk in front of the Crazy Cowboy Shirt and Hat Shop. Diane, Linda, and Patsy were nowhere to be seen.

The tourists cleared off the street. Our driver pulled away and parked the bus in a lot a few hundred feet north of the hotel. I stood helplessly in the middle of the road, surrounded by burros.

Like birds gathering on the power lines in the Hitchcock thriller, more burros trotted toward me. I didn't have anything for them. What would they do after they figured that out? I wondered. Do burros attack if they don't get what they want?

People stopped to watch, waving their arms and stretching their necks like freaking vultures. They pointed and laughed. One of the shopkeepers, to whom I will be forever grateful, approached with a handful of carrots and dangled them in the air. The burros abandoned me without even one menacing glance.

I was a little embarrassed.

Okay, a lot embarrassed, but I wasn't interested in dwelling on the subject. I strode through the crowd as though nothing had happened, pretending I wasn't pale and wide-eyed, pretending I had absolutely no fear of waist-high, furry creatures that might bite or kick if I offended them in some way.

I stopped to admire a magnificent, fire-red Harley Sportster, tempted to pat it on the fuel tank to show that I didn't like burros but I loved bikes.

"What do you think?"

I spun around, expecting to see a burly biker with tattoos covering his arms and piercings in tender places. Instead, a tall man with short gray hair, wearing leather chaps but no visible signs of body mutilation, gazed at the Harley, obviously the love of his life.

"Got her last week," he said. "It's the two thousand and seven model, but she's good as new. Set me back almost ten grand." He tore his gaze away from the Sportster and looked me over. "You ride?"

"Used to," I said.

"Why'd you give it up?"

"Don't have time. Sold the bike a few years ago."

I didn't tell this perfect stranger that the bike had belonged to my husband, Andy, and that I couldn't bear to ride again after he died, even though his accident had nothing to do with motorcycles.

Apparently I didn't pass the enthusiastic fan test for this Route 66 biker. He opened his storage pack and pulled out a black leather jacket with fringe on the sleeves. He put it on and fastened the snaps, then topped off his ensemble with a red helmet. A quick glance in my direction, presumably to make sure I was watching, and he walked the bike backward into the street, started it with a roar, and cruised out of town.

Pompous ass. Too tidy to be a real biker. I looked up and down the street, realizing then that most of the motorcycles were slick newer models with only two or three showing the wear and tear of years on the road. I stood by the hotel entrance. Bikers came and went, every one looking like a closet professional. I'd stake my reputation, such as it was, on nine out of ten riders being lawyers or doctors.

Inside the lobby of the Oatman Hotel was a collection of memorabilia, an old-fashioned pickle barrel, and a very modern snack counter. Sweet Sally's featured all the foods I love. For once Willie wasn't around to give me a hard time. I was thinking that a slice of pizza with a mint chocolate chip ice cream chaser would make me very, very happy.

Instead, I was yanked around by the elbow and pushed toward a door leading past a flight of stairs and into the bar.

"Go on, through the other door," Mom ordered. She gave me another shove. "We grabbed a table. Place is filling up fast."

I pointed toward Sweet Sally's. "I was going to—"

"You'll love this, Sylvia. The menu is great—burro ears and buffalo burgers. And they have bread bowls for their homemade soup."

I went down the steps into the restaurant, wondering what the heck a burro ear was, then stopped in my tracks so abruptly that Mom bumped into me. I hardly noticed, since I was staring at the walls, which were covered with bills, mostly one-dollar bills, autographed with names and dates.

Mom prodded me toward the table where Marianne, Patsy,

and Linda were already seated. "Did you see where Gail and Diane went?" she asked me.

"No. I was surrounded by those vicious animals and you guys passed right by me, didn't you?" I looked at each of them in turn. "Well, what do you have to say for yourselves?"

"They were only burros, dear," Mom said. "They won't hurt you if you don't feed them from your hand or stand too near their hind legs. Like horses—you like horses."

I do like horses. I even don my girlie-girl white straw cowgirl hat and go riding from time to time. But I don't ride wild ones that fancy biting and kicking people or furry ones that might be full of fleas.

A stunning blonde in black jeans, a cowboy hat and boots, and a wide leather belt with a huge silver buckle, strolled up, announced her name was Jo, and offered to take our orders. Gail and Diane walked in from the bar and created a few moments of chaos while they commandeered chairs from nearby tables and forced everyone to scoot around and give them room.

"You worked here long?" I asked, once all the ladies were studying their menus.

"Near five years. Live upstairs, oversee the whole place, including the ghosts."

"Ghosts?" Too bad Willie wasn't along. Ghosts would be right up his alley. As far as I know he's never seen or communicated with one, but I know he wonders if he could.

"Sure. Whole upstairs is haunted," Jo said. "Some people come running right back down because they feel stuff. You know, cold places in the rooms, tingly feelings on their skin. You been up there yet?"

"Not yet," I said. "Maybe after lunch." *In a pig's eye! I have enough trouble with flesh-and-blood goofballs in my life. I'm not about to introduce myself to a potential ghostly stalker.*

"Might run into Oatie if you're lucky," she said.

What luck. A ghost with a name. I didn't know if I was in

for a few tall tales or what, but the ladies were still debating items on the menu. What the hell, I'd bite. "Who's Oatie?"

"Irishman who drank himself to death right in there at the bar. Couldn't handle the grief of losing his whole family at one time."

Everyone at the table fell silent. All eyes were on Jo, waiting for her to continue.

"You guys ready to order?" I looked around the table.

"Hush, Sylvia," Mom whispered. She patted my hand, never taking her eyes off Jo. "What happened to Oatie's family?"

"Not sure. Oatie was a miner. He'd been squirreling away his money so he could bring his wife and kids over from Ireland, but something bad happened on the trip. I don't know if it was a disease or what, but they all died."

I'd read that a girl whose last name was Oatman was kidnapped by one of the Indian tribes in the mid-1800s, maybe the Yavapai. "This Oatie," I said. "Was he related to the Oatman family?"

"Nah. Oatie's real name was Ray Flowers. I don't know if he was called Oatie back in his time. Might be a nickname the town gave him later. I reckon it sounds more like a ghost than 'Ray' does."

"I'm going up there," said Gail, "right after we eat. Who's coming with me?"

Mom, Marianne, and Diane agreed. Linda paled, but said maybe. They all looked at Patsy and me, waiting.

"Good grief. Okay, I'll go," I said. Patsy concentrated on her menu.

"Room fifteen," Jo said. "If the door's locked, come down and tell me. He does that sometimes."

"Who does?" Linda seemed more apprehensive than intrigued.

"Oatie."

I looked up to see if Jo had a twinkle in her eye, but she'd said it with a straight face.

Linda's eyes opened a little wider.

It wasn't more than twenty minutes later that our table was

covered with burgers, baked beans, homemade potato chips shaped like burro ears, and beer, and we were happily munching and sipping while a scruffy long-haired cowpoke standing outside the restaurant door strummed his guitar and wailed cowboy songs. When he sang "Red River Valley," however, I remembered the old Johnny Cash recording that begged someone most vehemently not to play *that song.* I shared the sentiment.

As soon as we finished, most of the Flippers wanted to tackle room fifteen. I always thought older folks wanted to nap after a meal, especially a meal with beer, but this chipper bunch of dames was as energized as a pack of new motorcycles with full tanks of gas. I followed along, not sure why I was going to look for a ghost. My time would be much better spent if I topped off my lunch with a coffee ice cream cone from Sweet Sally's.

Upstairs the ladies tiptoed along the corridors, perhaps hoping to catch an unsuspecting ghost doing whatever ghosts do when they're not scaring humans half out of their wits. Mom peeked in rooms, but I noticed she didn't go inside two of them. I walked up behind her and tapped her on the shoulder, then jumped as she screeched and whirled to face me.

"Oh, Sylvia, why did you do that?"

"You didn't go in. Look, your buddies are milling around inside. There's nothing there."

Mom hung back. "I can't."

"Oh, Mom, for Pete's sake." I walked around her and strode to the door of room fifteen, started to walk through, felt a prickling sensation across my shoulders and the back of my neck, and slowly backed up to stand beside Mom.

"Okay," I said.

She glanced down the hallway. "I wonder where Linda is. Did she come upstairs?"

"I didn't notice. I'll go find her."

"Me, too," Mom said firmly as she hurried to catch up.

NINE

Linda was already on the tour bus, which the driver had brought from the parking lot. I climbed aboard while Mom waited for the others, who were drifting toward the bus from all directions.

Patsy was not with them. Nor had she been on the second floor of the Oatman Hotel, at least not while I was there.

A burst of gunfire came from in front of the bus. The sheriff had returned and was creeping toward the hotel with his gun drawn. Two desperados carrying bags marked with huge dollar signs burst through the door, firing their six-shooters into the air. They saw the sheriff and grabbed the two nearest women as hostages.

Marianne shrieked with delight as the bad guy snaked his money-toting arm around her waist and yanked her close. Gail saw what had happened to Marianne and stopped her own attempted abduction in its tracks by yelling, "My gawd," stomping on the villain's toe, smacking him over the head with her purse, and then kicking him in the shin with one of those heavy orthopedic boots.

He yelped in surprise and doubled over with laughter.

Marianne's robber tried to save the show by walking her forward so they'd be in between the crowd and his co-outlaw, but Gail wasn't having any of it. She grabbed Marianne's arm and pulled while she flailed away at the bad guy with her purse. I glanced at the sheriff. He was still in a semi-crouch, still pointing his gun, but his shoulders were shaking. He wasn't going to make it either.

Someone in the crowd literally crowed, and that's all it took to break up everyone else. Marianne freed her arm of Gail's grip and muttered something I couldn't hear. Gail huffed and drew her chin up, squared her shoulders, and stormed away. She whispered one more "My gawd" and climbed inside the bus.

By then, Marianne had both robbers and the sheriff off to the side, patting their arms and talking a blue streak. When she squeezed the sheriff's bicep, I had to stop watching. Marianne hung out with randy old Florida cowboys in rowdy saloons where the Texas two-step substituted for foreplay, and I didn't like where my mind was going.

Gail plopped down in the seat next to mine and tucked her purse between us. She looked straight ahead, never cracked a smile, and said, "What's next on the agenda?"

Diane boarded the bus in time to hear Gail's question. "Gold mine's next." She sat down behind us and made strange little noises that might have been giggling but I didn't dare turn around to check. Gail didn't seem to notice.

Linda moved up to sit by Diane. They whispered, cleared their throats, snorted, and finally burst out laughing. Gail turned around and gave them a look that would have stopped a mad dog in its tracks. Linda and Diane sat up straight and tried to look serious.

Then Marianne got on the bus.

"What the hell's the matter with you?" she shouted the minute she was in the door.

The three riders from Memphis stopped at the bus door and stared.

Marianne barreled down the aisle and plopped into the seat across from Gail. "You hit those guys. They were playacting, you silly old woman."

Gail's only response was to grab up her purse and clutch it in her lap.

The whole thing made no sense to me. Gail knew it was staged fun for the tourists. She's one of the bravest people I've ever met. She faces down those monstrous mosquitoes in the Everglades, for heaven's sake. Something else was going on and I had no idea what it was.

"You're jealous," Marianne stage-whispered as she leaned across the aisle. "Aren't you?"

Gail gave Marianne some kind of look, but I couldn't tell what since I was staring at the back of her head.

"Hah, I'm right," Marianne said out loud. "You're blushing."

What the hell? Jealous of whom?

Gail got up and walked to the back of the bus where she scooted close to the window. I'd bet a silver dollar she'd stuck her purse on the other seat so no one would sit there.

Marianne moved over by me. Before she could say anything, however, Linda asked the same question I'd pondered a few minutes earlier.

"Where's Patsy?"

The bus driver said, "You talking 'bout Miz Strump? She's walking around talking to people. Said to tell you she found out her friend that's missing was over here in Oatman this morning about the time the hotel opened for breakfast, so she's trying to find out more. Said if she wasn't here in time to go to the gold mine that I was to pick her up on the way back."

Damn. I hadn't thought about Sandra once since we got to town. By the sudden silence on the bus, I was guessing no one else had thought about Sandra either. Gail slid into the seat across the aisle from Marianne and said, as though no words or dirty looks had been exchanged between the two, "What do you think Sandra was doing here so early? Why would she come by herself instead of with us?"

"Maybe her friend from Needles met her here," Marianne said.

"Maybe she was meeting up with that cute outlaw," Diane said.

"Or the sheriff. Did you see the muscles on that young stud?" Marianne nodded her head as though she'd seen that and lots more.

I shook my head. That stud was at least sixty-five years old. Not that he didn't look mighty good for his age, with his thick white hair and rugged features. I tried not to let my feelings show. Apparently I failed or Mom's radar was working overtime as she walked past me toward the rear of the bus.

"Sylvia, don't act like such a prude," she whispered.

She was right. I had been known to look at a physically fit and handsome younger man myself from time to time. Boy FBI agent Damon Falls came to mind. Decorum dictates that a judge not blurt out comments about a guy's studliness, no matter what his age. Now that I was no longer a judge, however, maybe I needed to loosen up a little. I know my friend Tequila thinks I'm wound too tight, but she's a Latina with her own ideas about who a woman should be and how a woman should act. She swears I have an inner Latina, and she's promised to help free her if I'll try harder. That's why I'm taking those dance lessons. Cha-cha-cha.

The driver closed the doors and crept along the narrow main street. Random signs reminded me of the historic path we followed. In minutes we were wending our way toward the Lone Cactus Mine on a lonely road through unpopulated desert with miles and miles of nothing but hills and rocky bluffs and scrubby vegetation. And sand. There were a few other things out there, like scorpions and rattlesnakes, but when viewed from the inside of an air-conditioned bus, the desert seemed a benign and peaceful place, although a bit on the lonely side in my opinion.

I relaxed and let my mind wander. Hopefully, Sandra would turn up soon, safe and sound. I wasn't sure what we would do if we hadn't found her by the time our plane was scheduled to leave on Sunday morning.

The bus slowed and pulled through the entrance of the metal fence between the mine office buildings on the right and the parking area and outbuildings on the left. Gail, sitting on the left side of the bus, had a clear view of the cars in the lot.

"Look," she called out. "Is that Sandra's car?"

She was pointing at a little silver thing. And it was a Ford.

But Patsy was the only one who knew the license number, and Patsy was still in Oatman.

Linda, the first one off the bus, hustled toward the Ford and looked in the windows. She shook her head to tell us no one was in the car.

Gail took the lead into the mine office. "There's a silver Ford out there in your parking lot," she told the lady behind the counter. "Do you know who it belongs to?"

"Does it belong to a woman?" Linda said.

"Blonde, short, mid-sixties, square chin?" Mom added.

"Sounds like her," said the counter lady. "She said she was meeting up with friends who would come on a bus and that she'd wait and take the tour with them. Is that you?"

"Thank the Lord," said Linda.

"Where is she?" asked Marianne.

"Don't know. Said she'd wait around outside 'til y'all got here. Saw her talking to a couple of guys that was standin' by a fancy black Cadillac. Then I got busy and next time I looked out, I didn't see her. Ain't seen her since."

"The black car was gone when you looked?" I asked.

"Yep." She glanced at the clock on the wall. "You got to get on our shuttle wagon in the next five minutes. Otherwise you have to wait an hour for the next tour."

"Do we wait for Sandra or take the tour now?" Gail said.

"She might have ridden on an earlier wagon—could be waiting for us at the mine. Let's take the tour now and look for Sandra after, if she doesn't show up," said Diane.

"I agree," said Marianne.

Linda said nothing but filed out the door with the others.

I had a passing thought that Sandra might have gotten in the car with the two men, or perhaps been forced into the car, but I didn't bring it up. Mom and I exchanged a glance, then followed Linda.

The shuttle wagon resembled a buckboard with a canvas awning over the top. It chugged up the hill on the rock-strewn dirt road, bouncing in and out of deep ruts, slamming our teeth together, rattling our spines, and bouncing our unpadded rumps against hard plastic benches.

I stepped down from the wagon with a sigh of relief and offered a helping hand to those Flippers who needed assistance. We followed our driver to the mine.

A long history lecture came with the tour. We looked up when the funny guide, Crash, told us to look up, and peered into dark places when told to peer, from time-to-time examining tiny streaks of real gold in the mine walls. Lulled by the coolness of the place, we let ourselves be led farther and farther into the mountain, farther and farther down the mineshaft, until we finally stood at a dead end.

A ladder went up one wall, ending at a man-sized opening that tunneled into the mountain above our heads.

A wooden fence guarded the shaft that plunged downward. The air had a weird rank odor, like spoiled milk and decaying roses. Linda sniffed the air and frowned, then whispered to Marianne.

Crash motioned us toward the fence and held his lamp over the black hole. I reached out to test the strength of the barricade, giving it a little tug to see if it moved. It seemed sturdy enough. He kept talking, turned toward the shaft and looked down, inviting me to see for myself.

He stuck his hand out to stop me, muttered, "Shit," and then said, "Wait."

He faced us and held his hands out as though to usher a gaggle of geese away from his lawn. "Could you ladies move back a little? I need to check this fence again." The lamp quivered. Crash's hands were trembling. I tried to make eye contact, but he looked away.

Sweat broke out on my forehead and turned cold as ice in the chill air of the mine. "Is something wrong?"

He ignored me and once again extended his lamp over the hole. He stood very still for a long time, finally bending and lowering the light to get a closer look.

I joined him and peered over the fence. At first, all I saw was something yellow stuck on the ladder that descended into the shaft. The guide adjusted the angle of the light. My stomach lurched. Someone was down there. Someone whose yellow scarf had caught on a metal bolt protruding from one of the ladder's rungs and prevented her from falling into the darkness below. The scarf had caught her in a strangling hold which she could not possibly have survived…if she was still alive when she fell.

I looked at Mom and her friends. They watched me, waiting. "It's Sandra, isn't it?" Linda finally said. "I smell her perfume."

"I'm sorry, guys. It is Sandra. Her scarf is caught on the ladder."

"Is she dead?" Marianne asked.

"We can't know that," said Gail. "We have to get her out of there."

"My radio doesn't work down here," Crash said. "We need to go topside."

"I'm not leaving her here alone." Linda thrust her chin forward and furrowed her brow, daring him to tell her she couldn't stay.

"Me neither." Diane glared at the guide.

Gail and Marianne nodded.

"I'll get help," I said. "Give me your helmet and your radio. I know how to use it. What frequency?"

"You can't—"

"Of course I can. You won't get them out of here, and you can't leave us down here alone. I'll be fine."

He grudgingly handed me his helmet and the two-meter radio, gave me the regular and alternate frequencies to use for the mine office and the site manager. Then he flipped off the portable lamp. I knew why. If the power failed, and those lightbulbs strung along the mine ceiling went out, this little corner of the world would be mighty dark. I crossed my fingers and hoped the battery in the lamp on my helmet was fresh. I made sure I knew where the light switch was, just in case.

TEN

WILLIE STOOD IN the library's nonfiction stacks between two rows of bookshelves, but stared toward the end of the row where one permanently sealed window framed a small garden of deep pink azaleas and white impatiens. He saw neither books nor flowers, instead focusing inward, watching his sister plod along a dark tunnel. She followed the pale yellow light that bobbed along the path in front of her. She wasn't running. She kept a steady pace as though she knew where she was going and had no fear of losing her way.

Willie looked at the books on the shelves in front of him. What was he doing in a section on geology? Gold mines? He was looking for a book on the Everglades. Had he written down the wrong call number?

Okay, there's something going on, he thought. He returned to the table on which he'd deposited his book bag and the two books on Florida wildlife that he intended to check out. He sat down and planted his feet flat on the floor, placed his hands palm up on his thighs, and closed his eyes. With a few deep breaths, Willie relaxed. Images wandered in and out of his mind. An airboat whirled through the 'Glades. An alligator cruised along an irrigation canal and poked its snout above water.

Then total darkness. Lights flickered, flickered again and came on, revealing a string of bulbs stretched across the ceiling of a dimly lit room. Several people sat on the floor. Willie's eyes adjusted to the light. His mother and some of her friends made up most of the group. There were others he did not know. He did not see Sylvia.

The gold mine tour. But why was Sylvia alone in one of the mine tunnels?

Willie unconsciously squinted in an effort to see more clearly. Was someone in the group injured and unable to walk? He clenched his jaw, frustrated that he could not zoom into his vision and examine each person, especially his mother, who sat leaning against the tunnel wall, her legs extended into the center of the room. The lightbulbs flickered and went out. Willie was left with nothing but darkness.

Unable to call the moment back, unable to visualize more than a river of grass through which long-legged birds waded and searched for a late afternoon snack, Willie gathered his books, stopped briefly at the self-check machines, then biked home. As soon as he stepped into his apartment, he dialed his mother's cell phone. Her voice mail answered.

Willie shuffled through his notes until he found the phone number of the Laughlin hotel. He left additional messages with the front desk and on voice mail for his mother and Sylvia's room. After a minute or two of pacing back and forth across his tiny kitchen, Willie made a cup of chamomile tea and threw together a light meal before perching on a stool at his breakfast counter. He ate while he debated whether or not he should call his father.

Finally, he cleared his dirty dishes, washed them by hand, and set them to air dry in the drainer. He was once again standing by his telephone, trying to decide what to do next, when the phone rang.

"Willie," said his father, "I've been trying to reach your mother all day but either her phone's turned off or she can't get a signal. Do you think something's wrong? Have you talked to Sylvia?"

Well, that solves my dilemma, Willie thought. He'd never been able to lie to his father if asked a direct question.

"I haven't talked to either one of them, Dad. I was trying to decide whether to tell you. I was feeling uneasy. I—"

"You saw something, didn't you? What was it? Tell me."

Willie described the scene in the mine, reassuring his father that no one seemed upset, frightened, or injured. "But the lights went out, and I couldn't tell if the power failed at the mine or it was just my mind closing down the vision."

His dad didn't say anything.

"Dad, you still there?"

"Yeah. I'm thinking. Wait a minute. I want to look something up."

A few minutes passed during which Willie heard nothing from the other end of the line except a few thumping noises.

"Here it is," his dad shouted, nearly scaring Willie to death. "I knew I had it. I'll call you back in a few minutes."

"Dad? What did you find?"

But there was only the empty silence of a dead phone.

During the next two hours, Willie tried to call his father seven times but the phone was always busy. He dialed his mother's phone four times but she didn't answer. Then he called her Laughlin hotel again and asked whether the tour bus to Oatman had returned.

The desk clerk put the receiver down with a clunk. There was a sound of lowered voices, too low to hear the words. Another clunk and rattle as the phone was picked up.

"I don't have any information on that tour, sir."

"You don't know if the bus is back?"

"There's nothing I can tell you. I'm sorry."

"Does that mean you know something but can't tell me? Or does it mean you don't know anything?"

"I'm sorry, sir. Perhaps if you call later this evening? A couple of hours?"

"But my mother and sister are on that tour. I need to—"

"I'm so sorry but I have another call and someone waiting to check in."

And once again Willie listened to dead phone air as he wondered what the heck was going on. Where earlier he didn't want to assume trouble where trouble might not exist, he was now convinced that his family was in danger. He had to do something. And he had to do it from more than halfway across the country.

Who could he call? Did he have the name of the mine, or the mine's office phone number? He riffled through the information his mother had given him and found nothing except the schedule's reference to a gold mine tour.

Maybe calling the police was a better idea. Did Oatman have a policeman? Or was it covered by the county sheriff? What county, for that matter?

He turned on his computer and, while it booted up, he pulled his atlas out of the bookcase and flipped it open to the state of Arizona. After jotting down all the information he needed to report his concerns and ask for information about his family, Willie began making calls. Thirty minutes later, after talking to people at two of the three gold mines within twenty-five miles of Oatman in northwestern Arizona, failing to get an answer at the third after seven attempts, and getting nowhere with a county sheriff's dispatcher who sounded very much like she'd been trained at the same evasive answer school as the Laughlin hotel's desk clerk, Willie slammed his phone into its base.

The phone rang before he had time to remove his hand.

"Willie? I've been trying to reach you. Has your phone been off the hook?"

"No. I've been making calls. Who've you been talking to, Dad? I tried to call you a bunch of times."

"No time to chat now. I'll tell you when I get there. Pack some underwear and your toothbrush in that little green backpack you have. Don't take the big one. Pick you up in twenty minutes."

"Wait, Dad. What's going on?"

"No time. Pack."

Dead air again.

Twenty minutes later Willie threw his bag into the backseat and climbed into the passenger side of his father's car. "Where are we going?"

"Wait. Traffic's terrible. Gotta concentrate 'til we get on

I-95." Willie waited until they'd escaped onto the northbound interstate, although he had a hard time thinking of any time spent on Interstate 95 as escape. He had a harder time traveling south on 95 toward Miami, a ride comparable, in Willie's eyes, to racing in the Indy 500. He did not take that trip very often.

"Okay, Dad, we're on I-95," Willie said a few minutes later. "Tell me what we're doing."

"This is awful. There's a truck trying to climb up my tailpipe." His father yanked the wheel to the left and sped forward in the passing lane.

Willie cringed, then leaned his head against the side window and tried to visualize a slow stroll along the beach. His father finally pulled to the right and reduced his speed, so Willie spoke again. "Can you talk to me yet?"

"Sure. About what?"

"Tell me where we're going."

"Wait. Is that our turnoff?"

Willie shook his head as his father squinted and leaned forward, trying to read the signs. "Dad, shouldn't you have your glasses on while driving?"

"What does that sign say? You're not navigating worth squat today, son. Pay attention. You're looking for the airport exit."

Finally. The airport. West Palm Beach.

"You have a ways to go, Dad. I'll pay more attention."

"I'd appreciate it."

Willie waited a few minutes and then said, "Dad? What are we doing?"

His father reached over and patted Willie on the knee. "Don't worry. I've got it all figured out. Whoops. Traffic's getting jammed up. Shoot. Hope there hasn't been a wreck or anything. We've only got ninety minutes to park and get through security. You watching for that exit?"

"Yep. I'm watching."

ELEVEN

IT WASN'T THE FIRST TIME I'd been in a dark scary place, surrounded by strange noises and an eerie feeling that someone, or something, was stalking me. My rational mind said the noises were the echoes of my own steps, or maybe bats rustling around in the dark recesses. *Do bats hang around old mines? Or rats?* I shuddered.

It was unrealistic to think anyone was following me—unless he'd been lurking in one of the side tunnels or cubbyholes while the tour moved along the main shaft, or he wanted to delay discovery of Sandra's body and was willing to interrupt my hike to the mine entrance. A small rock clattered across the tunnel floor. I jumped, then realized I'd kicked it myself.

Stop it, Sylvia. I was being silly. This was nothing like the time I'd been confined in a root cellar with the trapdoor closed. Now that was dark. And since I'd been unconscious at the time and didn't know there was another person confined with me, I was justified in being frightened out of my wits when I heard noises floating out of the blackness as I came to. This walk was nothing like that, thank goodness. There were lightbulbs strung along the ceiling all the way to the mine entrance.

But then the bulbs flickered, flared, flickered again for a few seconds, and died.

I stopped in my tracks and waited fifteen seconds to see if the power came back on. Fifteen seconds during which I heard drops of water splash against the tunnel floor. Heard a rustling sound. Thought I heard the scrape of shoe against rock.

With a slow intake of breath, I prepared myself to see and

fight whatever was in the tunnel with me. As quietly as possible, I transferred the radio from my right to my left hand and reached up to switch on the helmet's headlamp. My eyes took a second to focus, but there was nothing within the lighted arc before me. I bent my knees and slowly pivoted to look back the way I had come, ready to lash out with a kick or bop someone up the side of the head with the radio if necessary.

Still, there was nothing to see within the range of the lamp. I straightened up, shifted the radio to my right hand, and turned toward the mine entrance. It was slower going since visibility was now limited to the lamp's reach, which had decreased from when I'd first switched the lamp on. I should have asked for spare batteries.

No, I thought. *Please don't let this happen.*

Nervous now, I picked up my pace. Ten minutes—I'd only been walking ten minutes. I was sure it had taken the tour group at least twenty minutes to reach the end where Sandra hung precariously over a deep vertical shaft. The group had traveled slowly on the way down, the Flippers dawdling as they stopped to listen each time the guide recited some new piece of mine history or tried to explain outdated versus modern mining techniques.

Maybe ten minutes is good. Maybe I'm almost there.

The lamp on my helmet dimmed and the arc of light tightened around me. I moved faster now, praying I wouldn't trip and fall as I tried to outrace the dying batteries. The light went out. My forward momentum pushed me three steps into the darkness before I could stop.

Okay. Now I'm in trouble.

I closed my eyes and listened while my optical memory erased the helmet's glow. Water dripped like a bathroom faucet that needs a new washer. Nothing else. I opened my eyes and peered straight ahead, or at least what I thought was straight ahead. There was a faint light in the distance. I reached out my left arm and touched the wall. With my fingers gently brushing rock so I wouldn't stray into one of the auxiliary shafts I knew were on my right, I continued up the gentle incline. Each step led me closer to the light and to point-to-point radio contact with a mine employee.

I was a few steps from the entrance when static crackled from the radio. I now had enough light to adjust the frequency and make my call, but no call was needed. There were voices just outside. I burst out of the mine and ran into three helmeted men toting bottles of water and energy bars, ready to escort the tour group to the surface.

"Lights are out all over," said the older one, who I was guessing to be about my age.

"Even the office," added another, who looked like he was about eighteen.

"You came out on your own?" The first man handed me one of his waters. "Crash shouldn't have let you do that. You stay here." He walked toward the tunnel and the other two fell in behind him.

"Wait," I yelled. "We have to call for help." The three men looked at me, then at each other.

"There's someone down that deep shaft at the end of the tunnel," I explained. "A woman hanging from the ladder."

"One of your bunch fall?" the third guy asked, his broken nose clearly obstructing his nasal passages. The in-charge guy stared at me like he was trying to figure out who the hell I was and why I was complicating his life this way.

"No," I said. "Well, she was one of our group originally, but she wasn't with us when we started the tour. Look, we're wasting time. You need to call the cops and an ambulance, and somebody's got to bring ropes and stuff to pull her up."

"You think she's alive?" the third guy said.

"It didn't look like it, but we need to hurry, just in case."

The in-charge guy finally took charge. "Phone's out in the office. Kelly, get down to my car and call the sheriff on my cell phone. Bring a couple of ropes with you. We'll go on down."

"I'm going, too," I said. "My mother's down there."

These guys moved a lot faster than the original tour,

covering the distance in less than ten minutes. I hustled to keep up, my step more confident on the path, now lit by their powerful lanterns.

"Crash, you down there?" one of them called out near the end.

"Hell's bells, what took you so long?"

"This lady here said you were all doing fine so we went over to Oatman and had us a beer first." The in-charge guy chuckled at his own joke, then strode over to the shaft, looked down, shook his head, and returned to his men.

Mom struggled to her feet and walked straight up to the jokester, standing on her tiptoes in an effort to look him in the eye. "Young man, our friend is hanging from that ladder over there with nothing more than her scarf to prevent her dropping into a hole so deep no one would ever find her body so she could have a decent burial."

Linda gasped and pressed her hand over her mouth.

"And that's if she's dead," Mom continued. "If she's still alive, and her scarf doesn't hold, she's going to drop into that hole. What if she's still alive? What if she's conscious when she hits bottom?"

Marianne jumped up and stood next to Mom, giving the two rescuers a dirty look. The men held their ground but didn't say anything.

"Do you think you could pay some serious attention to our problem now?" Mom said. "How do we get Sandra out of there?"

"Kelly'll be bringing ropes," the in-charge guy said. "And deputies. Strong men," he added as he looked over the elderly members of the tour group. "I'll climb down the ladder myself to get her good and secure so she can't slip out when we bring her up."

"There's nothing we can do?"

"Not a thing, ma'am. We'll need a lot of room to work. We came down to escort you to the surface."

Mom and Marianne consulted with the other three Flippers, then they all moved as one, creeping close to the railing, as close as they could get without actually leaning on it. They peeked over the edge and stared for a long time.

I finally walked over to join them. "What're you looking at?"

"I'm trying to figure out if she's dead," said Diane.

"I was wondering how she could have fallen down there without breaking this fence," said Marianne.

"I was saying a prayer," Linda said.

Marianne pointed at Sandra and motioned me closer. "Look at the way her scarf is knotted. Sandra always wore her scarves loose, the knot fastened on her shoulder with a brooch. That scarf is tight around her neck. She wouldn't do it that way."

I studied the scarf and what I could see of Sandra's face and neck, but couldn't tell whether the scarf might have been used to strangle her before she was hung from the ladder.

"Let's go," Crash said. "We want you up top before Kelly gets here with the sheriff."

Marianne, Gail, Linda, and Diane took one last look at Sandra. As the others left the fence, Mom joined me. "I think she was hung down there on purpose," Mom whispered.

I took a closer look. "Why would you say that?"

"Hush. Might be one of these guys who killed her." She pointed at Sandra's head and then I saw what Mom was talking about. The scarf was knotted in two places—once in a double knot at the front of Sandra's neck, and the second in a secure triple knot toward the ends of the scarf.

"No one wears a scarf like that," Mom said. "And without that big knot at the end, she wouldn't be hanging there at all. The scarf is too tight around her neck to catch on anything."

"Why would a killer hang her on the ladder? Why not just dump her into the shaft?"

"Someone wanted her dead, but not gone missing forever. Lots of complications when a person just disappears." Mom raised her eyebrows and gave me a knowing look.

"You mean, like settling her estate? You think her husband did this?"

Mom answered by putting her finger to her lips and whispering, "Shhhh."

WE REACHED the mine entrance at the same time a Mohave County truck arrived, followed at a distance by an ambulance that crept along the bumpy road as though the driver was fearful of destroying shocks and tires. I told one of the deputies about the body found in Sandra's hotel room and the interview with the Laughlin detectives. Maybe I shouldn't have said so much. The deputy ordered us into the bus and sent us to Oatman to wait while he called the Laughlin cops from Nevada, the sheriff of Mohave County in Arizona, and the county coroner. It was a kindly act on the deputy's part, since waiting in the hot mine office, where there were very few chairs, would have been tough on all of the tourists, but especially the older ladies.

As the Flippers straggled off the bus and milled around in front of the hotel, it was clear they weren't in the mood to have fun. The hotel restaurant was closing, but the saloon across the street was open, so we went inside the cool, dark room and sat down.

"What do you think Sandra was doing at the gold mine?" asked Linda.

The others shook their heads.

"I'm wondering what happened to Patsy," said Diane.

"Wasn't she supposed to be here waiting for us after the tour?"

I glanced at my watch. "We're almost an hour late. Maybe she caught a ride to Laughlin."

Diane and Linda were staring toward the door as though they wanted to make a run for it. Gail and Mom had their heads together, whispering.

Marianne, on the other hand, had perked up and was looking decidedly less somber than she had a moment before. She jumped up and strode briskly toward the bar, where Oatman's fake sheriff was nursing a beer. Marianne climbed onto the vacant stool to his left and two minutes later they had their heads together, giggling like a couple of kids.

I shook my head and tried to make eye contact with Mom, but she was busy patting Gail on the hand. Gail's lips were squished together and her brow furrowed—I could almost imagine a little smoke coming out of her ears. She slammed her purse down on the table and scooted her chair back, took a deep breath, and stood up. Mom reached out to touch Gail's arm, but Gail shook her off. Lifting her chin and smiling so broadly it looked as though she'd pasted the expression on her face, Gail sauntered to the bar and climbed onto the stool at the fake sheriff's right.

The rest of us released a collective sigh and leaned back in our chairs to watch. The poor man's head swiveled between Marianne and Gail for a couple of minutes before he slipped off his barstool and ambled out the door. Gail carefully avoided Marianne's glare and returned to her seat at our table, plopping her purse onto her lap with a satisfied nod.

Marianne stomped off to the ladies' room, but when she returned, it was business as usual. She dropped into her chair and said, "God, I had to pee so bad. You all order yet?"

Before we had a chance to respond, the real sheriff, his deputy, and Laughlin detectives Dunbar and Trilby walked in and advanced on our little group of defenseless ladies like a pride of lions going for the kill.

I looked at my watch. *Oh, hell,* I thought. The waitress was busy chatting up a couple of young guys at the bar. My stomach growled, but one glance at the expression on Detective Dunbar's face shut me up.

TWELVE

"YOU AGAIN." Detective Dunbar planted his hands on his hips and looked around the table before settling his gaze on me. "You…oh, hell!" He gestured toward me and muttered to Trilby, "You take 'em. I'm going to the mine." He walked out of the saloon, followed by the Mohave County lawman.

"Mind if I sit down?" Detective Trilby asked, even though he was already sitting before he finished the question. "I understand you ladies were the first to see the body…again."

Mom spoke up first. "No. Our guide found Sandra. He tried to make us stand back but we wanted to see."

Trilby stared at Mom. "Wasn't Sandra your friend? The one you couldn't find?" He pulled his little notepad out of his breast pocket and flipped through the pages. "Yeah, Sandra Pringle." He gave me a searching look, as though he thought I might have the full story written across my face.

"That's who it is," Mom said. "Our Sandra."

Trilby looked confused.

I explained the sequence of events, including what the lady in the mine office had told us.

"We hadn't talked to her since yesterday, Officer," Linda added.

"Detective." Marianne patted Linda on the hand to soften the correction.

"What?" Trilby said.

"Nothing. I was just telling my friend here to call you 'detective.' She called you 'officer.'"

Trilby focused on me again. "No one had talked to Mrs. Pringle since yesterday?"

"Except for the cashier in the casino." I reminded him of that last known encounter as Patsy had reported it.

Trilby glanced around the group again. "Patsy Strump, that's the lady who gave me the license number and description for Mrs. Pringle's car. Where is she?"

"We're not sure." Again, I told him what little we knew, that Sandra was seen in Oatman earlier that day, so Patsy opted to investigate instead of going to the gold mine. "We haven't seen Patsy since." I was sure Detective Trilby was about to lose his patience, but he seemed at a loss for words.

"Have you found out whose body was in the tub at the hotel?" I asked.

He nodded his head. "He was a PI from Vegas."

A private investigator?

"Hotel security said the guy was down here a lot. They thought he was running the take on a scam to someone in the city, but they couldn't figure out who he was dealing with at either end."

"How long had he been dead?"

"Not sure. Coroner thought maybe eight hours. We'll know more after the autopsy."

"So he couldn't have died in the hotel room?"

"Don't know for sure yet."

"That guy couldn't have anything to do with Sandra, could he?" asked Diane.

"I know for a fact that Sandra has never been to Las Vegas," said Linda.

"Why are you quizzing him about that, Sylvia?" Mom said.

Marianne sat up straight and opened her mouth, closed it, then opened it again.

Gail's eyes lit up as if she thought the fun was about to start. "My gawd. Sylvia thinks Sandra's death has something to do with that body in Laughlin."

Marianne looked at the detective. "What do you think?"

"Don't believe much in coincidence." Trilby pushed his chair away from the table and stood up. "You ladies stay here in case the sheriff has more questions. I'll check around, see if I can find Ms. Strump."

"We'll go with you, Detective," Mom said.

The Flippers jumped to their feet. Surprised that Trilby didn't order them to stand down, I let them go. At least they should be safe with a cop. The waitress watched the group straggle out the door before she finally sauntered over to take my order.

With an ice-cold longneck in my hand, I leaned back to think, stretched my legs out in front of me, and crossed them at the ankles. Thinking lasted about three minutes before Patsy strode in the door—sweating, flushed, and out of breath.

"Whoa, am I ever glad to see you," she said. "I figured I'd be hitching a ride across the river behind some big unwashed biker with greasy hair and bad breath." She waved at the waitress to get her attention and pointed to my beer.

"How was the gold mine tour? Did Sandra meet you there?" She glanced around the room. "Where's everyone else?"

"Patsy, I have some bad news."

"What? Sandra still not here?"

"We found Sandra."

Patsy emitted a sigh of relief. "Where was she?"

"But it's not good news. Sandra's dead."

I expected Patsy to be shocked and appalled, perhaps devastated by this news. Instead, she froze and studied my face as though wondering if I'd cracked an incredibly tasteless joke. Then she sat back and began a sequence of small movements—tilts of her head, mouth scrunches, tiny shrugs—that signaled an internal dialogue. "What happened to her?"

Trying not to leave out any details, I described the scene at the mine, the discovery of Sandra's body, my lonely trip to the surface, and what little I knew of the recovery efforts.

"Who's investigating? Must be Arizona. County?"

"Yeah, but those Laughlin cops are here, too. Dunbar's at the mine. Detective Trilby's out looking for you, and the rest of the Flippers are on his trail, trying to help."

"He took them along?"

"I reckon they'll be back after—"

"Patsy's here!" Marianne led the ladies through the front door and plopped into the chair next to mine. She squinted her eyes, checking out Patsy's sweat-soaked blouse and matted hair. "Where the hell have you been? That cop wants to talk to you."

"What happened?" I asked Marianne over the noise of sliding chairs. "Did Detective Trilby send you back?"

"Too hot, and Gail had to butt in every time the cop tried to ask someone a question. He was getting steamed."

"Don't start," Gail snapped.

Mom patted Marianne's hand. "Gail was trying to move things along. The detective would do a lot better if he'd cut to the chase while he's asking questions."

My mom, the self-appointed expert on police interrogation. Like me, she reads a lot of mysteries, but she prefers police procedurals over private eyes or amateur sleuths.

"I was telling Patsy about Sandra," I said. Everyone at the table fell silent.

They stared at Patsy for a moment, then all talked at once, each vying for Patsy's attention so they could tell their version of the story.

"Stop," Mom ordered. Some would have chosen that moment to take offense, but they quickly realized it was the waitress's approach that triggered Mom's abrupt command.

Trilby returned a few minutes later, followed by Dunbar and the sheriff of Mohave County, who Trilby introduced as Tony Yamato. Dunbar cussed and stomped around like a crazy man while Trilby was quiet and mostly stared at the floor. The sheriff grudgingly approached our table and told us the bad news. The in-charge guy had gone down the ladder as soon as he had the ropes, just like he promised. He tried to tie the first rope around Sandra's waist, but the bottom knot on her scarf gave way. The guy had his arms around Sandra's body when she suddenly dropped, almost taking him with her. Mine employees had told the sheriff that the ladders only went down to the small ledge in front of the first side tunnel. They were pretty sure Sandra had slid off that ledge and fallen deeper. Maybe her body would be recoverable, but they weren't sure yet.

Linda began to cry, and the rest of us became teary-eyed as well. The cops didn't give us much time to weep, however.

One by one, each of us were escorted to a table in the corner, where we gave our statements and answered questions from the three cops. During my turn, I gave them my observations about the condition of Sandra's body and what I thought the actual cause of death might be. I also squeezed in a few questions about a possible connection between Sandra's death and the body found in her hotel room. The cops weren't giving up much, but then I figured they didn't know much.

Trilby slipped in one comment about the PI's body being found in Sandra's room. Dunbar gave him a vicious glare, but Trilby turned in his chair so his partner couldn't see him and winked at me.

I decided to borrow Mom's cell phone and give Detective Trilby a call later.

Mom's cell phone! I'd completely forgotten about Willie. With everything that was going on, I was surprised he hadn't called a dozen times by now.

The detectives finally let me return to the group, and I took the empty chair next to Mom. "Have you heard from Dad or Willie today?" I asked her.

Without a word, she retrieved her phone from her bag and turned it on.

"You had it turned off?" I asked. "How long?"

She furrowed her brow as though trying to remember.

"Did you have it on at all this morning?"

"You know, I just don't remember. We used it in the restaurant last night." She started pushing buttons with her thumb, then held the phone to her ear. "I have messages," she said. She bent her head and listened. She looked up, studied Patsy's face for a couple of seconds, then exclaimed, "Oh, bother, it's beeping at me." She punched a couple more buttons, sighed, pushed another button and snapped the phone closed. She stuffed it into her purse. "Battery's going," she said. "Have to charge it when we get to the hotel."

I opened my mouth to ask if she'd heard even one message, but she gave a little shake of her head. I wasn't sure whether she'd read my mind and the answer was no, or if she was warning me off. I looked around the table at the weary, bedraggled group of ladies. They'd had a long and trying day and they looked so sad.

Diane, the last to be questioned by the cops, returned and collapsed into a chair. "We can go now."

"You guys wait here," I told them. "I'll find the driver and have him bring the bus to the door."

"Thanks, Sylvia," Mom said. "I'm pooped." Patsy and Linda nodded. The rest sat there, staring at their empty plates as though wondering how they could have eaten the whole thing.

"Do you think they have any dessert in this place?" asked Gail.

I escaped out the door before I heard what the others had to say about dessert.

It was late afternoon, still hot outside, but the sun's intensity was fading. Poised to begin its plunge toward the hills, it would soon balance precariously on a ridge before melting into the horizon. I strode up the street toward the parking lot, hoping I wouldn't have to search the whole town to find the driver. Patsy caught up with me.

"Did the cops tell you anything about Sandra?" she asked.

I shook my head. "I don't think they have anything. Without a body, what can they do? For all they know, Sandra fell accidentally."

A tiny beep from a car horn let us know we were in the way, and we veered toward the wooden walkway that formed a continuous porch along the storefronts. The car crept along the nearly empty street, keeping pace with us for a few steps. I glanced right, past Patsy, to see if the car's driver was trying to get our attention. The windows were tinted and I couldn't see inside. I audibly sucked in my breath.

"What?" Patsy said.

I shook my head and walked a little faster.

"You started to say something." The car sped up and then slowed again.

Patsy looked at it curiously. "What the hell?" She charged toward the Cadillac and rapped on the driver's side window.

The car accelerated, made a three-point turn using the parking lot entrance, and cruised past us again without slowing, driving southwest toward Bullhead City. I tried to get the license number but the plates were covered with mud.

Mud? Where did they find any mud out here? This place is dry as a bone.

"What do you think that was all about?" Patsy said.

"Could be the same car that was at the mine this morning. Maybe it's the guys who were talking to Sandra."

The car glided away in a cloud of dust.

"I'd better mention this to Sheriff Yamato before we go to Laughlin," I said.

"I can tell him. I have to gather Sandra's stuff and turn it over to the sheriff so he and the Laughlin cops can go through it."

The bus driver was leaning against his front bumper, waiting for us. I pointed out the saloon. The Flippers were already waiting in front of the door.

It was a subdued bunch of women who rode through the dusky light. They were exhausted and sad, but I thought they also looked a little scared. A member of their group was dead, probably murdered. There was a lot to think about. A lot of questions to ask.

Patsy tapped on my shoulder and pointed out the window at the rear of the bus.

I noticed first that we had passed three trailers set well back from the road on a long gravel driveway. Then I saw the black car that sat at the end of that driveway, facing the road. The car pulled out and followed us onto the Bullhead

Parkway, around the city, across the Colorado River, and south toward the casino. The Cadillac stopped at the entrance into the circle drive, its headlights spotlighting the Flippers one by one as they stepped down from the bus and filed into the hotel lobby.

Patsy and I stood in the light and watched the car. "A few pointed questions?" she suggested.

"Fine."

Before we'd taken two steps, the car pulled into the circle and drove forward.

"Hey," I yelled, waving at the tinted windshield.

The car glided past, pulled onto Casino Way heading north, and disappeared.

THIRTEEN

WILLIE HAD QUESTIONED his father's plan for getting from Las Vegas to Laughlin, but his father had doled out answers sparingly. Willie tried again after they changed planes in Chicago. "You didn't book a car rental?"

"Nope. Didn't need to."

"What are we doing, hitchhiking?" Willie's tone was more sarcastic than serious.

"Listen, young man," his father said with a mock tone of parental severity, "I can still drag you out behind the barn and give you a whuppin'."

Willie laughed. He'd never been whupped in his life, although the threat had been made more times than he could count. Not for anything real serious, thank goodness. Nothing that got him in trouble with the law or permanently damaged his body or brain. Probably the worst—at least the worst his father knew about—had been the day Willie convinced Sylvia to climb the old cherry tree with him, against their father's explicit orders. They'd broken two limbs off the tree, Sylvia fell and sprained her ankle, and the tree eventually died.

Noting how effectively his father changed the subject, Willie concluded that there was no plan at all, or there was a very specific plan his father didn't want to reveal until the last minute.

Why doesn't he want to tell me? What's the big secret?

"You didn't book a helicopter ride, did you, Dad? You know I won't ride in a helicopter ever again."

"Don't be silly. I don't like 'copters any better than you do. Did I tell you about the time I—"

"Yes, Dad. How are we getting to Laughlin, then?"

"There's a shuttle bus from Vegas to Laughlin. I checked."

"We're booked on the shuttle?"

"Well, not exactly." Willie's father pointed to the flight attendants advancing on their row with the beverage cart. "Would you please get me a diet soda? One with no caffeine. Wait, make it orange juice."

As Willie opened his mouth to mention his father's tendency to get acid indigestion from orange juice, his dad said, "No, better not do orange juice. See if they have diet ginger ale. Or ice water would be good."

"I read that ice cubes on most airplanes are full of bacteria, Dad. How about plain water?"

"I've been drinking iced drinks on airplanes for years. Hasn't killed me yet."

"I know. But the water's already cold. You don't need cubes."

"Fine."

Judging by his dad's pursed lips, Willie decided his concerns with healthy eating and drinking were interfering with his father's quality of life. The flight attendant handed a bottle of water and a cup to Willie, but instead of taking the cup, his dad leaned forward. "Could you please put a little ice in that cup for me?"

Willie took the cup of ice from the attendant's hand and passed it over without another word. He relaxed for a moment with his own bottled water, then reached into his shirt pocket for the unsalted peanuts he'd grabbed at one of the airport's newsstands. He offered some to his father, who wrinkled his nose, shook his head no, and pulled a bag of chocolate-covered peanuts from his own pocket.

He changed the subject again. Willie glanced at his dad thoughtfully, contemplated asking one more question, then decided against it. He took his paperback book out of the pocket in the seatback before him. His father closed his eyes and within minutes was snoring softly.

After an uneventful flight, during which Willie stubbornly

refused to ask any more questions, he and his dad grabbed their packs and headed toward the passenger pickup level.

"Dad, if we're taking the shuttle—"

"Won't need the shuttle."

"Car rental desks are—"

"Not renting a car. Come on, we're being picked up."

"By whom?"

"By an old friend of mine, that's whom. She'll be waiting by the escalator."

She? His father had an old female friend in Las Vegas? "I didn't know you'd ever spent time in Vegas. Does Mom know this friend?"

His dad hesitated, then said, "Nah, I don't talk about her much."

Willie swallowed nervously, wondering if he'd been given information he'd rather not have. He couldn't wait to see this mysterious woman, however. He scanned the crowd around the escalator, looking for attractive but not-too-young ladies who appeared to be waiting for someone. The only woman who paid any attention to the escalator's passengers was close to six feet tall, probably weighed in the neighborhood of two hundred pounds, and had coarse gray hair that was brushed back on the sides and short enough to stand straight up on top. She planted herself squarely in front of Willie's father as soon as he stepped off the escalator and grabbed him in a bear hug.

His dad hugged back, then pulled away and looked at her face. "You are a sight for sore eyes," he said. He reached up and wiped at his right eye, then yanked the handkerchief out of his back pocket and blew his nose.

Tears ran down the woman's cheeks. She looked to be about seventy, seventy-five, Willie thought. Skin brown and wrinkled, like she spent a lot of time outdoors. She moved well, no limping or shuffling. Maybe she was younger than he first thought, his age maybe.

"Frieda, this is my son, Willie. Willie, I want you to meet the very last one of my friends who's left from the war.

Least, the last one I know the whereabouts of. This is Frieda Schneider."

Confused, Willie looked at Frieda again as they shook hands. "You're friends from the war? You can't be talking about World War II. You must have been a kid."

"You bet it was World War II. And she was no kid, just doesn't look her age. Frieda was one of the nurses sent right up to the front. She spoke German and she could handle a truck, so she ended up driving an ambulance and doctoring in the field. I was a medic so we worked together a lot. This woman here, she single-handedly saved seventeen guys by piling them inside that ambulance of hers and blasting straight through enemy lines." Willie's father wiped his eyes again. "This woman's a bona fide hero."

"Oh, hell, this is getting totally out of hand," Frieda snapped. "Let's get out of here, and later on, young man, I'll tell you about what your old man did to save his buddies and exactly why we all got so close." She turned to Willie's dad. "I guess you heard Jamie died?"

"Yeah, I heard. That leaves you and me, Frieda."

"Yeah."

The two fell silent. Frieda pointed toward the door and led the way through, across the bus and van lanes, and into the short-term parking lot. "Hope you don't mind riding shotgun, Willie."

Shotgun? Was he riding in the bed of a pickup truck? "No problem," he said.

However, Frieda strode up to a big black motorcycle with a second seat astride the bike and a single sidecar attached. Then Willie understood. He was to ride in the sidecar.

"Helmet's tucked in the front with one of those Velcro fasteners." She used a key to open the lid of a storage box and pulled out two more helmets. She handed the red one to Willie's dad. "I know you guys are anxious to find your kin, but I've given up night riding since my eyes got so damned old. We're getting some shut-eye at my place and headin' out at first light."

Willie didn't protest, but walked straight to the sidecar and reached in to retrieve and examine his helmet, noting the built-in ear protection that would make the motorcycle noise bearable. Frieda also handed him a new pair of foam earplugs in a little plastic package. Willie nodded his appreciation. After securing the helmet in place, Willie climbed in the car and fastened the seatbelt. He stared straight ahead and waited, hoping the noise that did get through wouldn't send him careening back through time to his own war, the war that had changed him so much, both physically and emotionally. But then he thought of his father and Frieda, who also bore memories of explosions and blood and screams and death, and he told himself he'd be okay.

Right now he needed to focus on the mission. He had to find Sylvia and his mother and rescue them if they were in trouble. He wasn't happy about the delay, but neither did he want to end up in a tangled heap of machine and bodies if Frieda's night vision wasn't up to the trip. Willie placed his hands in his lap with the palms up, stretched his legs forward in the tiny car, and tried to relax.

As Frieda drove out of the parking garage, Willie hummed a mantra to the muted roar of the bike and tried to empty his mind of all outside thoughts.

FOURTEEN

MOM AND HER FRIENDS, grim and teary-eyed, trudged into the hotel and drifted toward the small lobby tucked into an alcove near the registration desk. A forest of live succulents, interspersed with philodendron arranged in tall planters, vainly tried to create a sense of privacy, but the noisy slot machines set inside the front doors and the cloud of cigarette smoke invaded our space and assaulted our already jangled nerves.

"This is driving me nuts," Marianne said. "Life is too damned short to mope about something we can't change. Buck up, girls. Who wants to meet me at the seafood buffet in an hour?"

I felt a surge of beer-flavored acid with a distinctly greasy edge. An hour? Would I be able to eat again in an hour?

"Fine with me," Mom said.

Patsy nodded and the rest of the group added their solemn responses. I'd go with the flow. Just because I joined them in the restaurant didn't mean I had to eat anything. Of course, if I had to pay the buffet charge to get in the door, maybe I'd opt out at the last minute—unless I was hungry by then.

Mom grabbed my elbow and nudged me toward the elevator. "I have to talk to you," she whispered. Obviously, whatever she had to say wasn't for the rest of the Flippers, because Mom clammed up when they followed us into the first elevator that opened its doors.

I looked at her, waiting, but she squeezed my elbow and stared straight ahead. These women were accustomed to the constant banter and sniping of old friends who'd grown as close as sisters. It was almost eerie to stand in the silence, as if I'd popped into an elevator full of strangers.

The secret Mom was dying to tell me would have to wait a little longer. Linda and Diane followed Mom and me to our room and asked if they could sit with us for a while. Marianne and Gail went to their own rooms, displaying no interest in their roommates' whereabouts.

Patsy went straight to her room, presumably to gather Sandra's effects and Barry Pringle's cell phone number for the detectives. I had a fleeting thought about the sealed self-addressed envelope in Sandra's luggage. Maybe if I asked Detective Trilby later, he'd tell me what it was.

I forgot about that envelope once we were inside the room and Linda said, "We don't actually need to sit with you because we're upset."

"Not directly anyway," Diane added. "We think there's a problem, but we didn't get anywhere talking to the others. Marianne said we're silly old women with too much time on our hands and we'd be better off taking some blackjack lessons in the casino, and Gail said it sounded like a conspiracy theory and wanted to know when we got to be so paranoid. So now we're talking to you to see what you think."

I took a deep breath, worried that they had a valid concern that would bring Detectives Dunbar and Trilby back to focus on our little group. My mother stared at them, her brain busily sorting through her own thoughts on the matter.

"What's the problem?" Mom said.

Linda took a deep breath, but before she could say anything, Diane blurted out, "The problem is Patsy. We think Patsy knew the dead guy."

I frowned. "The guy they found in their room? What makes you think that?"

Linda and Diane exchanged glances again, and Diane nodded encouragement.

"Remember the day we checked in," Linda said, "and we heard all that racket, and then Patsy came down the hall to get you, and we all rushed down to their room?"

I nodded.

"And we found Sandra on the floor?"

I was still nodding.

"Well," Diane said, apparently growing impatient for Linda to get to the point, "later on, after Sandra and Patsy were moved to their new room, I stopped by to see how they were doing, but I figured Sandra might be resting, so I leaned my head against the door to see if I could hear anyone inside, and they were yelling at each other. I couldn't decide whether I should knock or not, so I listened a minute to see what they were arguing about, but then the elevator doors opened and I didn't want to get caught lurking around their door, so I hightailed it to my room."

Mom didn't say anything, but she had her head slightly tilted, like a robin listening for worm sounds, and she watched Linda and Diane as though the ladies were centered on a specimen slide and Mom was viewing them through a microscope. "What did you hear?" she asked, getting straight to the point.

"Sandra said, 'Why did you hire him to do what I'm paying you to do?' and Patsy said, 'I thought we should have someone here, someone who knows Vegas.' Then Sandra said, 'I'm scared.' And Patsy asked her if she wanted to give it up, and then I heard the elevator, so I took off."

Mom nodded her head, as if she'd heard nothing more or less than she expected.

I was stymied. Detective Trilby had said the dead guy was a private investigator from Las Vegas who was suspected of shady dealings between unknown parties in Vegas and Laughlin. Now Diane thought—and had convinced Linda— that Patsy hired this PI without Sandra's knowledge to do something for her on Sandra's behalf.

"There's more," said Linda.

Mom raised her eyebrows expectantly.

She's eating this stuff up, I thought.

"Last night I heard a noise outside our door so I looked out that little peephole and saw Patsy walk by."

I pictured the lineup of rooms along the corridor. Patsy and Sandra's new room was at the opposite end of the hallway from the original room. The room I shared with Mom and the room occupied by Linda and Marianne were the only rooms between the elevator and the dead body room.

"She wasn't coming to see you?" I asked Linda.

"No. And she wasn't coming to see you, either. I opened the door a crack and she was almost to the end of the hall, by the room where they found the dead guy."

"That door has crime scene tape all over it. She didn't go in, did she?" Mom said.

"I don't know. I was afraid she'd see me, so I jumped back and shut the door. I wanted to watch out the peephole for her to return, but Marianne made me get out of the way so she could go downstairs. I guess I don't make a very good detective."

"That's it?" Mom frowned.

Diane nodded. "What do you think?"

"Well, it's certainly odd," I said. "But unless I go to Patsy and ask her—"

"Oh, no, don't do that." Linda shuddered. "She'll think we were spying on her. If she's a bad person, she might come after us."

"Let me talk it over with Sylvia," Mom said. She glanced at her watch. "We need to get ready if we're meeting the others for dinner."

Mom shut the door on Linda and Diane, then hurried over to me and whispered, "Patsy Strump is a Florida PI."

"And you figured that out how?"

"I didn't have to figure it out." She picked up the purse that she'd tossed on the bed and reached in for her cell phone.

"I thought the battery needed charging," I said.

Mom gave a wave of her hand to dismiss that silly notion. "I made that up. There's a bunch of calls, but the first one is from Willie and…here, listen for yourself while I check the room messages." She pointed toward the blinking light on the bedside phone.

She'd been punching cell phone buttons while she talked, and she handed the phone to me as she poked one last key.

Sure enough, Willie was delivering the report on his personal investigation of Patsy Strump.

So now we had a not-very-successful Florida investigator who was very much alive and a dead PI from Vegas. And both somehow connected to the recently deceased Sandra Pringle, who may have hired Patsy to do something, and Patsy may have hired the Vegas scumbag to do something. But what?

I handed the phone to Mom, and she punched more buttons as she walked across the room and settled into a chair by the window. "That hotel message was also Willie," she said. She put her cell phone to her ear.

What the heck was this Patsy/Sandra connection all about? I tried to think of all the reasons Sandra might hire a private detective, but the only thing that seemed likely was that Sandra and Barry Pringle were having marital problems and Sandra suspected him of infidelity. I'd heard that she could reach him only by cell phone, that she never knew exactly where he was. Maybe she knew which city he was in, maybe it was Vegas or Laughlin, but maybe she didn't know where he was sleeping. Maybe he didn't want her to know. Probably a simple thing for a private investigator to find out. There didn't seem to be any alternative but to ask Patsy. I couldn't believe she'd be a threat to any of us… *Or could she?* I wondered. Would it be better to quietly investigate the investigator? Could I do that without making her suspicious?

"Oh, dear," Mom said.

"What?"

She shushed me and pointed to her phone. A few seconds later, her lips firmly together and her brow creased in a fierce frown, she pressed a couple more buttons and put the phone back to her ear.

"Your father," she muttered.

"Dad? What happened?"

"Peter," she said into the phone, "I don't know what you think you and Willie are doing in Las Vegas or why you're not answering your phone if you're so worried about us, but we're fine. The last two days have been quite stressful, and now Sandra's dead and lying at the bottom of that horrid mine shaft, and we haven't had time to decide whether to stick it out until Sunday or come home tomorrow. Oh, bother, how could we leave tomorrow if you're on your way down? Just call me when you get this message."

"They're in Las Vegas? Why?"

"Willie saw you in the mine tunnel, and he saw us, and then the lights went out."

"Oh." I should have known that might happen. I should have made sure Mom had her phone on and that we'd called Dad so he and Willie wouldn't panic. "Are they driving down tonight?"

"He didn't say. Just said someone was picking them up at the airport and he'd call again later."

"Mom, is your phone still on?"

She glanced at the display. "Yes."

"And the battery is charged."

"Yes."

"Would you please leave it on the rest of the evening?"

"Of course, dear. Why would you think I'd turn it off now?"

I also took the time to listen to and delete the additional message Willie had left on the room's voice mail, so Mom and I were the last to arrive at the seafood buffet on the hotel's lower level. I planned to get my money's worth, even if I suffered for it later. Besides, I thought it would give me an opportunity to chat with Patsy. Since all of us were still less than lively, I didn't notice the tension that had resurfaced between Marianne and Gail until they approached the giant bowl of cut fruit and tried to spear the same hunk of watermelon. Marianne got the melon, but she stood frozen, staring at the marks from the fork's tines that clearly showed on the back of her hand. With an angry toss, Marianne hurled the piece of fruit off her fork and onto Gail's plate.

Playing the peacemaker, Mom wedged herself in between the two and set her tray on the serving table ledge. Then she grabbed Marianne's hand and rubbed the marks with her thumb while patting her on the shoulder. "It's okay," Mom said. "It didn't break the skin."

Marianne's face was red. She glared at the back of Gail's head. Gail continued filling her plate as though nothing had happened. Oblivious to the watermelon incident, Linda and Diane followed Patsy through the line. I overheard their attempts to strike up a conversation with our resident PI, asking how long she'd known Sandra. Patsy, who was right behind me, answered most of their questions noncommittally, probably unaware that she was now a suspicious character in their eyes.

I pulled out of line and stepped in between Patsy and Diane, claiming I needed more crackers to go with my cheese cubes. Diane briskly stepped around me and filled in the space I'd left between Mom and Patsy.

Patsy made eye contact with me, and whispered, "We have to talk."

Linda leaned past me and asked, "What about?"

Diane leaned around Patsy to see Linda's face. "Are you talking to me?"

Patsy shook her head in apparent frustration and bent over the serving table to load her plate with boiled shrimp. "I'll find us a table," she said. She backed away from Linda and Diane.

But I saw Patsy out of the corner of my eye, and she wasn't going anywhere. I tried to follow the direction of her gaze to see what she was looking at. I couldn't figure out what had grabbed her attention. There were plenty of tables with room enough for seven, including a couple of corner booths.

"Something wrong?" Mom said.

Patsy looked helplessly in my direction.

I grabbed the serving fork and plunked a generous serving of salmon onto my plate, then joined Patsy.

She gestured with her chin toward the far side of the restaurant where two men had entered the buffet line. They were big, but they were dressed like ordinary businessmen. They could be anybody.

I didn't understand Patsy's concern. "Do you know them?" I asked.

"No. But I saw one of them today in Oatman while I was looking for Sandra. I noticed him hanging around and tried to get a good look at him, but he walked up the street and got in a black car that was parked by the bus parking lot. I think he's the guy who was stalking us."

"Great. What do you want to do?"

"We're doing nothing," Mom said firmly. "The others don't need to know anything about this, or about you, young lady, until we've had our dinner."

"What's wrong?" Marianne asked as she joined us.

"Nothing," Mom said. "Where should we sit?"

"Over there, in the corner." Marianne led the way with Diane bringing up the rear. We ended up seated in the order we'd arrived—Marianne first, then Patsy, me, Mom, Gail, Linda, and Diane—so that Marianne and Diane sat at each end of the semicircular booth.

FIFTEEN

AT LEAST MARIANNE and Gail were separated so they could do no more than throw visual daggers across the table. Everyone concentrated on ordering drinks, salting, peppering, spreading butter on rolls, followed by a few moments of silence while most of the ladies attacked their food as though they hadn't eaten in a week. Patsy shoved her boiled shrimp and grilled vegetables around her plate with her fork. I stared at my salmon, wondering why on earth I'd paid twelve bucks for two bucks' worth of poached fish, cheese and crackers, and a wimpy little side salad.

"Those guys are still watching us," Mom said in a low voice, having apparently changed her mind about waiting until after dinner to talk about new developments.

Gail dropped her fork on her plate. "Where? Over there? My gawd, they are watching us."

Marianne, Diane, and Linda looked up. This elder group had no problem whatsoever hearing low or whispered conversations, although certain members wore hearing loss like a suit of armor whenever they needed protection from unwelcome ideas or advice.

"Don't stare at them," Mom said. "Who do you suppose they are?"

I looked at Patsy, but she was diligently attacking her veggies with a knife and fork, as though she'd heard nothing. The next thing I knew, everyone's eyes were on Patsy.

Unwilling to alarm the Flippers, or to unleash their curiosity and detecting skills again, I tried to change the subject. "Patsy, did you find everything of Sandra's that the police wanted?"

She nodded, pointing at her mouth to indicate she couldn't talk.

"You gave them Barry's phone number?" Marianne asked.

Patsy nodded again, still chewing vigorously.

"Did you try to call him yourself?" Gail said.

Patsy swallowed, probably convinced the Flippers would pelt her with questions whether she continued to eat or not. "I left him a message this morning, before we knew what happened to Sandra. He didn't call back, so I let it go."

Mom poked me in the ribs, but I didn't have a clue what she was trying to tell me this time. The two creeps across the room seemed content to remain in their seats, watching us.

"One of us must call Barry," Linda insisted. "The news about Sandra should come from one of her friends, not from the police."

"You call him, then," said Gail. "I never met the man."

"I don't really know him. Anyway, I don't think he likes me." Linda looked at Marianne expectantly.

"Hey, Sandra and I never saw each other anymore, except on these trips. I didn't even know her old man's first name."

"You should call him then, Kristina." Linda nodded as though she'd solved the problem.

Mom shook her head in protest. "I know his name, but I've never met him either."

How odd. "Wait," I said. "I thought all of you, including Sandra and Velma, have been friends for years. Weren't you neighbors in Deerfield Beach? Didn't you all go to football games together?"

"Ah," said Marianne. "You never heard the story about Sandra's divorce?"

I glanced at Mom, who shrugged and muttered something about "gossip" and "Sylvia was always so busy" before focusing her attention on Marianne, who'd leaned forward, ready to tell me the rest of the story. Patsy set down her fork and listened.

"Well, about the time that my Bobby was eaten by the alligator—"

"Oh, my gawd!"

"Marianne," wailed Linda.

Diane and Mom exchanged a glance, and Diane shook her head.

Patsy stared at Marianne, probably hearing of Bobby's fate for the first time.

"So, what happened to Sandra's marriage?" I asked, hoping to get the conversation back on track.

"Sandra was married to a drunk," Marianne said.

Linda rolled her eyes, but the rest of the Flippers nodded, ignoring the blunt nature of the announcement.

"She'd been putting up with his benders for over thirty years, but she finally got sick of cleaning up after him— especially after he puked all over her new carpet—and she literally shoved his ass right out the door. He lay sprawled out in front of their condo for about two hours while she made an appointment with a lawyer, packed a couple of bags, and called me to come pick her up."

"So…Sandra wasn't married to Barry Pringle very long?" I said. "What, a couple of years?"

"Not much more than that."

Now I was definitely getting curious. "Where did she meet him?"

Marianne looked at each of the Flippers in turn, but all shrugged or shook their heads, including my mother.

It was Patsy who finally cleared her throat and spoke. "She met him at a poker tournament in Miami Beach."

My first thought? That a friend of Sandra's had taken her to one of those Texas Hold 'Em tournaments like they show on television. That she'd gone for fun. Maybe the friend who took her was Barry Pringle. I was wrong.

"She had a gambling problem," Patsy said. "The trouble was, she usually won. She didn't have an incentive to cure her addiction, especially since she hid her winnings from her first husband, who would have sucked up every bit of it in booze if he'd only known it was there."

"Wow," Marianne said. "I had no idea. So she didn't disclose all her assets when she filed for divorce?"

"Nope. Her lawyer told her to keep her mouth shut. And then ten days after the divorce was final, that same lawyer introduced Sandra to Barry and the two of them—the lawyer and Pringle—hung around to watch Sandra rake in another fifty thousand dollars."

"My gawd." Gail's pseudo-whisper was probably heard by the two thugs across the room. "Do you suppose Pringle killed her for her money?"

Patsy shook her head. "He already has it. She invested everything in his new business. Part went into an account in her own name, but she gave him most of it. Didn't even make him sign a note."

The silence lasted a couple of minutes while the Flippers digested all this new information about Sandra Pringle, the woman they thought they'd known for nearly seven years.

Diane looked at Patsy. "How long have you known Sandra?"

"Not long." Patsy stirred uncomfortably, now that the conversation was focused on her.

"Yeah, right," Linda said. "If she never told us about all that stuff, how did you learn so much?"

"Girls," Mom cautioned. "Who Sandra chose to confide in and why is really not our business."

"I don't know why not," Marianne said. "Sandra invited Patsy to come on this trip. Insisted on it, as a matter of fact. I'd say we have a right to know how that came about, especially since Sandra's dead and we've got a couple of creepy guys watching us."

Once again, everyone turned to look at the two men who sat across the room. The two stared back, making no effort to disguise their interest in our little group.

Mom elbowed me again, and this time I passed it on in an effort to persuade Patsy to do a little more sharing. "Mom and

I already know your occupation," I said. "You might as well tell the rest of them."

"Okay. I wasn't Sandra's friend. I met her for the first time the day she showed up at my office without an appointment and told me she needed help."

"If you're a psychiatrist," Linda said, "you can't tell us stuff about Sandra."

"I'm not a psychiatrist. I'm a private investigator."

That stopped the Flippers cold for all of two seconds.

"Still, don't you have to keep stuff like that confidential?"

"Oh, hush up, Linda," said Gail. "I want to hear it all."

"There isn't much more I can tell you," Patsy said. "Sandra wanted to know more about Pringle's company and he wasn't talking. She knew the business had an office in Vegas and one in Laughlin, because that information was on the papers she'd signed. She thought having the rest of you along like it was any normal Flippers vacation would give her some cover, make it less likely that Pringle would suspect her of checking up on him. The story about her friend in Needles was supposed to give her an excuse to sneak away from the tour and check out the Laughlin office."

"What were you supposed to do?" I asked.

"I have a few connections out here. Mostly in Vegas."

"You mean like that dead guy you and Sandra found in your tub?" Diane's eyes narrowed. "You hired him to do something, didn't you? Linda and I heard you talking to Sandra."

"What was he, then? A hit man? Was he going to knock off her husband?" asked Gail.

"*You* hush now. You didn't believe us before," said Linda.

"And *you* could have been more convincing, instead of fluttering around like old biddies who thought they heard a fox outside the henhouse."

Diane pressed her lips together. I had a feeling she was holding back a few choice words in the interest of promoting peace and harmony. She turned her attention to Patsy. "So, was he a hit man?"

"Of course not." Patsy heaved a deep sigh. "He was a PI. I hired him about a month ago to check out the business address in Vegas in case Sandra and I couldn't get up there. If he found Pringle, he was supposed to follow him."

Marianne frowned. "But he died before he could tell you anything, right?"

Patsy nodded.

"What about those two over there?" Mom gestured toward the men across the room. "Do you know who they are or why they're here?"

"Maybe they're watching her," said Gail, pointing at Patsy.

"Easy enough to figure out," I said. "We'll split up and see what happens. But no one goes wandering off alone, okay? Especially not outside."

"What if I want to go back to my room?" Linda said.

"Find Patsy or me to go with you. I'll stay with Mom."

Mom nudged me with her elbow again. I reached down to rub my side, wondering if this frequent nudging and poking was bruising my ribs. She slid a small piece of paper into my hand. I unfolded it in my lap and glanced down to read the block letters: WE NEED TO FOLLOW HER. An arrow pointed to my left, toward Patsy.

I nodded.

Marianne announced that she was going to the restroom before dessert and told us to order her a piece of carrot cake. Patsy slid out of the booth and followed as though she'd also heard nature's call.

Marianne returned in minutes. Patsy did not.

I watched the two guys who sat across the room. If these guys had anything to do with Sandra's death, why hadn't they followed Patsy? After all, she was the person with the big connection to Sandra, the person who shared Sandra's room. Yet they continued to sit there, relaxed, watching me watch them, long after Marianne had returned and it was obvious Patsy had flown the coop. I grew increasingly uneasy, wondering if I should call Detective Trilby and report these guys. But Patsy had already reported the incident with the black car—at least she was supposed to. I needed to check on that.

If my mom and the rest of the Flippers are in any kind of danger—

One fact that had only amused and somewhat annoyed me earlier was now a comfort. Dad and Willie were less than two hours away. I wanted to talk to Willie, but I wasn't sure I should call him in front of the whole group. Then again, I didn't want to let any of them out of my sight until we were on our way home.

"Mom, may I borrow your phone, please?"

"Now?"

"Yes. I think we need to tell Dad and Willie what's going on."

"Calling that detective would be better, Sylvia," said Diane.

"Your dad and Willie can't do anything from Florida, except worry."

"They're already worried," Mom said. "They flew to Las Vegas, and they're on their way here."

"Willie must have had a visitation." Linda nodded knowingly, although she knew less about Willie's occasional bouts with clairvoyance than any of the others.

"Vision, not visitation," snapped Marianne.

Gail scowled. "Oh, Miss Perfect Person, do you have to correct every single thing we say?"

"Enough, you guys," I said as I called Dad. The phone rang several times before voice mail picked up, so at least he had his cell turned on.

Why doesn't he answer?

I was certain Dad would check his messages often, so I left one, asking Willie to call as soon as possible.

The Flippers were listening to every word I said. I debated whether to say more, decided I would, changed my mind, then changed it back again in the matter of a few seconds. "There were two guys over in Oatman today, and now they're here in the restaurant, and we think they're watching us. They haven't done anything I can tell the cops about." I glanced at Diane to make sure she heard why I wasn't calling the detective. "But to play it safe, the Flippers are going to stick together this evening. Just so you know, though, we'll be real happy to see you."

As I set my mother's phone by her plate, I glanced around the table at the solemn women who stared at me as though I'd sentenced them to a few years in prison.

Marianne waved the waitress away. "I think this development calls for liquid dessert," she announced. "To the bar, ladies?"

I couldn't remember a moment of my sixty years that I'd felt so little control over my life. These five elderly women were going to lead me around by my nose for the rest of the trip. I only hoped I could keep them together and safe until reinforcements arrived.

SIXTEEN

THE MOTORCYCLE'S forward movement stopped. Its rhythmic vibration became a shudder, then pulsed in time to a sharp cough. The bike's engine seemed reluctant to end its ride.

Wasn't so bad. Willie finally opened his eyes and glanced at his watch. The trip to Frieda's place had taken fifteen minutes. Their ride to Laughlin would take a couple of hours. He sighed.

I'll do it. I'll be fine.

The bike was parked in front of a double-wide trailer in a classy-looking trailer park boasting well-kept lawns and wide streets lit by electric lamps of an old-fashioned gas lamp design. Frieda pointed them toward the door. "Go on in. It's not locked. I need to cover my bike."

Entering the trailer was oddly like leaving one stage set and stepping onto another, since the inside resembled Willie's apartment more than any mobile home interior he'd ever seen.

"You boys'll be sleeping in the guest room," Frieda said as she strode in the door. "Down that hall. Got bunk beds since the room is so small, but you look spry enough, Willie. You shouldn't have any trouble with the upper bunk."

"That's fine," Willie said.

"Anybody hungry? Peter?"

"You bet. I could eat a horse."

"Willie, what about you?"

"Oh, sure. No horses, though."

She chuckled. "Not one of those animal rights folks, are you?"

"No, ma'am."

"Good. Put your stuff in the back room and do what you need to do. Bathroom's right there."

"Dad, have you checked your voice mail?"

"Oh, Lordy, your mother's probably fit to be tied." Willie's father felt in the side pocket of his pack, then checked his shirt, pants, and windbreaker pockets. Finally he pawed through the few items of clothing he'd brought along.

"Dad, did you lose your phone?"

"No. Here it is." He flipped the phone open, frowned, pushed a couple of buttons, then flipped it closed. "Battery's dead." He stood wide-eyed for a moment, his mouth askew.

"You forgot the charger, didn't you? Maybe Frieda's charger—"

"Nope. Saw her mobile. It's one of those old-fashioned things. Different kind of battery. She has a land line, though."

Willie's dad tried to call several times during the next hour, but the phone went directly to voice mail. Already feeling fatigued from the day's travel, and anticipating the early morning departure for Laughlin, Willie and his dad went to bed soon after they ate.

SEVENTEEN

We had settled into a cluster of comfortable chairs in a dark corner of the bar, all looking as though we'd been sucking lemons, most likely all thinking the same thing. *Am I going to be stuck with these women for the rest of the evening?* I love Mom and her friends to death, but their endless bickering exhausted me. I was ready for some serious silence and a good book. Maybe I wasn't the only one.

At least we didn't have much evening left. The one who would suffer most from the togetherness was Marianne, since I knew she'd planned to spend a couple of hours at the blackjack tables. I could only imagine the effect a table full of Flippers might have on the casino. How many times per hour would a casino manager rotate the dealers who claimed they were about to suffer meltdowns on the spot?

So far, not one of the Flippers had mentioned Patsy's conspicuous absence. I wondered why. I was certainly curious.

The women brightened considerably after the waiter delivered their drinks and a large bowl of peanuts mixed with crunchy brown things I couldn't identify. The ladies unfolded their tiny cocktail napkins and covered all available space with the snack mix.

I'd resolved to stop eating, and decided to forego my gin martini in the interest of staying alert. I had overcome that moment of silliness, however, and was slouched into the comfy cushions of a large easy chair. I pulled the toothpick from my drink and chewed off the first of three pimento-stuffed olives.

The Flippers were sucking up the hard stuff now—two Jack Daniel's on the rocks, a gin and tonic, one full-calorie beer, and a frozen strawberry daiquiri, the last sitting on the table, sweating profusely, while my mom once again rummaged through her purse.

"Sylvia."

Mom's right hand continued to bob and weave inside the bag while she visually inspected my pockets, lap, and hands. "Do you still have my phone?"

I raised my hands to show them empty, then stuck my hands in my pockets to show there was no need to pat me down. I'd goofed, though. I'd turned off the phone, contrary to my own instructions, and set it on the table next to Mom's plate, but I hadn't said anything to her at the time. I told the Flippers to stay put while I performed the search and rescue.

Our two stalkers were outside the entrance to the bar, talking to a third man. The new addition stood with his back to me, but it didn't matter. I'd recognize FBI agent Damon Falls in the dark. That's how powerful the attraction I felt toward this man who was way too young for me, who shamelessly flirted in an attempt to recruit me back into the service of my country, and who I hadn't seen in months, ever since I refused to infiltrate the social circles of retired crime boss Vincent Vortinto.

I didn't want anything to do with Vortinto. Retired or not, he was one bad dude. He'd set me up, hoping to force a legal decision to benefit his family. The way I saw it, there was only one way to escape his trap—gnaw off my foot. At least that's what it felt like at the time. I stepped down from the bench, gave the full story to the press, and tried to step out of Vortinto's life. But now this aging mob boss wanted to teach me how to play chess because he admired my game-playing skills. Agent Falls also thought learning chess would be great mental exercise, keep all my synapses firing. He said that Vortinto was good, won trophies at tournaments. How's that for a complicated situation?

What the hell is Damon Falls doing in Laughlin? Surely he's not following me around the country with his goofy employment offers.

Only one way to find out. I tapped him on the shoulder.

"Judge Thorn," he said, as if he had eyes in the back of his head and saw me coming. "I'd like you to meet Agents Frank and Billings."

I'd discovered his association with two thugs and he introduced us like we were about to do business. *Wait a minute. Agents? What the hell?*

"Men, this is the lady I told you about."

Frank and Billings. I pictured their names on a poster announcing a vaudeville act. Neither spoke, but they set their heads to rocking, keeping perfect time to the same beat. If they had moved their arms and legs in unison, I wouldn't have been surprised, but it didn't happen. Either Frank or Billings held out his hand to shake mine, and the other one delivered a mock salute. Both murmured "Judge Thorn" as they did their thing. I didn't want to know what else Falls had told them besides my name and title...former title.

"I scared those five little old ladies in there into thinking you mean us harm. I wish you'd told us you were Feds." About to vent my annoyance on the real culprit, Agent Damon Falls, I made eye contact with him. My brain fogged over.

Man, he looks good.

Falls grinned and waved his hand in front of my face.

The fog lifted. I focused on his ear lobe. "What's going on, Falls? Why aren't you in Florida where you belong?"

He took my elbow. "We need to talk. Guys, take a break. Come back in an hour."

As perceived danger made its exit, I had a strong feeling that real danger was about to make a dramatic entrance. I pulled my elbow free so the little electric prickles would stop shooting down my arm. I dried my damp palms on my slacks by pretending to straighten the creases.

"Stop calling me 'Judge Thorn,'" I snapped. *Too obvious?* Probably. His grin was so smug, I wanted to bring him down. I wanted to kick him in...well, his knee would be sufficiently satisfying.

I had to find out why Falls was here and how it might affect my innocent little travel group, but I had a priority mission to complete first. "I have to find my mom's cell phone. Get a table in the bar, Falls, far away from my mom and her friends. I'll be right back."

Moments later I returned, empty-handed. I reported to Mom, told her the staff was alerted and would look for her lost phone, mentioned that our mysterious stalkers were Feds, and motioned toward Agent Falls.

The Flippers leaned forward to inspect this new player, nodded their approval, and waved me and my martini off. I figured they'd move across the room and shamelessly eavesdrop if they thought they could get away with it. Apparently, they had something else on their minds. They scooted their chairs closer to the table and bent their heads as though inhaling fumes from their drinks. They didn't fool me. They were up to something.

Falls tapped on the table until I gave him my full attention. "Judge…Ms. Thorn, for the last month I've been working out of Las Vegas, temporarily assigned to MLU."

MLU was part of the Asset Forfeiture/Money Laundering Unit managed by the Criminal Investigative Division. Vegas seemed a good place for this wing of the FBI to have a strong presence.

But what does that have to do with me? I tasted my martini. It had lost its chill. "I'm listening. Continue."

"Barry Pringle has set up a hedge fund and established offices in Atlantic City, Las Vegas, and Laughlin. He has official-looking investor statements and stationery naming his corporate officers, including Sandra Pringle, by the way. The company uses retirees to establish a seemingly legitimate clientele to receive regular checks they think are dividends or capital gains."

"Most of the retirees I know don't have enough money to support a big operation. He either picks very rich retirees or he pulls in an awful lot of them," I said.

"The fund itself is bigger than you can possibly imagine. But only a few of his investors of record are real people, maybe ten percent. Those are the retirees. Makes the company look real, even though the rest of his client accounts are fictitious."

"And the investments for these fictitious accounts come from where?"

Falls smiled.

"Oh, I get it. You think this has something to do with Vinnie Vortinto, don't you?" I pushed my chair back and stood up. "Don't even think about it."

Falls stuck a piece of flypaper in front of me as I tried to get away. "One of the company's investments is the gold mine where you found Mrs. Pringle's body. Doesn't it make you the least bit curious how your mother's friend was involved, and who might have killed her? What if the killer thinks Mrs. Pringle might have confided in one or more of the Florida Flippers?"

He knows the name of my mother's little travel club?

Random thoughts and questions got all tangled up in my head. Feds were watching us. Was that because they thought we needed protection? Or because they suspected one of the Flippers of complicity in Pringle's crimes? Was one of Mother's friends an investor? Was my mother an investor? Or was one of the Flippers Sandra's confidante? I quickly scrolled across their faces, then focused on Linda, who was watching our every move.

Aha. Gotcha, baby!

She looked away.

I fought the temptation to learn more before launching my own personal investigation of the Florida Flippers, who were still conferencing and seemed to be in full agreement. All that nodding was making me real nervous.

I shrugged off my irritation with Damon Falls, as well as the uneasy feeling that the Flippers were plotting something. "Are the investments that feed the fictitious accounts cash payments?"

"Most are."

I tapped my knuckles on the table, wishing I had another martini. "Dividends and capital gains paid out by check?"

He nodded.

"Each transaction that goes through the bank kept well under ten thousand dollars?"

Falls nodded again.

"Not very original, is it?"

"Barry Pringle is not a great thinker."

"What do you want from me?"

He motioned me to sit down and then leaned forward, signaling me to do the same. Our heads nearly met across the tiny table.

God, he smells good.

"I want you to sit down with those ladies and find out what they know about Pringle's company and the gold mine. Most of them invested in this fund, Ms. Thorn, including your mother."

I hadn't wanted to hear those words, but they didn't surprise me. The sneaky way I'd been maneuvered into coming on this trip was now so obviously a Flipper plan that I couldn't believe I'd been that gullible. I was tempted to march across the room and wring some necks.

"By the way, where's Ms. Strump?"

Magic words. Ms. Strump. Now I remembered where I'd seen Patsy Strump before. It had been less than a year ago that Patsy had taken the stand in my courtroom as a witness in an identify theft case. She'd solved the thing herself while investigating a husband's suspicion that his wife was siphoning off funds from their joint accounts. Turned out it wasn't the wife at all. Because Patsy had access to everything her client owned and all his financial records, she easily traced the fraudulent transactions and presented the evidence to the district attorney's office for prosecution. No cops needed.

Or so I'd thought. Identity theft falls under the jurisdiction of the FBI. Had the suits been lurking in the background, maybe running the investigation? Did the PI get all the credit so undercover agents didn't have to testify?

"Does Patsy Strump work for you?" The last olive slid down the toothpick that still lounged in my empty glass. I popped it into my mouth while I waited for his answer.

"She works with us if we ask."

Unlike me, he means. "Fine. I'll talk to Mom and her friends."

"Not talk, Judge Thorn. Interrogate."

"I'll talk to them. You want more, do it yourself."

Oh, bite your tongue, Sylvia. Did I want the FBI to turn its full fact-finding force against the Florida Flippers? Would I do something that cruel to my former coworkers, my country's premier crime fighters? Of course not. I did as I was told. I returned to their table and surveyed the five innocent faces that stared at me expectantly.

"He's adorable," said Diane. "Do you think he'd mind being a character in my book?"

Marianne fanned her face to cool the hot flash she fancied herself young enough to have. "I'd rather he be the character in my be—"

"Marianne!" Linda squealed. Then she giggled. "Wish he'd stand up so I can check out his butt."

Gail's eyebrows hiked an inch closer to her hairline.

Mom nudged me in the ribs. "Is he the same one—"

"Ouch! Mom, stop poking—"

"Same one what?" Diane, ever the romantic, ignored me and honed in on Mom's words. "Does Sylvia know him, Kristina? Have they—"

"Oh, for gawd's sake," Gail said. "He's half Sylvia's age. She's not like Marianne."

"Stop it." I waved my hands in the air to shush them up, hoping to pinch the head off this discussion before it seeded a full-blown cross-examination of the wrong party—me. I briefly described how I'd previously met Agent Falls, then segued into what he'd asked me to do.

I glanced at his table, but he was gone. Agents Frank and Billings were there, nursing drinks from foam cups with lids.

The Flippers had gone uncharacteristically quiet. I tried

to interpret their expressions. Thoughtful? Alarmed? I wasn't sure. "Why don't we go upstairs, kick off our shoes? Mom and I have snacks."

Marianne grabbed her drink. "Bottoms up, ladies. Time to toe the line. Face the music. Pay the piper."

"Can we take these upstairs?" Mom's plaintive appeal accompanied a woebegone expression as she eyed her no-longer-frozen daiquiri.

I hated to do it, but I knew I'd get more cooperation by bribing the lot of them. "I bought two bottles of Arizona pinot gris at the wine shop in Oatman. And I have a big bag of chocolate, both milk and dark. I'll share if you will."

"Pinot gris should be chilled." There wasn't a one of these gals who wouldn't drink warm white wine when offered, so Gail's grumbled protest drifted away like a puff of hot air.

Diane, a self-proclaimed wine connoisseur who could recite all the finer points of each of the best-selling boxed wines, stuck her nose in the air and sniffed. "An Arizona vintage? How quaint."

I glared at Linda and Marianne. "You two have nothing to add about my wine?"

Linda shook her head as she watched her right hand scratch the knuckle on her left thumb.

Mom patted Linda's shoulder, then reached for her strawberry goop.

I shook my head no. "No time, Mom. Let's go."

Mom jerked her hand back, clasped her bag to her chest with both hands, and marched out of the bar, the rest of the Flippers scurrying to catch up.

EIGHTEEN

OUR BODYGUARDS WEDGED their bulk into the elevator with us, presenting a formidable barrier against anyone else who might want to come aboard. The elevator doors opened and the Feds peered out, each checking both directions of the hallway before letting us disembark. While the rest of the Flippers and I headed to the room I shared with Mom, Diane went the other direction to knock on Patsy's door. Our guards lurked near the elevator.

This vacation was turning into one wacky escape from reality. Impossible to take seriously, the plot was over the top, the characters out of control, and the setting contrived. Only when I reminded myself that two very real people were dead and that I escorted five women who could also be targets, did I stop viewing the case as though it were the debut novel of a novice crime writer.

"Okay, ladies." I shut the door after Diane returned from her unsuccessful mission. "I hope you have your stories straight so this doesn't take all night."

Mom was already tossing bags of snacks on the bed. Linda, uncharacteristically eager to break out the booze, had found the wine and was gathering cups and glasses. The rest of the Flippers sat down, but I'd never seen a less relaxed group of vacationers. Backs rigid and hands fidgeting in their laps, they waited.

Feeling a bit like Hercule Poirot during a climactic gathering in the drawing room, I paced across the room and back, hoping one of them would leap nervously to her feet and tell everything she knew. Instead, the Flippers sat, each one displaying an enormous amount of interest in her fingernails, shoes, or, in Mom's case, the nutritional information on a bag of mixed nuts.

"Mom, let's start with you." Seemed fair that I not give my mother special treatment.

"Me?" With a haughty lift of her chin and a tone so snooty I flinched, my mother tried to put me in my place.

I didn't back off. "Agent Falls told me you invested in Barry Pringle's hedge fund. When did you find out the setup was crooked?"

"For heaven's sake, Sylvia. I only invested a thousand dollars because Sandra asked me to."

"You were flimflammed, Mom, and you know it. When did you first figure out there was something fishy about this deal?"

"Me, too," Gail said. "One thousand. Sandra wanted us to pitch in ten grand apiece, but I told her she could suck eggs because I wasn't doing it."

I offered the three remaining Flippers a chance to spill their guts. "Marianne?"

"Don't look at me. I'm not as gullible as some people I know."

"Diane?"

"One thousand."

"Linda?" I'd saved her until last because I was convinced she knew something that was making her very uncomfortable. Maybe I was being mean, but I wanted her to worry about what the others might say. Wanted her fear to grow until it pushed the whole story out in a flurry of words. She was, after all, a Flipper, and the Flippers have a lot of trouble with verbal restraint. After the last couple days of holding it all in, Linda's head should have been ready to explode.

Instead, she burst into tears.

"Look, guys," I said in an effort to combat their reproachful looks, "I hate this, but the FBI needs to know. Who are you protecting? Sandra's dead. Maybe you have information that can help track down her killer. Even if she did something wrong, she didn't deserve to be murdered and hung from a hook like a piece of meat. And if you're protecting her husband, don't bother. He's a crook and, for all you know, he murdered his wife."

Every one of the Flippers now wore a pained expression. Linda busied herself hunting through her bag until she found a handful of tissues to sop up the tears, but she stopped when she saw that everyone was watching her. I could almost see her thoughts as she ran through her options.

One quick glance at the expression on Mom's face told me that she already knew the full story. For some reason, she wanted Linda to do the talking. I checked out the others. No matter how innocent they tried to look, the Flippers were plainly keeping their mouths shut to protect their friend. But it had become obvious they weren't protecting Sandra at all. They were protecting Linda.

I grabbed the second bottle of wine and made the rounds, this time grabbing a coffee cup and pouring some for myself. "To the truth."

There were a few mumbled "truths" in return.

Linda chugged her wine and set the glass on the bedside table. "I didn't do anything wrong."

"Of course you didn't."

Linda acknowledged Mom's sympathetic words with a faint smile before continuing. "It's just that I was so suspicious of Sandra, thinking she was as big a crook as her husband, and she was in so much trouble, and when I tried to help, I only made it worse. It's my fault she's dead." With that pronouncement, Linda collapsed backward onto the bed and grabbed one of the pillows to stifle her sobs.

I made a mental note to remove that particular pillow from my bed as soon as I could do so without attracting the group's attention. I had no desire to bury my face in a puddle of Linda-tears, if I ever managed to get to bed. So far, however, this question-and-answer session had all the signs of becoming an all-nighter. "Please, please, please, would someone tell me what the hell is going on?"

"Okay, okay." Linda threw the soggy pillow aside. I watched it bounce off the headboard and onto the floor.

The rest of the Flippers sighed and relaxed as Linda sat up on the edge of the bed.

"It's a long story," she said.

Great.

And it was indeed, when told Linda's way. It took her two hours to finish, and by then I was mentally exhausted from my efforts to keep the facts straight. Maybe "facts" wasn't quite the right word, since Linda's knowledge was almost all hearsay. The only fact to which she could attest was that she'd invested a full ten grand in Barry Pringle's hedge fund. Her motivation for doing so was a bit shaky, since she stated once that Sandra was very persuasive, but later said she felt bad for Sandra when she found out the rest of the Flippers were being so stingy.

At one point I interrupted Linda's rambling account in an effort to unscramble some comments she'd made earlier. "Why do you think you caused Sandra's death?"

Linda's eyes widened as she focused on the real source of her distress. She took a deep breath and made a visible effort to hold back another flood of tears. "I called Barry and told him the Flippers were on to his shady deal and that if he didn't return our money, we'd go to the cops."

"What did he say?"

"He said, 'Whatever Sandra told you is a goddamned lie, and if you repeat one word of it, I'll sue you for so much money you'll be eating cat food the rest of your life.' And he said some other stuff about Sandra being paranoid and a jealous bitch and if she didn't watch her step she was going to be out on her ass because he wasn't going to put up with it anymore."

"What did you do then?"

"I called the rest of the girls, and we decided to come to Laughlin like Sandra insisted and then keep an eye on her to see what she was up to. We wanted to know for sure if she was a victim, like she said, or if she was Barry's partner, like we suspected. We thought Velma would be here and that I would room with Sandra since I knew her better than anybody.

"Then all that happened with Velma breaking her hip and Sandra hiring a PI that we thought was just a friend. That's when I got mad at Sandra. She said there was something funny about Barry's investment in the gold mine, and I told her there was also something very funny about her and her friend Patsy. I even told her it might be dangerous to be alone with Patsy."

Linda swallowed hard. "That conversation took place before we left Florida. Even after Sandra disappeared, it never crossed my mind that she'd actually go out to the mine all by herself. I believed her story about the friend in Needles, and I thought maybe she had something going on with a guy just so she could get even with Barry for what she thought he was doing. And I didn't have a clue that Patsy was a private eye. I just didn't like the way she was always staring at me and asking nosy questions, and I couldn't understand how all of a sudden Sandra had a new best friend that we'd never heard her talk about before."

"Well, we were all a little jealous," Mom said. "But you can't blame yourself for what happened to Sandra. She hired Patsy, so she knew who and what Patsy was. If she chose to go out to the mine alone, she must have had another reason."

Like what? What would get Sandra down in that mine alone, especially with no emergency light or a way to summon help? But what if Sandra had no intention of going into the mine? What if she wanted to get into the mine office, maybe the files? Or more likely, what if she'd arranged to meet someone there? Either way, perhaps she chose to leave Patsy behind because…well, maybe she thought Patsy was a law-abiding PI who wouldn't break into an office after hours and snoop through financial records. Maybe I'd read too many PI novels, but I didn't believe that was the reason. So maybe someone else had been in touch with Sandra, someone who claimed to have information, but insisted that Sandra be alone when they met. I nodded to myself.

"What, Sylvia?" Mom, with her sharp eyes and mind, had caught the slight movement of my head.

"Would you please try to call Patsy's room?" I asked Diane. "Maybe she's back by now."

Mom was still watching me, but she didn't repeat her question.

"Not there." Diane was leaving a message for Patsy to call, when we heard a knock at the door.

Marianne jumped up at my nod and yanked the door open, revealing Patsy with Agent Falls standing close behind her. Both seemed reluctant to enter the room when they saw the Flippers.

"Everyone still up?" Patsy's raised eyebrow made it clear that she thought it was long past the Flippers' bedtime.

I was a little surprised that no one bristled at the remark. I was not surprised, however, that none of them offered to leave. What interested me the most was that Patsy and Agent Falls had shown up at my door together. I wanted to know why.

When I saw Falls take a step backward as though he planned to bolt toward the elevator, I contemplated a dash into the hall to bring the man down with a flying tackle. But an alternative approach seemed more appropriate for a former judge and current escort of an elder ladies' travel club. "Agent Falls, I need to speak with you. Could you come inside?"

Talk about your little boy dragging his feet as he grudgingly does what his mommy asks. He even sighed as he walked across the room. I summarized in five minutes the information it had taken Linda nearly two hours to communicate. She continued to sniffle in the background. When I finished, I told the ladies they were free to leave and suggested they get some rest since they still had the Saturday bus tour to Hoover Dam scheduled for the next day. The grumbling was audible, but I couldn't tell if it had to do with the early start time for the tour or that they'd been dismissed and wouldn't hear what Patsy and Agent Falls had to say.

By then, I didn't give a rat's ass about much of anything. But two things I did know for sure—I wasn't getting on that bus the next morning, and I was most definitely going to the gold mine.

Did I want company? Patsy? Agent Falls? My mom?

Am I out of my mind?

"Thanks for sending them off to bed," Falls said. "We need a few minutes alone."

I might have taken that differently if Patsy hadn't been standing there, watching us like the trained observer she is. Not to mention my mother, who had scrunched into her chair—the only comfortable chair in the room, I might add—as though to make herself invisible. I dropped onto the edge of my bed as I realized how tired I was.

"We want the Flippers out of harm's way tomorrow," Falls said. He glanced toward my mother. "That includes you, Mrs. Grisseljon."

Mom didn't say anything for a change.

"I want to send Frank and Billings along, but the tour is full, so I need you, Ms. Thorn and Ms. Strump, to give up your seats."

I exchanged a glance with Patsy. Even though we'd purchased tour tickets in advance, Patsy and I no longer planned to go anyway. Mom caught the look and pursed her lips in disapproval, or maybe envy. I made a childish face at her and she laughed.

"Oh, but your brother—"

"We're scheduled to leave on Sunday." I interrupted Mom before she could finish, guessing she was about to remind me that Dad and Willie were somewhere in or around Las Vegas and most likely on their way to Laughlin. Unless Mom's phone was found before morning, or Dad gave up on the cell phone and left another message on our room voice mail, we wouldn't know their plans until they actually showed up.

Falls looked at me curiously. "I know you're scheduled to leave on Sunday." He turned to Mom. "What were you going to say, Mrs. Grisseljon?"

"Nothing."

"What's happening tomorrow?" I said. "What do you want me to do?"

"We're conducting a raid on Pringle's headquarters in Vegas and Laughlin. I want you to stay out of the way." He turned to Patsy. "You, as well."

"Okay if we go other places, act like tourists?" Patsy asked.

"Like where?"

"Lake Havasu, or drive up to Hoover Dam on our own."

"Or back over to Oatman. I'd like to buy a painting I saw over there," I said, lying through my teeth.

"Okay. Don't go anywhere near Pringle's offices in either city."

"Fine," Patsy and I said in unison.

After Falls left, Mom sat quietly in her chair, clearly waiting to see what happened next.

I turned to Patsy. "Are you really going to Havasu? And do you just happen to have the phone number for that mysterious friend of Sandra's from Needles?"

Patsy reached in the pocket of her slacks and pulled out a small green address book, waving it in the air.

"Weren't you supposed to turn that over to the sheriff?"

"Apparently that has slipped through the cracks with the sudden jurisdiction shift. When the FBI showed up, the locals backed off, and I'm not sure what was communicated to the Feds and what wasn't. I gathered Sandra's things and left a message for the sheriff and for Dunbar, but nobody ever came by."

"Did you tell Agent Falls?"

"No, didn't think of it."

"Oh, for heaven's sake," Mom said. "Do you think anyone ever called Barry Pringle?"

"Not unless the FBI called him," I said. "Falls requested that the locals make no contact with Pringle, and he ordered me to butt out."

"The man's wife is dead," Mom insisted. "He should be notified."

"Maybe they haven't tracked him down yet. Or maybe they're assuming he already knows."

"You mean because he killed her?"

"Possibly."

"What are you doing tomorrow, Sylvia?" Patsy said. "I know you're not going to Oatman to buy a painting."

"I'm really going to Oatman, and I really might buy a painting. But first I'm going to the gold mine. Interesting country out there. The hills, winding roads."

"Sylvia," Mom said, "you be careful."

"I'll be careful."

NINETEEN

PATSY HAD BEEN GONE for more than five minutes before I forced myself off the bed, gathered my pajamas, and headed for the shower. A room key card went skittering into the bathroom. I'd kicked it with my toe.

"Mom, is this your key?" I reached for my purse and checked the pocket of my billfold. My own key was right where it belonged.

Mom held up her key, then tucked it inside her bag. She didn't look as though she planned to move out of that chair for a long time.

Before I kicked it, the key would have lain about where Patsy stood when she pulled Sandra's address book out of her pocket. Maybe her card had snagged on the edge of the little book and fallen to the floor. But if that were true, why hadn't she come back to see if the key was in our room when she found it missing? Unless, she hadn't tried to get into her room yet.

Something was nagging at me...not the key card...what was I missing?

The little green address book.

The book I'd found in Sandra's suitcase was a larger day planner with an address section in the back. But the book Patsy had waved in the air was a tiny green book about the shape and size of the object inside the sealed brown envelope Sandra had stashed among her clothes. I wanted to know if Patsy had opened the envelope, and if there was anything in that little book that Sandra might have wanted to hide. With a sigh, I threw my pajamas on the bed and took off down the hall.

Patsy didn't answer when I knocked. I stuck the key in the slot to see if it worked. All I got was the little red light. I tried again, but no luck.

I stared at the card for a moment, then looked toward the other end of the hall where the door to Patsy's old room was still crisscrossed with yellow crime scene tape. I looked at the card again.

What the hell! Why not?

I trotted down the hall and slipped the card into the slot. Green for go. Another slipup—the old room cards had not been deactivated. Faced now with overwhelming temptation, I took one tiny precaution before blatantly breaking the law. Returning to my own room, I leaned in the door and told Mom what I was going to do.

She perked up, her eyes brightened, and she jumped out of her chair like a teenager. "I'm going with you."

"Mom, I don't think that's a good idea."

She marched across the room with such determination that I stepped aside without a word and even held the door for her. "The cops let Patsy and Sandra transfer their stuff to their new room that first day," she said. "What do you think we're going to find?"

"Probably nothing. But if this key card slipped through the cracks, maybe they missed something else. Can't hurt to check."

Mom glanced down the hallway toward the elevator. "Where are the cops?"

"When Agent Falls was here earlier, he sent them on a break. They're probably downstairs. Let's get this over with before they come back."

Mom peered at the yellow tape as I pulled a strip free of the doorjamb. "You want me to stand guard?" She eagerly leaned forward, ready to hurdle the remaining strips at the bottom of the door, clearly hoping I'd say no.

"No. If we're going to get caught, let's get caught after we've been through the room. If you're hanging around out here when the Feds show up, they'll know right away something's going on."

With some expert maneuvering, and using a couple of tissues to guard against leaving fingerprints, we stepped inside, reattached the tape to the doorjamb, and shut the door.

"Wow."

"No kidding," I said.

The room was a mess. Drawers hanging out, television armoire doors open, bedding thrown in the corner, mattresses pulled sideways and half off the beds, and one bed itself askew. One thing was odd, though. The front half of the room had clearly been dusted for prints, but the back looked clean.

Mom looked at me with raised eyebrows. "The police did this?"

"The crime scene crew, I guess. But I don't think they completed the job."

"Why?"

"For one thing, it doesn't look like the whole room was dusted for prints, just this part. It was Looper who told Patsy the crew was on its way. They should have finished with the whole room before they moved the body." I kicked at the empty wastebaskets. "No discarded evidence baggies, no latex gloves or paper booties."

"We haven't seen the Laughlin detectives around this evening. Only the FBI agents."

I peeked in the bathroom door. "Don't touch anything, Mom. Just look around, in those drawers, check the corners."

It was the bathroom that interested me the most. After all, Sandra had discovered the body in the tub almost immediately upon entering the room. There'd been no time for Sandra or Patsy to empty their suitcases or hang things in the closet. If there was anything here, it was most likely left by the killer or killers who'd placed the Vegas investigator's body in the tub, unless, of course, the scene had been contaminated by the Flippers, ambulance guys, Looper, or the cops.

I nudged the bathroom door inward with my hip and stepped inside. The shower rod had been replaced in its brackets and the curtain partially pulled. Other than a few handfuls of wadded tissue stained with dark brown, probably Sandra's blood, there appeared to be nothing else in the room. I looked behind the toilet, behind the door, even lifted the lid from the toilet's tank. Then I leaned over and peered into the tub, elbowing the curtain out of the way to check the soap tray and then the drain. Something was wedged between the drain opening and the tub stopper. I tucked the tissue around my fingers and reached down to retrieve it.

"Sylvia. Someone's coming." Mom flipped off the lights and scrambled past me, climbed into the bathtub, and yanked on my arm, nearly tumbling me forward head first.

I knew it was a stupid thing to do, but I stepped the rest of the way into the tub with my mom and pulled the curtain closed. Mom scrunched herself down as far as she could and tugged on my arm to pull me down beside her. I sat, then fumbled around until I found the object from the drain, wadded it into the tissue, and stuffed it in my pocket.

The door from the hallway opened and the light came on in the tiny entryway outside the bathroom door. Someone tromped a few steps into the room. There was silence that seemed to last a long time. The tromping was repeated, moving the other direction.

"Hey, Trilby. Come look at this."

It was the Laughlin detectives. What were they doing? Sneaking around the FBI, conducting their own investigation? Could there be a jurisdictional rebellion in the works? Had the FBI pissed off the local cops by charging in and taking over with no offer to coordinate their efforts?

Oh, goodness, surely not.

"Looks like the Feds chased off the lint pickers before they were done." Dunbar's voice.

"You were here, weren't you?"

"Yeah, I was here. Standing in the hall getting my ears chewed off by some asshole citing fifty different reasons why I should have known this dead guy was part of a federal case.

By the time he was finished, the room was empty and the door was locked and taped."

Detective Trilby didn't answer.

Sounded like Dunbar and Trilby had problems. I was having second thoughts about calling Detective Trilby to get more information. If he was at odds with Dunbar, and if those two were trying to follow up on their investigation without pissing off the FBI, then I'd probably get the cold shoulder, no matter who I talked to.

"Who do you think killed the guy?" Trilby said.

"How the hell would I know?"

It was quiet for another long time, probably a good forty-five seconds. I imagined the two detectives nose to nose, fists clenched at their sides, glaring at each other. Then I heard the outside door open…and slam shut. The light was still on.

I motioned Mom back when she grabbed the side of the tub, afraid one of the detectives might still be in the room. We waited, and waited. There were no sounds other than the usual distant hotel plumbing noises. I finally forced my stiff, resistant knees to push my body into a standing position, and helped my mom out of the tub. I was more than ready to get out of that room.

The peephole in the door didn't help much. Since the room was at the end of the hallway, I couldn't see the elevators or the space in front of the other rooms. Mom eased the door open and held it so I could put my ear to the crack and listen. I didn't hear anything.

She pulled the door open wider, and I stuck my head out.

Frank and Billings stood in front of the elevators, looking straight at me.

They exchanged a glance, and then, without a word, turned their backs.

I didn't get it, but I wasn't going to fight it. After hurrying Mom through the door and pointing her toward our own room, I did my best to replace the yellow tape the same way the detectives had left it. That wasn't hard since they'd left two strips hanging loose. No doubt, Dunbar was the last one out the door.

One quick glance down the hall as we snuck back to our room confirmed that our bodyguards were ignoring us. One of them was talking on his cell phone. I'd bet a hundred bucks Agent Falls was getting an earful.

Mom and I scooted inside and collapsed onto our beds.

"That was fun," she said.

"It was not."

"Yes, Sylvia. That was fun."

I retrieved the wad of tissues from my pocket, unwrapped the bundle, and set it on the bed.

"What's that?" Mom said.

I pulled the tissues closer to the bedside lamp and bent down to get a better look. Mom scooted over to see what I was looking at.

"It's a rock," I said. Disappointed, I moved it with my finger so it flopped over onto its side.

"I have one just like that." Mom trotted across the room to pick up the purse she'd left on the floor by the chair, but this time she didn't try to dig through its contents. Instead, she dumped her possessions onto the bed and poked around until she found her little rock.

It was exactly like the one I'd pried from the tub drain.

"Where did you get that, Mom?"

"See this streak? That's gold. The tour guides at the mine have pocketfuls they hand out to the tourists when the tour is over. But if you didn't get it on the tour, where did you find it?"

"In the tub."

Her expression went from confused, to thoughtful, to *aha* in seconds. "This whole mess has something to do with the gold mine, doesn't it? The dead PI, Sandra's murder. You don't think that nice tour guide was responsible, do you?"

I hoped not. Could I have left my mom and the rest of the Flippers in the hands of a killer while I fumbled my way to the surface to get help? Wouldn't that be ironic? I shuddered at the thought.

"Oh, my goodness, look at the time." Mom thrust her arm in front of my nose as though her watch was the only timepiece in the room. It was two o'clock. In the morning. Mom and the Flippers, along with the two FBI agents, were scheduled to leave for Hoover Dam at nine. And Patsy and I were heading in separate directions to do a little investigating on our own. That's investigating spelled S-N-O-O-P-I-N-G. The local cops and the Feds were pussyfooting around, and God only knew how long it would take them to establish a joint task force of some kind. Maybe Patsy and I could turn up something useful to help them out. I wrapped the little rock in the wad of tissue and stuck it in my pocket.

TWENTY

I HEARD KNOCKING, but I couldn't attach the sound to a meaningful thought telling me how to make it stop.

It kept knocking and knocking.

There was also whispering. "Sylvia, you're closer to the door. See who's there."

I came fully awake when my mother got a tight grip on my shoulder and shook my body so hard my teeth rattled. Tangled in the sheets, I thrashed around until I was free, switched on the light, and then sat on the edge of the bed and stared at the clock. It was a little after five. In the morning. Three short hours after I'd gone to bed.

The persistent knocking was getting on my nerves. It took an enormous amount of effort to stand up and stagger across the room. I planted my face against the door, my eye to the peephole.

No way.

I lurched to my bed, turned off the light, and burrowed into the rumpled sheets. The knocking continued.

"Sylvia, who is it?" This time Mom didn't bother to whisper. As loud as she was, I thought her lips must be right next to my ear. I tried to swat her away.

She switched on the light. "Sylvia Lucille."

I sighed. *Suck it up, Sylvia. You've had all the sleep you're getting this morning.* And talking to myself wasn't going to help much, either.

"It's Agent Falls, Mom." FBI Agent Damon Falls. He was going to be so mad. I was sure he'd come here to bawl us out. I had sleep in my eyes and my hair was a mess and I was wearing old flannel pajamas with frayed cuffs and a torn collar.

Oh, what the hell does it matter?

I forced myself to get up, walk to the door, open it, and motion Falls inside.

For the next fifteen minutes, he lectured my mother and me on our responsibility to obey the law and avoid interfering in a police investigation. Then we got an extra tongue-lashing for putting ourselves in danger.

I tried to change the subject. "You know, Trilby and Dunbar were in there. Dunbar said—"

"I know. The guys told me. They were in the hallway when the cops strolled out of the room."

"What are you going to do?"

"Forget it. It has nothing to do with you, Judge Thorn."

"I'm not a judge anymore."

He threw up his hands, then pointed his finger at Mom. "Mrs. Grisseljon, you be on that bus when it leaves for Hoover Dam." Then he pointed his finger at me. "You stay away from the raids on Pringle's offices."

"Fine," we answered.

Falls stomped out of our room, apparently angrier than when he came in.

"Bossy dude," Mom said with a sniff.

"No shit." Anyway, I didn't know what he was so huffy about, especially the part about me putting myself in danger. Working undercover to find out what Vinnie Vortinto was up to in his professed retirement couldn't be any less dangerous, could it? Why was Falls working so hard one minute to get me to spy on a known criminal, and the next minute he was acting like a cranky old lady because I was mixing in FBI business? I was thinking he was one mixed-up kid. *He must be hell on wheels when he's hunting down criminals and terrorists,* I thought. Made me wonder whether I should laugh or cry.

Mom was still sitting up in bed, her back against the wall.

"I think he likes you, Sylvia."

It's too early for this.

With luck, I could squeeze in another hour of sleep before our alarm went off. Ignoring my wacky mother, I turned off the light and rolled back onto my bed. I pictured myself as I must have looked. Sleepy eyes, the smudged eye makeup I hadn't removed the night before, slept-in hair.

Nah. Not a chance.

AS WE SIPPED OUR room coffeemaker's brew and rotated in and out of the bathroom, my mom didn't repeat her less-than-astute observation about Agent Falls.

I, on the other hand, couldn't quite put it out of my mind, though the rational side of my brain reminded me that the guy was at least twenty years younger, and even if he did like me, there was a sixty-year-old lady looking back at me from the mirror. Her features were a bit refined without appearing haughty or ultra-sophisticated, hair gray, short professional haircut, skin tone good for her age, no jowls, no bags, not too many wrinkles. To me, she looked old enough to be someone's mother, without looking too motherly, if that made sense. She could be Damon Falls's mother, for instance. That did it. I finished primping and told Mom I was ready for breakfast.

The Flippers gathered at the elevator before going downstairs. Even Patsy came charging out of her room, looking as if she'd had eight good hours of sleep. Was she in her room when I tried to return the room card? Was she already asleep? Did she sleep so deeply she couldn't hear me knock? And what did it matter?

Two men waited for us in the hall, men we didn't know. They introduced themselves as the night shift, escorted us to the dining room, and told us our regular keepers would return in time for the tour.

"Whew," Mom said. "That's sure a relief."

I didn't know whether she was being sarcastic or sincere. I didn't ask.

I tried to shake off the weird stuff clogging my thoughts so I could focus on what I planned to do in Oatman and what I was going to do at the gold mine. So far, I didn't have a clue.

The rest of the Flippers seemed happy about the day trip, although they were quieter than usual. Maybe they saw it as a chance to get their mind off Sandra's death. And with their bodyguards along, they'd feel safe.

"What are you girls doing today?" Diane said, after we were seated in the coffee shop.

Patsy and I explained we'd be sightseeing on our own, but that we weren't going together.

Five pairs of beady eyes focused on me. I felt as though I'd been targeted by a bevy of red-tailed hawks, ready to dive and pounce at the first sign of movement.

"What are you going to do?" asked Marianne.

"Explore," I said.

"Patsy's a PI," Gail said, as though it was new news. "She can take care of herself. But what about you, Sylvia?"

"Sylvia can take care of herself," Mom said. "She used to be with the FBI, you know."

"She worked in the office," Gail said.

"But she was trained just like agents are. She knows those kicks and jabs and things. And she knows how to shoot guns. Lots of different guns."

"Do you have a gun, Sylvia?" Gail wasn't going to let this go, in spite of my mother's intervention.

"No, I don't have a gun."

"I know where you can get one." Patsy smiled sweetly, enjoying the moment much too much.

The hawks fixed their beady eyes on Patsy. "Are you packing heat?" Gail said.

"Of course not."

But I caught the slight lowering of her eyelids to hide the almost imperceptible flick of her glance to the left. I know it's a royal pain in the ass for a cop to declare a weapon in his carry-on luggage, because of the paperwork involved. I'd bet there was even more red tape involved for private investigators.

None of it mattered. To the best of my knowledge, Patsy was a licensed PI only in the state of Florida, so there was no way she could have brought a weapon on the plane.

I, on the other hand, had no current status as a law officer in any capacity in any state. I didn't own a gun, though I always kept my Florida concealed weapon license current, just in case. If the Nevada or Arizona cops caught me carrying, I'd be in serious trouble.

"We're not going to do anything that requires a gun," I said.

"Do you have a can of hair spray in your purse?" Linda asked.

The Flippers all nodded. "Or a hatpin," Diane said.

More nods of approval.

There was an abrupt outbreak of purse-digging. Completely useless purse debris came skidding across the table from all directions. Diane did have a hatpin—an old-fashioned, extra-long pin with a black onyx head. Linda's travel-size can of hair spray rolled its way into the pile. Marianne added a two-foot length of bungee cord with hooks at either end. Mom, just to be funny I think, tossed a book of matches onto the table. Patsy sat and snickered. Gail, still rummaging in her bag and muttering an occasional "My gawd" to keep our attention, finally produced her contribution with a flourish.

I glanced down at the table. "A tube of glue?"

"Hell, yes. Did you know you can glue a man's—"

"Stop!" Linda stuck her fingers in her ears.

"—hands together with a tiny drop in the middle of the palm? You smack his palms together and, just like that, he's not going to get them apart for hours."

"I don't think—"

"Nonsense, Sylvia," Patsy said, trying to look sincere and failing miserably. "You never know when you might want to poke a man with a hatpin and then glue his hands together."

I thought it more likely I'd jab my hand on the hatpin, which would then necessitate a tetanus booster, or that the hatpin would puncture the incredibly toxic tube of incredibly

powerful adhesive, and I'd end up with all of this parapher-
nalia, including the purse, glued to my hand.

My mother correctly interpreted my concern and pulled
one more donation from her own bag—the hard leather case
in which she carried her sunglasses. She wrapped her glasses
in tissues and tucked them in the outside pocket of her purse,
then picked up the hatpin and matches and placed them inside
the case. She rolled the tube of glue in another clump of her
endless supply of tissues and secured the package with a
rubber band she also retrieved from her purse.

Something else slid across the table from Linda.

I raised both hands in protest. "Stop. Really, thank you
all so much, but this is enough to cover every possible
emergency."

My tone must have expressed my frustration more than I
intended, because Linda froze and grabbed back the last thing
she'd tossed on the table.

"Wait," Patsy said. "What is that, Linda? Let me see."

Linda flushed, but she handed it over.

Patsy snapped open the small plastic box, then snapped it
closed and handed it to me. I peeked inside. Finally, something
useful. I tucked it safely into my purse.

"What was that?" Marianne asked.

Linda shrugged. "Emergency kit. A little flashlight, Swiss
Army knife, a whistle, and a panic button, like the one for
your car remote, only this one has its own little siren."

Diane laughed. "You want to give the rest back, Sylvia? I
think Linda has the whole package."

"No, that's okay." I scooped the stuff into my bag. "You
never know."

An hour later, I saw the Flippers to their tour bus, then
ran to my room for a few minutes before meeting Patsy. The
message light on the phone was blinking, so while I sorted
through the contents of my purse, which I'd dumped out on
the bed, I listened to the most recent call from Willie. He'd
found out from the front desk that the Flippers were on the
road to Hoover Dam and that Mom had misplaced her phone.

He wanted to tell us that, although they had been delayed earlier, he and Dad were finally on their way, and they'd probably pass us if we traveled by way of Route 93 from Kingman. He was relieved to find out no one was in trouble, so he and Dad could sit back and cruise Route 66 like a couple of old easy riders. They'd meet us for dinner at the hotel. I left the message alive and blinking, in case Mom got back before I did.

Apparently, Dad and Willie never received our message about Sandra and were, therefore, in no hurry to get to Laughlin. That was disturbing, but even so, I chuckled at the thought of Peter and Willie Grisseljon tooling along Route 66 on massive motorcycles. Not a chance. It was more likely an old brown clunker of a car rented from a cheap off-site clunker lot. Dad would be driving, since Willie didn't have a license.

I sorted through the contents of my purse and stacked the things I hoped I wouldn't need on the bedside table. The good stuff went into the roomy fanny pack I wore when walking. A quick visit to the restroom to tend to the essentials, and I was off to meet Patsy.

TWENTY-ONE

WILLIE DID NOT TRY to call his mom before leaving Las Vegas on Saturday morning. According to his dad, his mother always turned her phone off at bedtime, and she usually got up around seven. By then, Willie, his dad, and Frieda would be an hour south of Las Vegas.

At least, that's what Willie had hoped. Stopped by a traffic jam that seemed to extend miles and miles to the south of Las Vegas, he doubted they'd be in Laughlin by noon. Other vehicles were gradually silenced, and Frieda in turn shut down her bike. Much to Willie's relief, the desert wind gradually dissipated the fumes that had settled over the highway.

There was no northbound traffic. Willie extricated himself from the sidecar and walked back and forth nearby to stretch his legs. After a few minutes, he ambled along the road and struck up a conversation with a truck driver. When he returned to his dad and Frieda, who now had their helmets off and were standing in the roadway, he found them engaged in what seemed to be a spirited debate.

They turned expectantly at his approach. "There's a wreck up ahead," Willie said. "Bad one. Totally shut down the highway. That driver recommends we go back to Vegas and head south by way of Hoover Dam. He says traffic probably won't start moving for at least an hour."

"See?" Willie's father said to Frieda. "There's no sense in waiting here that long. There's no other way to get to Laughlin on this side of the river? No side roads?"

"I wondered about that." Willie nodded toward the truck driver. "But that guy said the only one he knew about was

Highway 165, and it dead-ends at the Colorado River. We could wait here a little longer—"

"Heck, no. I told Frieda we should cut through these vehicles and cross over to the other side. She says the bike is too big, but I said if she's lost her nerve, then she could ride on the back and I'd do the tricky part."

Willie looked at Frieda in alarm and vigorously shook his head to establish his firm opinion that his father had no place maneuvering the motorcycle anywhere.

Frieda threw up her hands. "Okay, okay. Never could win an argument with you. But the other way takes longer. We go down almost to Kingman, which is way east, and then take Highway 68 west to Oatman. Or," she said, "if you want a scenic side trip, we can take old Route 66."

"I don't know," Willie said. "Maybe if we get hold of Mom and find out everything's okay..."

A few cars were doing U-turns onto the northbound lane, leaving plenty of room for Frieda to maneuver her bike across traffic. Willie and his dad donned their helmets and climbed aboard, waving their arms wildly to signal the bike's entry onto the now-busy route north to Vegas.

Frieda backtracked through the city, and they rode on to Hoover Dam before she stopped. Willie, stiff and uncomfortable from his tensed muscles, hobbled around the bike until he loosened up. His dad was bent forward at the waist, his hands pressed against his lower back as though trying to push his hips and buttocks into place.

"You okay, Dad?"

"You betcha. Just working the kinks out." Frieda looked the two of them over. "Old wusses. I'll get us some java." She strode toward the coffee shop as if she'd never experienced an ache or pain in her whole life.

"There's a couple of pay phones over there. I'll try to call Mom again."

His dad was standing upright now, but still rooted to the same spot next to Frieda's bike where he'd stood ever since he dismounted.

"Dad, did you hear me?" His father waved and took a tenuous step forward.

"Are you sure you're okay?"

"Will you stop asking me that? I just feel a little odd. Like I'm bowlegged and wobbly-kneed."

Willie offered his elbow. "Here. Let's walk it off."

"Didn't think it would feel this goofy. I used to ride all the time, but it never felt like this before."

"How long ago did you ride?"

"Ummm, maybe…holy baloney, nearly thirty years, I guess."

"Better now?"

"Much. Go on. Call your mother. You got change?"

Willie flipped through all the dividers in his billfold before pulling one piece of plastic out and waving it at his dad. "Phone card."

"Why on earth don't you get a cell phone? You're worse than your sister."

Willie sighed, unwilling to replay that conversation. He hated the darned things. His fingertips fumbled the numbers so he often misdialed. He didn't like the way they sounded when they rang, all those silly noises and songs. Nope. He didn't want one and he wasn't going to get one.

He dialed his mother's number, but once again it went directly to voice mail. He left a message explaining where they were and why it would be lunchtime or later before they finally arrived. From his pocket he retrieved the slip of paper on which he'd written the number of the hotel's front desk. The clerk told him that members of the Florida Flippers had boarded a tour bus to Hoover Dam and left the hotel ten minutes before his call, and that his mother had lost her cell phone but it had now turned up and would be at the front desk when she returned. Willie relaxed. He left one more message, this time on the voice mail system for his mom's room. He figured there was no more need to worry. *Old Route 66.* Willie nodded his head. *Sounds cool.*

The caffeinated brew Frieda handed him tasted the way

burnt rubber smelled, but Willie choked down a couple of swallows before he gave up. Then he told his dad and Frieda what he'd learned from the hotel and detailed the messages he'd left for his mother and Sylvia.

"Sounds like everything's hunky-dory," Frieda said. "You boys ready for some fun now?"

Willie's dad didn't say anything, but his shoulders dropped at least an inch. Willie hoped his father was feeling better as some of the tension disappeared. Although Willie thought his dad's crazy plan was well-intentioned, his dad had clearly given little thought to the danger he'd placed himself and Willie in by arranging to travel on an ancient motorcycle chauffeured by an elderly Amazon.

Anyway, it was a done deal. Willie had no intention of sabotaging his dad's ride by pointing out all the risks they were taking. Instead, he tried to anticipate the things they might need to make the ride more comfortable. "Frieda, will there be a place to stop between here and Kingman? Like a restaurant?"

Frieda dug in the duffel bag strapped to the back of the sidecar, retrieved her road atlas, and then declared there might not be any services for at least fifty miles. All three trooped into the coffee shop and visited the restrooms. They met at the counter with the food and drinks they'd gathered just in case, although Willie's dad had already eaten half of the sandwich he was paying for.

"This road from Hoover Dam to Kingman and on down to Oatman is marked scenic." Frieda traced the route on her map. "There are mountains on both sides, but not big ones, I guess. Looks like they're not much higher than the city of Denver, and Denver looks like it's sitting in a hole compared to the mountains it's next to."

"You've never ridden this way from the dam?" Willie asked. He couldn't imagine living anywhere in the country without exploring his world for hundreds of miles in every direction. In Florida, he'd covered the state from Key West to Jacksonville and Tallahassee to Naples and lots of places in between. He'd been to the big parks in Kissimmee, ridden airboats through the Everglades, and gathered shells on Sanibel Island. If he couldn't get where he wanted to go by air, he took a bus. And if the bus didn't go there, he loaded up his backpack and walked.

He'd never thought of getting a motorbike. He eyed Frieda's monster machine, thinking he'd go for something smaller and easier to handle. He'd have to take a course to learn how, of course. Pass a test and get a license. Get one of these helmets that blocked the noise. Willie imagined himself on such a bike as he climbed into the sidecar, imagined himself on the road, getting to more places he hadn't been, getting there faster. It was something to think about.

Frieda's bike developed a bad cough after they crossed under Interstate 40 on old Route 66. They still had twenty-five miles or so left before reaching the ghost town, which Frieda had heard described as a "crazy little place that's more fun than Sin City on New Year's Eve."

Willie figured most anything would be more fun than that. But he was ready to get off the bike for a while, no matter where they stopped. He just didn't figure they'd be stopping in the middle of nowhere, in the desert heat, while Frieda hauled out her toolbox and tinkered with the engine.

"Frieda, have you read *Zen and the Art of Motorcycle Maintenance?*"

"Aw, hell, yes, Willie. Hasn't everybody? That's where I got my inspiration to buy this thing."

She waved a tiny wrench at Willie and pointed at her toolbox. "I got a wrench in there that's a little bit bigger than this. Toss it to me, will you?" While Willie searched the toolbox, Frieda sat back on her heels and stared at the gas tank with a frown. "*Easy Rider* was good," she said. "You like that one, Pete?"

"Not much. Didn't like the ending. You seen *Easy Rider*, Willie?"

"Sure." Willie handed the wrench to Frieda. She once again fiddled with the bike's innards.

With the sun getting higher overhead, and the heat increasing by the minute, and with no shade anywhere, it wasn't long before Willie was parched and uncomfortable and desperately hoping Frieda would soon get her bike repaired and ready to face the hills and curves ahead. He retrieved the stash of food and drinks from the sidecar. He urged his dad to drink water and motioned for Frieda to take a break.

There were a couple of good-sized rocks a few feet off the road, none big enough to provide shade, but at least they were flat enough to sit on.

"You think you'll get it running?"

"Oh, sure, Pete. This happens all the time. Few more minutes and we'll be on our way."

Willie hoped Frieda was right. They only had so much water. If they got stuck in the desert more than a couple of hours, they'd be so dehydrated they'd keel over on the spot.

"Anybody ever come along this road?" Willie said. "Seems deserted."

"I don't know. I heard bikers from all over the world come here to ride this piece of Route 66. Haven't ever done it myself. More fun to do with a buddy. Like with you guys. Or it will be when I get this danged thing running again."

The rocks were getting too hot, so Willie, with his dad, followed Frieda to the bike and stood nearby, ready to help if needed. Neither attempted to offer advice or ask questions, Willie because he knew nothing about the inner workings of motorcycles. That was one more thing he'd have to learn if he got a motorbike.

An hour went by. Willie sensed his body drying from the outside in, regardless of the amount of water he sipped. Finally Frieda struggled to her feet and tossed both wrenches into the toolbox, climbed astride her bike, and started the engine. It roared to life without choking or gasping even one time.

Willie applauded. So did his father. Frieda took a bow. And they were on the road again.

For the next ten miles, the only signs of life Willie saw were one rattlesnake near the road, a hawk overhead, and a couple of wild burros ambling across the desert. Because of the noise from their own machine, and the helmet he wore, Willie heard nothing but a steady drone from the engine. He was startled when Frieda tapped him on the shoulder and used her thumb to indicate traffic was approaching from behind.

Willie glanced in the mirror that was attached to his sidecar and saw seven black bikes. Bikers dressed in black. Black helmets with tinted face shields. As they drew closer, the bikers moved into single file, as though waiting for an opportunity to pass on the curvy two-lane road.

Frieda pulled onto a hard-packed patch of ground. The seven bikes followed. All seven bikers flipped up their face shields. Willie, his dad, and Frieda did the same.

Amazed, and unable to hear a thing the others were saying, Willie gazed at the young women wearing black leather chaps, leather vests, and dangly earrings. His dad waved at the nearest girl. She grinned and waved back.

Frieda and the lead biker spoke briefly, then the seven girls moved ahead but stayed close by. Willie didn't mind the escort one bit. The thought of being stranded as the afternoon wore on and the heat increased was enough to make him worry even more about his father's cockamamie plan.

It was obvious to Willie that dying in the desert was not uppermost in his dad's mind. He seemed to be living in the moment, and for the moment his father was riding on the back of a big motorcycle, surrounded by a pack of pretty female bikers.

I'm getting too uptight, Willie thought. Sylvia was always telling him he needed to chill. That's what she'd say. "Just chill, Willie."

He tried. As long as he avoided stressful situations— avoided the big, bright lights and the loud noises, and crazy traffic—he did okay. But the last two days had been filled with more anxiety and pressure than usual, and it had been more or less continuous. It was getting to him, and his dad didn't seem to notice. Sylvia would have sensed his tension by now. His mom would have asked if he was okay. But what was his dad doing? He was flirting with lady bikers.

Okay, what's the worst thing that can happen? Willie decided that was a stupid question, because a list of potential disasters zipped through his mind so fast it made him dizzy.

He focused on what he actually feared the most when he felt anxious—nightmares. If the nightmares started up again, he'd be a mess. He couldn't let himself slip back to Vietnam. He needed to concentrate on something else. *Think about,* he mused, as he closed his eyes and placed his hands palm up on his knees. *Think about...what Sylvia is doing right now.*

Willie pictured his sister as she'd last appeared in his mind view. She'd worn a hard hat and carried a radio and she'd trudged along a tunnel in a cave. Gold mine, he corrected himself. Where was she now? His mind wandered past the phone calls, the messages. She should be at Hoover Dam with his mother and the rest of the Flippers. They'd be eating lunch, taking the tour, hearing the lecture. They'd be relaxed and having fun.

He guessed that was why he saw and felt nothing. His family was okay. They were happy, relaxed. The tension left his body as though it had traveled down his neck and shoulders and arms and flowed right out the tips of his fingers.

The weight of his dad's hand rested on Willie's shoulder. Willie glanced up, saw his dad smile and raise his eyebrows.

Willie gave his dad two thumbs up. He was fine.

TWENTY-TWO

PATSY AND I TOOK the hotel shuttle to the small and very crowded Bullhead City/Laughlin Airport with the Saturday departures who were rushing to check in and make their way through security. It was actually more like rushing to get in a long line, then checking in to get in the next long line. Unfortunately, there was also a long line of folks dropping off keys at the car rental counter, so it took us forty-five minutes to accomplish a ten-minute task.

While we were waiting, I thought about the little green address book Patsy had let me examine as we rode to the airport. She had indeed found it in the brown envelope, but couldn't figure out why Sandra had it sealed up and ready to mail to herself in Florida. Patsy also could not decipher the entries in the book. I studied the series of numbers on random pages, but couldn't make any sense of it either. I returned the book to Patsy, and she stuffed it in her day pack. She'd have to rely on the usable information in Sandra's calendar for her investigation.

We finally worked our way to the rental counter and received our cars. I wasn't happy about driving a bright red vehicle in the Arizona heat, but we didn't have too many choices. I didn't want to wait for one of the newly returned cars to be checked and refueled.

When I reached Oatman, I drove slowly through the main drag to get another feel for the place. A few cars already lined the streets, and tourists wandered aimlessly along the boardwalks, even though most of the shops were still closed. The sidewalk vendors had begun to unload their T-shirts, belts, and cowboy hats onto display tables.

The Oatman Hotel was open, as was the saloon across the street, both advertising breakfast specials on the boards displayed out front. I smelled bacon and coffee, but resisted the temptation to stop for a second breakfast. A brown and white burro, trailed by her colt, trotted toward my car, abandoning the family who'd admired and petted but offered no food. I had no goodies to give them, and I wasn't interested in making friends, so I cruised past the creatures before they could block my path.

It seemed logical to go to the mine first to see what I'd missed on the original tour that was cut short by the discovery of Sandra's body. What I might see in the mine, or discover by talking to the tour guide, was unknown. I had no plan—random thoughts, maybe, but nothing of substance.

Old Route 66 winds through and past Oatman, curving through the hills to the north and east, eventually leading to Kingman. There used to be several operating gold mines in northwestern Arizona, but many of them were now shut down. The Lone Cactus Mine was one of the two or three open to tourists. There'd been talk of mining the site again, but the locals said nothing was likely to happen for a long time. "Politics," Jo had told us the day before at the hotel restaurant, because the county wanted a piece of the action. "And water," she added, because one of the Indian tribes owned the water rights. "And money," she concluded, because the mine didn't have enough investors to bribe the politicians and pay for water, too.

I'd heard no one, even the tour guide, say there were definitely accessible veins of gold left in that old mine. Maybe if I could complete the full tour without any new surprises, I'd find out more.

I navigated the winding road toward the mine, thinking some more about Barry Pringle's hedge fund and the iffy investments the FBI knew he'd rolled into the fund's assets. Were investors so gullible they didn't even try to research high-risk funds? Or was it only the elderly who were so vulnerable they'd rely on the advice of a friend without checking on the legitimacy, age, and ranking of the investment, or the reputation of the fund's manager? I was darned sure none of the Flippers had asked for, much less read, a prospectus. For that matter, I wasn't sure a hedge fund was required to publish a prospectus, since they were not regulated in the same way that mutual funds were. My own broker had told me not to include hedge funds in my portfolio because they were too risky for financially conservative investors in my age group. Willie agreed, so that was that.

The tall chain-link fence, bordering the mine property, appeared on my left when I rounded the next bend. A few hundred feet farther on, the two gate sections were open and secured to the fence with wire. Dangling from one side was a length of steel chain and a brass-colored padlock, their shine conspicuous against the rusty fence. It was logical to secure the property at night. The office would have credit card information and cash from tours and the gift shop. Maybe they didn't do a bank run every day. And there was equipment about—a couple of the buckboards used to transport tourists to the mine entrance, probably a gas tank for the vehicles. There were radios, hard hats, lamps.

There were several cars and a couple of motorcycles in the parking lot, and at least a dozen people milling around. I went straight to the office to see if I'd arrived in time for the first tour. Minutes later, I was squished between a young woman, a thin ring pierced through one side of her nostril, who was trying to ignore the squalling baby she'd left at the office with Grandma; and a huge tattooed guy, with long hair and a beard, who wore a sleeveless black leather vest over a black T-shirt and a black bandanna wrapped around his forehead. The Mommy smelled like baby powder. Amazingly, so did Biker Guy.

I checked out his tattoos. His arms were covered with intricate designs that didn't seem to be anything in particular. He saw me staring and raised his pant legs to show me more.

"Cool, huh?"

I grimaced. "You must have a remarkable tolerance for pain."

"It was nothing." He shrugged, as though the memory of the needle poking at his shins and calves didn't bother him one bit.

I knew better. The application of that one tiny butterfly perched on my left hip was the first and last time a tattoo artist's needle would come within fifty feet of my body. Make that one hundred feet.

The guy sitting on Mommy's right leaned around her to see what we were talking about. "You get those in Phoenix?" he asked the biker.

"Yeah." Biker Guy stretched his arms out to better display the art. "You get one?"

"Show him," Mommy ordered the guy on her right. I guessed he was her significant other when he obediently unbuttoned his shirt and displayed the alligator ambling across his chest.

"Ouch." I didn't realize I'd spoken out loud until several other passengers chuckled and nodded.

"You ever get a tattoo?" Mommy asked me.

"Um—"

"Me, neither."

I left it there.

Our group numbered nine people in addition to the guide. This time we were escorted by the red-headed youngster named Kelly, who'd been sent to call the cops and fetch ropes the day before. I wanted to ask where Crash was but didn't want to call attention to myself, or the fact that I was present at the discovery of Sandra's body. Kelly didn't remember me, or chose not to mention it if he did.

The guide's spiel was the same. They must have memorized their lectures from a script. I listened carefully as we descended into the mine, but this time I spent less time watching where I placed my feet and more time examining the walls and ceiling and peering down exploratory shafts.

Kelly called me back to the group at one point when I took

a couple of tentative steps into a darkened tunnel that veered off to our left. "Dead end," he said.

Maybe. But unlit bulbs were strung along that tunnel's ceiling, and there was a switch near the entrance. I slowed my pace and dropped to the rear of the group, feigning interest in the multicolored striae of the main tunnel wall. As soon as the last tourist passed me by, I flipped the switch. The lights in the side passage came on. I flipped them off again.

I hurried to catch up with the tour while I mulled over what I had seen in that one quick glance down the tunnel—boxes. At the point where the tunnel curved off to the right, a stack of boxes stood at least as high as my shoulder. Whether the boxes were cardboard or wood, I couldn't tell. If there was writing on the boxes, I couldn't see it from where I stood.

What the heck would they be storing down there if the mine was only used as a tourist attraction?

I moved closer to the front of the group so I was directly behind the guide. "Kelly, are the exploratory tunnels and shafts used for anything?"

"Nah."

"You said something earlier about plans to bring in new equipment, drill out some samples."

"Yeah…well, not plans exactly. More like they're thinking about it."

"Are they thinking about doing it soon?"

"Dunno. Geologists haven't been here to figure out if it's worth the trouble. They might decide the mine's played out. And even if they want to run some tests, we have to find a way to pay for it. Don't come cheap. We'd have to close down the tours if there was equipment operating on site."

"Do you think there's more gold down here?" Biker Guy asked.

"Not that I've ever seen," Kelly said.

I touched Kelly's elbow. "You say 'we' like you're an owner instead of a tour guide."

He grinned sheepishly. "A figure of speech, ma'am. I'm a student. I come down from Vegas for the weekends during the tourist season. Sometimes I drive the buckboard, do the tours, and when I can, I help out in town with the gunfights."

"So you're not around the mine all the time."

"No, ma'am."

"Do you stay overnight in Oatman?"

"Nah. Go into Bullhead City. If I've had a long day, I crash on the couch in the mine office."

"Must be awfully quiet around here when they lock the gate and everyone goes home."

"It is."

"Anybody ever try to break in while you were here?"

"No, ma'am. Why would anyone do that? There's nothing much here to steal."

"Then I guess they don't bother to lock the place up."

"Oh, yes, ma'am, they do. I think the insurance company says have to. Keeps kids from wandering in and getting hurt."

I wanted to know if people came and went after dark, if the mine owners employed security guards or guard dogs, and if strange things ever went bump in the night while Kelly was sleeping on the couch in the office. But I couldn't think of a good reason I'd be asking those questions, and I was afraid Kelly would mention my nosiness to someone in authority.

I glanced at Biker Guy, and then Mommy and her man, hoping they'd jump in with a question or two, but they looked bored and fidgety, as though they wished I'd shut up so we could get on with the rest of the tour.

We were only a few hundred feet from the end of the tunnel by then, a few hundred feet from the railing where the day before I'd stared down at Sandra's body. I stayed behind, lurking at the rear of the group, reluctant to be the first one to peer down the shaft.

It wasn't reasonable to think another body would turn up in this mine. For that matter, it was totally unreasonable for bodies to turn up at all. Yet here I was, mixed up in a bizarre set of events that had nothing to do with me.

By the time it was my turn to step up and *ooh* and *ah*

over the incredible depth of that shaft, there was no reason to hesitate. Yet, I hesitated.

I reached out and touched the end wall, exclaiming over the cool, slightly damp rock.

I wondered why the rock would be damp when the air outside the mine was so dry.

I stepped back and looked overhead, toward the upward extension of the shaft. Another ladder was anchored there, leading up to a large opening that branched off at a ninety-degree angle from the main tunnel. The opening into this new tunnel was dark, almost black. I took another step back in an effort to see more. Another step.

"What are you looking at?" Kelly asked.

"Nothing," I said. "I'm a little afraid of heights. I was trying to talk myself into doing this." I walked forward to stand by the railing.

"You don't have to look down there if you don't want to," said Biker Guy. He gallantly stepped to my side and leveled a menacing look at Kelly.

"Heck, no. You should have said." Kelly looked at me curiously before turning to herd the group away from the edge and finish his lecture.

I returned to my vantage point and looked up, trying one more time to see into the tunnel's blackness.

"And here's the best way to show you how dark it gets when the lights go out," Kelly said.

And the lights went out.

Amidst the squeals from the ladies and a startled "Whoa" from at least one male, Kelly yammered on about mines and mine disasters for a few seconds before turning the lights back on.

What had seemed to be a pale ghostly glow from the ceiling as we made our way down the tunnel was now a blinding glare. I rubbed my eyes and waited for them to adjust to the light. I walked closer to the railing and let my gaze drift slowly down the ladder. Finally, I looked down. A tiny piece of Sandra's scarf was caught in the joint where the hook entered the side of the descending ladder. I tried to swallow, but there was a lump in my throat. I backed away with every intention of catching up to the tour, until I saw how far ahead they were, and that no one had noticed my absence.

I strolled along, checking out the rock formation as though I knew exactly what I was looking at, rubbing my finger on little deposits of light-colored porous material that had formed anywhere moisture was present. Dropping back far enough that I could no longer hear the group's chatter or Kelly's comments, I stopped. Once they'd rounded a slight curve just past the side tunnel where I'd caught a glimpse of boxes, we could no longer see each other. That suited me fine.

I flipped the light switch on and hurried down the passage toward the crates. The secondary lights went out just before I reached the boxes. Before I had time to panic, they came back on.

Crash, the guide from the previous day's disastrous tour, was at the switch. "You're not supposed to be here."

"Where does this tunnel go?"

"Come on out. We get in big trouble with the insurance company if a tourist gets hurt in the mine, especially if the guide lets someone wander off alone."

"There are boxes stored here, you know." As soon as the words were out of my mouth, I realized that was a stupid thing to say. Crash's expression went from concerned to pissed off so fast he looked like man turned werewolf. I expected him to snarl his next words and bare his teeth.

Instead, he marched toward me, grabbed my elbow, and pushed me toward the main passageway. I didn't resist, but suffered a brief moment of anxiety when I imagined Crash shoving me left toward the death shaft, instead of right toward my tour group. My fears were unfounded. Crash took me to Kelly's side, ordered Kelly to keep a better eye on his charges, and then stomped off.

Kelly gave me a reproachful look and watched me like a hawk until we reached the surface.

TWENTY-THREE

I HAD THE UNCOMFORTABLE feeling that all eyes were on me as I walked from the mine's buckboard to my car, just as I'd been the main item of interest during the ride from the mine entrance to the parking lot. The group had quickly shifted their attention from Biker Guy's tattoos to the nice gray-haired lady who'd drawn attention to herself, advertised her secretly nonexistent fear of heights, and then wandered off alone, thereby putting her safety at risk. They hadn't said much, but I was sure they thought I was odd. I sat and smiled, trying to look like a happy tourist experiencing a wonderful adventure.

Kelly didn't let me go off alone again, even to my car. "Ma'am, which car is yours?"

I pointed to my red sweatbox.

He made one of those sweeping gestures, graciously letting me lead the way. It was annoying, obviously sarcastic, and designed to show his employers that he had the unruly tourist under control. But as I brushed past him and started toward my car, I sensed him step closer.

"Don't turn around," he cautioned.

I slowed, but kept walking.

"What were you looking for in the mine?"

Well, I thought. *What's this?* A possible source of information? Or had someone given Kelly instructions to find out who I was and what I was up to? Better to err on the side of caution. "Honestly, nothing. It was stupid to get separated from the group. I'm sorry."

I unlocked the car door, and Kelly opened it for me. I

started the engine and cranked up the air conditioner, then got out to let the car cool down.

"You don't have to wait," I told Kelly. "I'll be fine."

"No trouble, ma'am. Do you have any water?"

"No."

"I'll get some for you."

Kelly trotted toward the office. He returned in minutes with a cold bottle of water that had already begun to sweat.

"Listen," he said, "I'm heading into Oatman in thirty minutes or so. If you want to, you know, ask any more questions about the mine, or rock formations, anything like that, I'll be at the hotel for lunch before the afternoon tours."

I nodded. "Sure. Maybe I'll see you there."

A couple of minutes later, I was on my way, my car semi-cooled and my mind abuzz as it tried to sort out Kelly's words and intentions. I had a feeling there was something he wanted to tell me, but I couldn't figure out why, since he didn't know anything about me, except that I was nosy and peculiar.

I hadn't driven more than a quarter of a mile before I noticed the big black 4x4 pickup coming up fast in my rearview mirror. Too fast for the winding road. There was no place to pull over, not even a wide shoulder. Holding as far to the right as I dared, I sucked in my breath as the truck rushed closer, the driver invisible behind the tinted windshield. Would he slam on his brakes at the last second? Or take a chance and pass on the upcoming blind curve?

As the truck loomed in my mirror, it lined up squarely behind my car.

I gripped the steering wheel and took my foot off the brake. The impact was deafening. Metal crunched. Glass shattered. Then the damned air bag blew up. I had an iron grip on the steering wheel and tried to hold my upper body back and my head forward to protect myself against whiplash. I slammed into the air bag with enough force to take my breath away. The car's momentum took me left, across the oncoming lane and toward a rocky hill. Using every ounce of strength I had, I forced the steering wheel toward the shallow ditch on the right that separated the road from the desert. At the same time, I tapped the brakes, hoping the car would not roll over when it hit the ditch. It left the road, tipped forward, and stopped.

I switched off the ignition and sat there, my whole body shaking, as I tried to assess the damage to myself before I dared move.

My left knee ached. Left shoulder, too. I took a deep breath. My chest was sore, but I thought my ribs were okay. I rubbed my neck and turned my head back and forth, stretched side to side. Everything seemed to work. There was a tender spot above my left ear. No sign of blood, thank goodness. After carefully checking my nose, I was convinced that none of my parts were broken.

I hadn't expected the air bag to inflate in a rear-end collision, but it was probably a good thing it had. I smashed down the now almost-deflated bag, tried the door handle, and pushed. The door screeched and clanked but opened far enough so that I could squeeze out.

For the first moment since landing in the ditch, I remembered the black truck. Maybe I'd hit my head harder than I thought. Staying close to my car, in the shelter of the door, I looked up and down the road and across the desert in all directions. I could hear every tiny hiss and ping as my car settled into the sandy bottom of the ditch.

A sudden wind blew a yellow wave of dust into the air and then died. From a far distance, I heard the steady sound of a vehicle moving closer. I ducked down and propped my knee on the driver's seat so I could peer out the unbroken side windows.

The sound grew louder, coming from the direction of the mine. As far as I knew, the truck that rammed me had roared on past and continued on the road to Oatman. Would I have noticed if he'd turned around and gone back toward the mine? No. I almost laughed. I hadn't even remembered the *truck* until after I landed in the ditch.

Maybe this vehicle was Kelly on his way to town. Or one of the tourists, like Biker Guy.

On the other hand, the truck's occupants might be coming back to find out if I'd survived.

Wondering wasn't going to do me any good. There was nowhere to go, nowhere to run. If I took off across the desert with my little bottle of water, a 4x4 could run me down. The rocky hill on the other side of the road was just that, a rocky hill. If I tried to scramble up the side, I'd be totally exposed. There was no cave or crevice where I could hide.

I sat behind the steering wheel and let loose with a muttered litany of all the cuss words I'd ever learned, including the really bad ones. With my arm across the back of the passenger seat, I bent forward to take another peek out the window toward the road from the mine. There was a large cloud of dust. The oncoming vehicle was definitely big. And it was black.

Hell and damnation. I reached down and turned the key in the ignition. When the engine roared to life, the surprise nearly took my breath away. I gently pushed on the accelerator a couple of times, but only raced the engine. Another glance toward the mine told me the dust cloud with the black center was getting closer. With a burst of energy, I jumped out of the car and ran around to the front end, where I skidded to a halt and stared at my car with dismay. Nose down, the two tires were sunk in the sand and the bumper rested against the ground.

I dashed to the rear to see if I could back out of the ditch, but the bumper and part of one fender were firmly wedged against the tires, which also happened to be flat.

There wasn't a single thing I could do to escape that black truck except dodge and weave and run around in goofy circles. I reckoned I'd wear out before the truck did. And if the driver was carrying a gun, then I might as well climb onto the hood of my car and present as big a target as I could to get it over with faster.

I trudged back to the driver's side, reached in to retrieve my water bottle, and took a couple of swigs while I kept one eye on the oncoming vehicle.

Or was it vehicles?

With my eyes squinted against the glare of the powerful Arizona sun, I stared into the dust cloud and tried to make out the image. Was I seeing double? I rubbed my head. Maybe I had a concussion.

Seconds later, I realized the dust cloud trailed two bikers dressed in black and riding black Honda Wings. I took a deep breath and let it out slowly. Two more bikes materialized as the group's speed slowed and they drew near enough to see my car's condition. By the time the dust settled and the lead bikers dismounted, I'd counted seven of the black-suited riders and another three people mounted on a huge hog equipped with a sidecar.

Everyone else stayed on the road with their engines idling while the leaders, two young women, who looked more like fashion models than bikers, came down the slight incline to check out my car, make sure I was okay, and offer me a lift into Oatman. I looked at the rest of the band, wondering if this was a safe thing to do, wondering who these women were, wondering if I'd make it to Oatman alive, when something struck me very odd about the three people on the big bike.

I stared at them for a moment. I assumed they were also staring at me, but with their face shields closed, I wasn't sure. All three of them looked bigger than the seven bikers in black.

"Who are you people?" I said.

"Bike club. We have ladies' day once a month while our guys babysit."

"What about them?" I thrust my thumb toward the strange trio that sat at the rear of the group. "They don't look like they'd qualify for a ladies' day."

The biker chuckled. "Actually, the one who owns and drives that bike is named Frieda. The one on the bike with the red helmet is an old friend of hers and the one in the car is the old guy's son.

Dad and Willie. But why were they sitting there like that? Why hadn't they rushed up to see if I was okay?

"Do you know them?" the biker asked.

"I think so. But if they saw me—"

"Their face shields are dusty. You want to talk to them now or wait 'til we get to town?"

I took the biker's helmet and pulled it on without another glance at Dad and Willie. We didn't need to waste everyone's time with a family reunion.

I waited for the biker to straddle her classy machine before mounting the seat behind her. One glance at the pathetic little red car sent a shiver down my spine. I looked away as my ride accelerated and the band of lady bikers headed toward Oatman, with the tagalong threesome bringing up the rear.

No one else was on the road for that last few miles. No tour buses, no black 4x4, no Kelly on his way to town. By the time we rolled into Oatman, I was more angry than scared. There really is something to that safety in numbers thing. Not that a big truck couldn't have ground the whole lot of us into mincemeat, but it definitely would be a lot harder for the driver to claim it was an accident.

The biker ladies lined up in a row and parked diagonally near the entrance to the hotel. It was weird watching them step off their bikes, pull off their helmets, strap helmets to bike handles—a routine so synchronized they must have practiced.

The big bike stopped. The lady driver chatted with the biker ladies. By then I was close enough to reach out and touch my dad on the shoulder. Instead, I walked around to stand behind the sidecar, and I focused on the back of Willie's head. With his bizarre ability to visualize where I am and what I'm doing when I'm under stress, I was a little surprised that he was riding along, calm as could be, seemingly oblivious to my run-in with the black truck and the bumps and bruises I'd suffered in the process.

I concentrated on a mental replay of my bad experience, recalled the anxiety I'd felt as the truck lunged toward the rear of my car, the fear during the accident, the terror when

I thought the truck was returning. I beamed the full range of emotions directly at Willie, working myself into a sweat.

He and Dad sat there, jiggling to the vibration of the motorcycle's engine. Then Dad looked around, saw me, and waved. He leaned down and tapped Willie's shoulder. Willie looked at Dad, saw him gesture toward me, then twisted in his seat. He flipped up his face shield and stared a minute before he put it all together and waved.

I mimed that he should take off his helmet. He shook his head no and pointed to his ears.

As I nodded and stepped away from the bike, I understood why Willie seemed unaware. When he'd returned from Vietnam, he'd been recovering from injuries suffered when a nearby explosion threw him into the air and killed some of his friends. After all these years, Willie still trembled at loud noises and cringed at bright moving lights. On the Fourth of July, he stuffs cotton in his ears, dons his best set of earphones, grabs a comforter and a pillow, and settles down to read in the bathtub.

Now here he was, riding in the sidecar of a big motorcycle, surrounded by seven other bikes, clearly doing his best to keep his wits about him while protecting himself from the noise. I could have run all over the desert, chased by that 4x4, without Willie sensing a thing until he stepped out of the sidecar, removed his helmet, and found a quiet place to sit and relax.

I could have been dead before Willie even knew I was in trouble.

TWENTY-FOUR

DAD'S FRIEND MOVED down the street and pulled into a space large enough to accommodate her bike. When she killed the engine, I realized how loud her motorcycle actually was, and how brave Willie had been to travel in the sidecar all the way from Las Vegas.

Both Dad and Willie walked toward the hotel like old men—short steps, stiff-legged, and bent forward at the waist. As soon as he reached the bench where I sat, Dad plopped down with a sigh of relief and began to knead his lower back.

"You okay, Pete?" Dad's friend patted him on the shoulder and gave me a friendly smile. "And who's this? Wouldn't be your daughter, would it?"

Dad straightened up long enough to introduce us, then leaned back against the hardwood bench and stretched out his legs. "You okay, Willie?"

Willie looked confused for a minute, then pulled the foam earplugs out of his ears. "Forgot they were there." He smiled sheepishly as he shoved the plugs into his pocket.

"I wasn't expecting to see you two until I returned to the hotel," I said. "How'd you happen to come this way?"

"Accident jamming up traffic," Willie said. "We went up to Vegas and came down by way of Hoover Dam. Thought maybe we'd see you and Mom up there, but I guess we were too early. Then we had trouble with the bike after we got on Route 66. That's when we met up with those girls."

"I'll bet you didn't mind that much."

"I sure didn't," Dad said. "I don't know about Willie. He didn't pay much attention."

"I was busy keeping my head straight. Putting me on that motorcycle was not a good idea."

Dad shrugged apologetically. "One-track mind, I guess. I was too worried about your mom and Sylvia. Wait a minute," he said to me, as he realized I wasn't where he thought I should be. "You must be the lady we picked up in the desert. What happened? And why aren't you at the dam with the rest of the girls?"

"Some creep hit me from the rear, knocked my car off the road, and then took off."

"Why the devil would somebody do that? Oh, I get it. You came nosing around where you shouldn't have been."

"Hey, you're my dad. How can you say such a thing about your loving daughter?"

"Easy. You're here, when we know the tour bus went up to Hoover Dam on schedule. We know you were supposed to be on that bus with your mother. Therefore, I have quickly reached the conclusion that you're snooping, probably something to do with the mine that Willie saw you wandering around in alone. And by the way, if the hotel desk hadn't known about the tour, Willie and I would have been frantic by now. What happened to your mother's phone?"

"We left it in the restaurant. What about yours? Mom was trying to call you, too. She left a couple of messages—"

"Battery's dead. I left the charger at home."

Frieda snorted. Dad gave her a dirty look. Willie made eye contact with me.

"How about getting something to eat?" Frieda studied the southwestern-flavored menu posted by the door. "Burro's ears. You see that, Pete?"

"What the heck would that be?" Dad struggled to his feet and hobbled over to stand by Frieda.

"Don't know. But they got buffalo burgers and iced tea, and that's good enough for me. You all gonna join me?"

Like I'd pass up a chance to eat. Not to mention an opportunity to learn the rest of Frieda's story. "Yeah, but there's something I have to tell Dad and Willie first."

All three gave me their full attention when they saw my serious expression and heard the catch in my voice.

"Is it Kristina?" Dad paled. "Did something happen?"

"No, Dad. Mom's fine. It's Sandra." I told them the story as briefly as I could and persuaded them to put off their questions until later, claiming I needed a little break since I was still shaky from my accident. I thought they gave in a little too fast, but then figured it was due to their heightened level of Route 66 biker excitement. I followed them into the hotel to see Willie's reaction.

Willie loves old things—old tools, old pictures, old buildings—so he stopped inside the door as though he wanted to soak up the feel of the place. The worn wooden floors that creaked with every step, the pickle barrel, posters and newspaper articles that had yellowed over time, even the smell of dried-out wood and must and oiled leather that spoke of the cowboys and miners who had walked on these floors over the years.

Dad and Frieda led the way through the lobby and disappeared into the narrow bar.

I was behind Willie and nearly ran into him when he stopped at the bottom of the stairway, looked up toward the second floor, waved at someone, and then went on. I glanced upstairs when Willie waved, then did a double-take. There was no one there.

"Willie," I muttered as I hurried to catch up. "Who did you wave at?"

He ignored me.

I wanted to talk about it. "Did you see something? It's creepy up there, and it's cold. Are you going up?"

"What do you mean, creepy?"

"You should go up, see for yourself. There's supposed to be a ghost or two."

"There was a man on the stairs."

"No, there wasn't."

Willie shook his head and walked on through the bar, refusing to say more.

"My son and daughter have a way of getting mixed up in other folks' business," Dad was telling Frieda. "They find bodies, try to figure out who the killer is, and nearly get themselves killed."

"Why?"

Well, now, that was a good question, I thought with a smile. Frieda, Willie, and I looked at Dad, fully expecting him to have the answer.

Dad thought for a minute, then gestured toward me. "Sylvia there takes after her mother. Reads too many mystery stories. And she used to work for the FBI. Willie, well, he's sort of psychic. Sometimes things pop into his head and off he goes, trying to fix whatever's wrong."

These explanations were a long way from the truth. Willie and I had been tangled up in one real case where we found our lives in jeopardy. Before that, each of us had stumbled over a body or two, but our involvement had ended when we called the police. And as far as I knew, Willie did his best to confine his psychic experiences to answering my telepathic distress signals.

Willie's afraid of his ability. He once told me he thought he might go mad if he opened himself up to any and all signals from the other side.

"The other side of what?" I'd asked.

"You know, spirits and stuff like that."

I didn't want to laugh. Lord knows, I wanted to understand and believe when Willie talked about his visions. And I did have to admit, he'd unexpectedly bailed me out of trouble a time or two because of those visions. But I had no frame of reference, no personal experience, except for one time—after my husband Andy died. Willie had feared I couldn't move past the grief, so he became alarmed one day when he couldn't find me anywhere. He beamed me a message. Somehow, I plucked that thought of his out of the air and sent one back to set his mind at ease.

That had taken place years ago. It hadn't happened since. I'm not real sure it happened then.

Dad was still explaining to Frieda about the adventure Willie and I had in Illinois several months ago, the one that led to my abrupt retirement.

"Nothing exciting ever happens around here," Frieda said.

"You live in Las Vegas," I said.

"I mean nothing exciting ever happens to me. Chauffeuring Pete and Willie down here because they thought you and your mom were in trouble got my blood going. I was ready to kick some ass, if you'll pardon the expression."

I hadn't seen Kelly come in, but heard him when he yelled across the room, "Hey, what happened to your car?"

Not interested in shouting back so everyone could hear, I waved him over to our table and introduced him as one of the mine's tour guides. Then I said, "Know anybody who drives a black 4x4, Kelly? Maybe has some damage to his front end?"

He looked away, then down at the floor. "One of the other guides has one. He took off after you did and said he was going to Laughlin."

"Which guide?"

"Crash. You know him?"

"I was on his tour yesterday."

"You're the lady who walked out of the mine by herself while Crash stayed with the tour, aren't you?" Kelly reached around behind him, grabbed a chair, and pulled it up next to me. "You saw something there in the mine, didn't you? Are you a cop? Are you going back in? Want me to go with you? I can get through the gate and in the office."

"Hey, I'm in," said Frieda.

"Me, too," Dad said.

"You're all going down in the mine?" Willie blinked, surprised. "Why?"

This time all eyes were on me to provide the answers. I now had team members—one with bad knees, one who was craving excitement, and one who, for all I knew, might be a bad guy. Lord help me.

"This isn't a good idea," I said.

"Honest, it's okay," Kelly said. "No one ever returns to the mine at night. We could take one other person, I guess. He could stay topside and send us a signal if someone comes." When he realized he'd contradicted himself, he added, "But no one will. It'd just be a precaution."

"How would you send a signal, Kelly? Crash's radio didn't work when we were in the lower tunnel."

"I don't know. I'll think of something. Come on, let's check it out. I know something funny is going on in that mine."

Willie said, "What makes you think so?"

Kelly leaned forward and lowered his voice. "I came in early last Saturday, and there was a flatbed truck creeping down the road from the mine. You know, ma'am, the road the buckboard uses to take the gawkers up for the tour? The truck had no business up there that I could figure out. And there was nothing on it except a dozen wooden pallets, some canvas straps, and a bunch of plastic that was all stretched out like shrink wrap."

"It's a mine," said Willie. "Maybe they hauled in equipment to dig, or cart out the gold."

"It's not a working mine, sir."

"What do you think the truck was doing up there?" I asked.

"That's what I'd like to find out. Whatever it is, it's a big secret. I asked about it, and the office lady told me I was full of baloney, because if there'd been a truck scheduled in for some reason, she'd know about it. And when I asked Crash, he told me they'd brought in supplies for a geologist who's scheduled to survey the area. But we've got a forklift and tons of space in the outbuildings. Why would they back a truck up the hill, break down the load, and haul stuff down there one box at a time? Doesn't make any sense to me."

"What do you think they carted into the tunnel?"

"Honest, ma'am, I don't know. But I was wondering about drugs or guns."

Dad said, "You haven't taken a look on your own?"

"Boss said the only time I'm supposed to go down there is when I'm conducting a tour. If I leave the gawkers for even a minute, I'll get fired. I almost got fired for letting you wander off today, ma'am. Crash was mad, and he told the boss about it. I figure my days are numbered anyway."

Willie shook his head. Dad's eyes were lit with eager anticipation. Frieda tapped her fingers on the table and bit her lip. Kelly was leaning so close I could have bitten his nose.

"No, Dad," I said, shaking my head emphatically. "Mom would kick my rear end all the way to Key West if I let you do this. She'll be in Laughlin with the Flippers before dinner, and she'll expect to see you and Willie there. You need to go to the hotel and explain to Mom what's going on, but no one else. There are two FBI agents with the tour and more agents hanging around Laughlin, a couple of local homicide detectives, and the Mohave County sheriff—so you have to keep this quiet."

Dad and Frieda deflated like balloons whose hot air had been turned off.

"But you're coming, right?" Kelly said. "Oh, man, I'm working on a case. This is cool."

"No," said Willie.

Before I could answer, I felt a hand on my shoulder and heard Patsy's voice. "Hey, Sylvia, I was hoping to find you here." She dragged another chair to our table and wedged herself between Dad and me.

I introduced Patsy to the others and explained who she was and what she'd planned for the day.

"You're back sooner than I expected," I said. "What happened?"

"Sandra's friend doesn't exist. The address in her book is a city park. I guess she really did give us that story so she could get away for a few hours without making anyone suspicious."

"But why wouldn't she tell you? She hired you to…exactly what did she hire you to do, Patsy?"

Apparently, Patsy didn't want to tell her story in front of

strangers. She shook her head. "Did I interrupt something, Sylvia? It looked like you were having a serious discussion when I came in."

I recounted the day's events again, ending with the topic under discussion—the late-night visit to the mine with Kelly, and Willie's resistance to the plan.

Everyone looked at Willie, but it was obvious that he wasn't paying one bit of attention to my story. Instead, he was looking at Patsy with the biggest pair of puppy eyes I've ever seen in my life. Patsy winked at Willie and grinned. He blushed and ducked his head like a schoolboy.

"Hey," Patsy said. "I'm game. I'll go with you."

We all looked at Willie. He mumbled okay but studied the table as though the menu was carved into the wooden surface.

That left Patsy hyper, Willie resigned, and me apprehensive. Dad and Frieda listened without comment as the rest of us made our plans. Kelly and Patsy eyed each other with distrust. I supposed that was to be expected, since they'd never seen each other before.

"Dad, whatever you do, don't tell the rest of the Flippers anything, okay?"

He nodded, but his attention was now focused on the dollar bills stapled all over the walls.

TWENTY-FIVE

A LONG AFTERNOON stretched out ahead of us. Willie told me he wanted to explore Oatman with Dad and Frieda before escorting them to the hotel in Laughlin. Kelly left with the promise to meet Willie, Patsy, and me at the mine gate at midnight.

I glanced over my shoulder before walking out the door of the Oatman Hotel. Dad and Frieda stomped up the stairs toward the second floor to view the room where Clark Gable and Carole Lombard spent their wedding night. Willie hesitated on the second step from the bottom. He shivered and moved closer to the railing, paused, and then dashed up the stairs.

A quick slap of cold hit my arm.

Patsy, walking ahead of me, rubbed the side of her neck.

We stepped outside into the glare of the hot Arizona sun. Refusing to analyze what had happened, I focused on the small gathering of burros outside the hotel.

Someone should write a scary story about Oatman, I thought. *The burro population slowly increases each day, soon outnumbering the town's occupants. Their gentle demeanors morph into belligerence, and their sweet brown eyes harden, their benign stares become menacing glares. Still the burros come. Tourists are forced onto the buses or into their cars by snapping jaws and brutal kicks.*

Still, the burros come.

Sort of like *The Birds,* only big, furry, and earthbound.

Patsy waded into the midst of the herd as she pointed across the street toward the saloon where her car was parked. She rubbed a burro nose here, scratched an ear there. I followed in her wake but didn't make any friends along the way.

Since I'd neglected to remove my rental papers from my red wreck, we had to go back. The car's front end now rested on its rims, the tires removed by some kind of magic, since no human could operate a jack in the sandy ditch bottom, especially with the car's front end half-buried. I tried to lift the hood to see if the engine and other parts were intact, but it wouldn't budge.

There was no oncoming traffic. Even so, a crawly feeling moved up and down my spine. I wiped the perspiration from my forehead, grabbed my papers from the glove compartment, and bolted toward Patsy's car, where she sat waiting, the air conditioner going full blast.

Patsy and I talked during the drive to our hotel, which meant that I asked a lot of questions and insisted that Patsy provide answers. "I was very suspicious of you at first," I told her. I then described the sequence of concerns before I hit her with that same old question. "Why did Sandra hire you?"

Patsy thought for a minute before answering. "Sandra's husband is a wheeler-dealer of the most corrupt kind, but Sandra didn't know that when she married him. She thought he was rich, that he'd made his money in speculative but legal investments, paid his taxes, and had brilliant entrepreneurial instincts.

"When he told her about his latest venture, a hedge fund that focused on natural resource and energy-related businesses, she fell for his line and said she wanted to invest. As you know, she was so enthusiastic that she persuaded some of her friends to invest as well. Convinced she could make a quick killing, Sandra also pulled money from her other investments and dumped the whole wad into Barry's new fund."

"How much are we talking about?"

"Around three hundred thousand dollars. Almost everything she had saved."

"Oops."

"Yeah. She received healthy dividend checks each quarter

on the part invested in her own name, along with official-looking balance sheets and profit and loss statements, so she thought everything was fine…until about two months ago."

"What happened?"

Patsy was silent while she maneuvered around construction equipment coming off a building site on Boundary Cone Road. I tried to imagine how Sandra discovered that something was wrong. Had the statements stopped coming? The checks?

"One day while Barry was out of town," Patsy said, "Sandra tidied up Barry's home office. She was shocked to find his briefcase tucked in the closet. When she pulled it out and looked inside, she found papers, his appointment book, calendar, some files. His cell phone, however, was not there."

"Could that be where Sandra found the little green book?"

"Maybe. But the first thing that crossed Sandra's mind was that Barry left his briefcase behind because he wasn't on a business trip at all. She thought he was having an affair. She panicked, convinced he'd stolen her money. She figured her cash was gone forever, and he was going to divorce her.

"When he came home from that trip, he acted the same as always, so she relaxed for a while, but then he was off on another mysterious jaunt without telling her where he'd be staying, accessible only by cell phone. She couldn't take it."

I nodded. "So she called a private detective to check up on Barry and find out where he was and what he was doing."

"Right. Since Sandra had left several messages, and Barry hadn't called her back, there wasn't much to go on. His newest business venture was the hedge fund, and the offices listed on his stationery were in Laughlin and Las Vegas, so I contacted a Vegas PI I'd worked with a couple of times and asked him to find out if Barry Pringle was out here. At the time I last spoke to him, he'd had no luck, but he said he still had some things to check out. I left a message on his answering machine to meet me Thursday afternoon and give me a report."

"The body in the tub."

Patsy nodded.

"Do Detectives Dunbar and Trilby know all this?"

"Hell, yes. Agent Falls, too. But I couldn't give them much help since I'd never met with my guy. If the Feds conducted a raid on Barry's offices today, they must have a lot more information than I do."

"You were expecting to find Barry shacked up with a Vegas showgirl. And the Vegas PI was only trying to find out where Barry was so he could initiate surveillance. Your investigation didn't have anything to do with Barry's business."

"Right…except in whatever way the business might impact Sandra's marital status and the loss of her life savings."

"Do you know if the cops ever got in touch with Barry? Does he know Sandra's dead?"

"No idea. But if Barry Pringle's here in Laughlin, or in Vegas, he could have read something in the paper. I assume he knew Sandra was coming on this trip, so even if the cops are keeping her identity a secret, you'd think Barry would call to make sure she's okay."

"Unless he already knew she was dead."

"Yes."

I had hoped to learn so much more from Patsy. Too much information had died with the Vegas PI, and much more with Sandra. I still couldn't get over the tremendous coincidence of Velma's fall occurring at the same time Sandra hired Patsy and brought her along on the trip, so I mentioned my suspicions.

"That's a fluke," Patsy said. "I had no intention of coming on this trip. That's why I'd hired a PI to do the legwork. He would have reported by telephone or fax, I'd have charged Sandra for my time as well as his, and then I would have paid him whenever he got around to billing me. It wasn't until Velma went to the hospital that Sandra and I discussed me coming along. I'm confident she had nothing to do with her friend's accident."

Another dead end. Sandra would have been the only one who could answer the question, and Sandra was no longer talking.

"What about tonight, Sylvia? How much do you trust that tour guide, what's his name?"

"Kelly. I don't know. He says he's a student, says he works part-time, but he's very intense about what's hidden in the mine. Why does he care so much?"

"Maybe he has a personal axe to grind with his bosses. Sounds like they're kind of tough to work for."

"True."

"Uh-oh." Patsy nodded toward her side rearview mirror.

"What?"

"Black truck coming up fast."

I flipped the visor down and positioned the mirror so I could see out the rear window without turning around. It sure looked like the same 4x4 I'd tangled with earlier, but I couldn't tell if the truck had any front-end damage or not.

"The driver couldn't know you're in this car, could he?" Patsy said.

"Not unless he was lurking somewhere in Oatman and saw us leave together."

Patsy glanced at me. "Or Kelly told him."

We weren't going to know if this guy—I assumed it was a guy—and his truck were after me again until the vehicle either hit us or passed us. I grabbed the armrest and scrunched down in the seat.

Patsy kept driving at the same speed, but when the truck was less than twenty feet behind us, she pulled to the right and coasted. The truck roared by. Her breath escaped in a rush. She stopped.

I sat up straight and pried my hand free of its grip on the armrest. "Did you see the front end? Did it look damaged?"

She gave me a look that could have melted an ice cube. "You think I was calmly analyzing the driver and inspecting the vehicle? You weren't the only one who was scared shitless, you know."

I shrugged off her hostile tone and motioned her to get on with the trip to Laughlin. "Sorry, Patsy, I thought you might have noticed."

After a couple of minutes, she shook her head and grimaced. "Actually, I did notice the front end. It's kind of hard to tell on a dirty black truck, and from that distance, but I didn't see any dents or anything."

"So it's probably not the same—"

"But there might have been something red, like paint, on the bumper."

Scared shitless, my foot. Patsy was one cool cookie. I'd bet she did her best detecting under pressure, and probably solved cases in her sleep. Not that her observations would do us much good unless we ran into the black truck again before it was cleaned up.

"Are you sure your car was rammed on purpose? Why would anyone at the mine want to hurt you?"

"I don't know, Patsy, but I'm sure it wasn't an accident. Maybe they want to scare me away because I'm showing too much interest. I've been to the mine twice, I was there when Sandra's body was found, and I was obviously snooping when I found the boxes in the side tunnel."

Neither of us spoke for several minutes, then I said, "What are we going to do after we get back to the hotel?"

"I don't know." She thought a moment. "We could drive by Barry Pringle's office, see if the raid actually happened. Then get something to eat."

That sounded good to me. I sure didn't want to go mine sleuthing on an empty stomach.

By the time we made it to Bullhead City and I'd bickered about insurance for a while with the car rental guy, another hour had gone by. It was after five when we drove past the three-story Laughlin building where Barry Pringle kept an office. We had to park and go inside the lobby to even find out which floor he was on.

There were no police or FBI vehicles near the building, at least not ones we could identify. There was no building security, no information desk. The floor directory by the elevator had Pringle's number listed as 302. Patsy and I exchanged a glance, eyebrows raised in a silent question. She pushed the button to call the elevator.

All was quiet on the third floor. Two glass panes on either side of the door into Suite 302 showed some light, but not the bright light of overhead fixtures or lamps. I reached out and turned the doorknob, but it was locked. I knocked, and we waited to see if anyone answered. Finally Patsy fumbled in her pocket and pulled out a credit card that she tried to slip between the door and the doorjamb. The fit was too tight.

I rummaged in my fanny pack and produced the Swiss Army knife I'd taken from Linda's emergency kit. "Can you use this?"

"Maybe." She flipped out each tool, one by one, and closed all except the corkscrew and a tiny screwdriver. I don't know how she did it without real honest-to-goodness lock-picking tools, but she had the door open within seconds.

"I have to learn how to do that," I whispered.

"Piece of cake. I'll show you later."

We stepped inside and shut the door. There was enough light from the windows that I didn't need Linda's emergency flashlight. Patsy motioned me toward the desk and files in the front room, while she assigned herself the attached office. Quickly moving toward my own target, I aimed a silent sneer at her backside for taking the choice job for herself.

The drawers of the desk were empty, and so were all four file drawers. There was a phone, however, and an answering machine with a blinking message light. I pushed the play button and listened to Patsy's voice leave her number and request someone call her. There were no other messages. In what I assumed was Barry Pringle's office, Patsy sat comfortably in a leather executive chair, a puzzled look on her face.

I said, "Nothing here either?"

"Nada."

"Do you think the FBI took everything?"

She shook her head. "They would have left the staplers and pencils, stuff like that. I'm guessing there was nothing to take."

"Why would Barry go to the trouble and expense of setting up an office if he wasn't going to use it?"

"Maybe he needed a legitimate mailing address, and a post office box would seem too fishy."

I looked around the room, hoping something would jump out and hand me a clue in a sealed envelope. That didn't happen. I spotted a picture on the wall that was hanging slightly askew, walked over to set it right, and checked behind the picture in case there was a wall safe. There was no safe, but there was a long piece of tape patching a tear in the painting's brown paper backing.

"Help me, please," I told Patsy.

We placed the painting facedown on the carpet and carefully pulled the tape away. I could feel the shapes of what was hidden there when I ran my fingers across the paper. I pointed to the spot where I'd slid one of the items close to the opening, and Patsy reached her fingers inside. One by one, through the paper, I manipulated the pieces close to the tear so Patsy could retrieve them.

"Now what do we do?" I said, as we studied the gold coins, all Krugerrands, that the Feds had missed in their raid.

TWENTY-SIX

WITH A SENSE of anticipation, Willie watched his dad and Frieda nonchalantly climb the stairs of the Oatman Hotel. The nerves in his shoulders tingled, and the hairs on his neck and head lifted as though from a chill breeze, an unlikely occurrence in a non-air-conditioned building in Arizona.

Willie's father followed Frieda around the corner without a backward glance, and with no indication he or Frieda had sensed an otherworldly presence. Willie dashed up the stairs and joined them as they wandered down the first corridor, reading the articles and documents, framed and protected by glass, displayed on the walls.

The door into the room where Gable and Lombard had allegedly spent their first night as a married couple was locked, but the curtains on the glass pane in the door were drawn back so visitors could see inside. Old furniture, a worn comforter, a faded gown draped across a chair, old dust.

The tingly feeling Willie had on the stairs was gone. The air was hot and stuffy.

He moved on down the hallway, walking into rooms that were open to the public, glancing around, walking out. Then he returned to the junction with the second corridor, where he resumed his inspection. A bathroom, modernized so long ago the fixtures now seemed as old as the hotel itself, and a shower stall, opened into the hallway—improvements apparently made to accommodate the occasional overnight ghost hunter.

The second corridor was short, and only one room was of any interest to Willie. Frieda had gone inside, and Willie's dad stood in the doorway. The man Willie had seen on the stairs earlier was stretched out on the bed, his hands under his head, his booted feet crossed at the ankles. He winked at Willie, and then he got up, crossed to the doorway, walked through Willie's dad, and disappeared into the hall.

Willie looked at Frieda, who was peering at a tiny framed photograph hanging on the wall over the bed. Willie's father crossed the room and stared out the window.

"I'm going downstairs now," Willie told them.

"Right behind you," his dad said.

There was nothing else. Nothing in the corridor. Nothing on the stairs, or in the hotel lobby. Willie stopped at Sweet Sally's and perused the list of ice cream flavors posted on the wall. "I'd like a cone, please," he told the young woman at the counter. "Vanilla. What about you, Dad?"

"Vanilla for me, too."

"Me, three," chimed in Frieda.

"Are you Sally?" Willie asked the woman at the counter.

She grinned. "I am."

"Do you ever feel the ghost moving through here? Do you ever see him?"

"I've never seen him. Never seen any of them. But sometimes I hear things I can't explain. It can be a little creepy around here after dark."

"Any of them? You mean there's more than one?"

"Three or four, from what I hear."

"More than one what?" Frieda said. "You talking about three or four ghosts? Here in the hotel?"

"Sure. That's one of the reasons the tourists come. They all want to see old Oatie."

Frieda looked around the lobby, then stood with her back to the counter, as if she figured any and all ghost sightings had best be faced head-on. She handed the money for her cone over her shoulder, took her ice cream, and headed out the door.

Willie's dad chuckled and glanced at Willie. "You don't believe that stuff, do you?"

Willie wasn't interested in debating the existence of ghosts with his father. From his point of view, there was nothing to debate. He'd seen the ghost in the hotel twice, but he doubted his dad would believe the sighting was anything other than Willie suffering from dehydration and heatstroke. If pursued, the debate might end with his dad dragging him off to the emergency room.

My first ghost. Willie smiled to himself, then quickly looked around, fearing he might now see ghosts everywhere. That would be intolerable. He had to shut down the receptor, block the pathway. A man could go mad if he let his mind become a Grand Central Station for anything and everything that wandered through his space.

By the time he arrived at the hotel in Laughlin, Willie had put the encounter completely out of his mind. The Flippers had just stepped off their bus when Frieda zoomed into the circular driveway, skidded to a stop, and killed the engine.

"Kristina!" His dad yelled and waved frantically, making no effort to dismount.

Willie's mom turned around when she heard her name, stared blankly at the three bikers, turned away as though she planned to ignore them, then turned back and planted both hands on her hips. With a glare that could have struck a more cowardly man speechless, she advanced on the bike.

Willie removed his helmet and earplugs. He didn't want to miss anything his parents said to each other.

"Peter, is that you?" his mom said. "Did you come all the way from Las Vegas on that contraption? What in the world were you thinking?"

Willie's dad untangled himself from the bike and stood up as tall as his aching back would allow. He removed his helmet and gestured toward the sidecar. "Willie's here, too."

Frieda removed her own helmet. Her hearty handshake nearly yanked Willie's mother off the curb. Willie had to grin.

The other four Flippers charged into the scene like a flock of old hens scrabbling after a handful of ground corn.

"What's going on?" Diane said.

"My gawd, is that Peter? And Willie?" Gail marched over and slapped Willie on the back. "Good for you, Willie-boy. You'll be a soldier yet."

Linda tsk-tsked Gail's faux pas, but said nothing.

"Don't pay any attention to her," Marianne said. "If she ever showed signs of having manners, we'd keel over in a dead faint."

"What did I say?" Gail looked at Marianne, who merely rolled her eyes and didn't answer.

"Nothing. It's fine," Willie said.

"Hey, who wants a ride on my bike?" hollered Frieda. "Guaranteed to give you a thrill."

"Me, me," Linda squealed as she elbowed her friends out of her way.

"My gawd," Gail said. "If that little scaredy-cat can do it, so can I."

Frieda roared out of the drive onto Casino Way with Linda riding behind and Gail in the sidecar. Marianne and Diane stepped to the curb, putting themselves next in line.

"What about you, Mom?" Willie sidled up to his mother and poked her with his elbow. "You know you want to."

"Look at your father." She pointed to Willie's dad, who stood with both hands pushing against his hips, trying once again to stretch the stiffness out of his back. "You want me to look like that—unable to stand up straight, probably not able to sleep tonight?"

"Come on, Mom. You're afraid of what Dad will say if you go for a ride after giving him such a hard time. It won't be a long ride. Look, they're already coming back."

The last thing Willie saw before he walked into the hotel lobby was his mom, helmet already in place, climbing into the sidecar.

Inside the hotel, the roar of the bike was replaced by the distressing lights and sounds of slot machines. Casino equipment had even invaded the lobby. There would be no escape on this floor. Willie checked into a room to share with his dad for one night, one floor down from his mom and Sylvia. He left a key at the desk and headed for the elevator. With a strong suspicion that the hotel's floor plan was designed to channel people toward the casino at every opportunity, Willie checked to make sure his earplugs were still in his pocket. He might need them to go from his room to one of the restaurants.

It wasn't long before Willie's room was full of people, destroying his chance to take the nap he longed for. His dad and mom looked as tired as he felt. The rest of the Flippers bubbled over with excitement at their great motorcycle adventure. They cornered Frieda and pelted her with questions, both personal and technical. Frieda seemed to be having a ball and didn't look in the least tired.

Then Sylvia and Patsy showed up and told of their afternoon, especially their visit to Barry Pringle's office, which had nothing in it but the telephone and a bit of furniture. Willie listened attentively, aware the two women seemed excited, though they reported nothing of consequence. He paid close attention to everything Patsy said, though he knew he was being observed in turn by Sylvia and his mom. Willie's father, in his usual detached way, didn't notice anything, or pretended not to.

Patsy talked directly to Willie when she spoke. "You still going with us tonight?"

"I guess so. Not that it's a good idea, but if you two are determined to go, what can I do?" He shook his head. "Listen, when you have time, could I talk to you?"

"Sure. What about?"

"Detecting. Financial stuff. Banking, fraud cases, embezzlement audits. Maybe when we get back to Florida?"

"You know how to reach me." She raised her left eyebrow and gave him a somber look.

Willie ducked his head and blushed.

Someone pounded on the door, and Willie rushed to answer, happy to escape Patsy's knowing stare. When he pulled the door open, he was certain he would not get the nap he wanted.

Agent Damon Falls of the FBI stepped through the doorway

and strode into the room. "I have knocked on every one of your doors, canvassed the casino, the bar and the restaurants, looked everywhere to find you. What the devil is everyone doing down here?"

The room grew as silent as a church after the pastor utters the words, "Let us pray."

"Judge…Ms. Thorn, Ms. Strump, may I speak to you?" He looked around the room as though taking inventory. "Alone."

"Alone separately?" Sylvia said. "Or alone together?"

"Alone together is fine. Outside?" Patsy and Sylvia followed him out of the room.

"What's that all about?" Willie's dad looked at Willie, then Kristina, then the other Flippers.

"Well," Gail sputtered indignantly. "Why would we know? We were banished for the day."

"What do you mean, banished?" Willie said.

All of the Flippers spoke at once about how they'd been ordered to take the tour and accept the FBI escort.

"Didn't you see those two guys get off the bus?" Marianne said. "Big guys, had guns in shoulder holsters."

Linda gasped. "Guns? They had guns?"

"Oh, can it, you ninny. Of course they had guns." Gail looked to Diane for confirmation. "You knew they had guns, didn't you?"

"Well, of course."

"Peter," Willie's mom said. "It was okay. Really, dear. They were very sweet and they watched over our every move. We couldn't have been any safer."

Willie's dad was clearly distressed. "But why were you ordered to go on the tour? Why did you have guards?"

"Oh, dear, we don't know. There's some kind of problem with that business Sandra's husband started. Barry is being investigated and—"

"You invested in that business. Are you in trouble?"

"No, it's okay. I only invested a thousand and one of those

nice agents assured me we didn't do anything wrong." She frowned. "We might lose our money, though."

Linda paled and muttered, "Oh, no."

"It'll be okay," Gail told her, with an uncharacteristically sympathetic pat on her knee. Then Gail destroyed it all by gleefully saying, "I know for a fact that bag ladies live longer in Florida than in any other state except California."

Linda wailed, clearly not comforted by Gail's words.

"Nice, Gail," said Marianne. "You'd give the Wicked Witch of the West a run for her money, wouldn't you?"

"Why? Was she rich?"

Diane groaned.

"That does it. I'm going to the casino. Anyone coming with?" Marianne sailed out of the room without waiting for an answer.

"Come on, girls. Let's give these folks some peace." Diane herded Linda and Gail out the door.

"What's the deal now, Pete?" Frieda said. "Do you need me to stay over and take you up to Vegas in the morning?"

"It would sure help."

Willie's mom stared at the ceiling, her lips pressed firmly together.

Willie slumped in his chair and felt his pocket to make sure the earplugs were there.

"Then I'm going to my room for a while to rest up for dinner," Frieda said. "You folks all eating together?"

"Probably," Willie said. "We'll talk to Sylvia and give you a call."

"Okay," Frieda said. "I'm outta here. See you later."

With only his parents left in the room, it now seemed remarkably spacious. Willie stretched out on one of the beds.

His dad cleared his throat. "I need to tell you the plan, Kristina. That PI and Willie and Sylvia are meeting up with one of the tour guides over at the gold mine tonight. Sylvia and the guide think there's something hidden in the mine, maybe something illegal."

"You're going along?" she asked Willie.

"Yes. They talked me into it."

She scoffed. "You mean Patsy Strump gave you the eye and you caved like a—"

"Mom!"

She sniffed. "Is this going to be dangerous? Should your father and I go along to be, you know, lookouts?"

Willie tried not to laugh. "It won't be dangerous at all. This guide says the mine people never return at night."

"We'll be here, at the hotel. Call us if you need us."

"Absolutely, Mom."

His parents exchanged a glance, but Willie didn't try to interpret. They had been able to communicate with a look as long as he'd been old enough to notice. He'd tried from time to time, but he'd never cracked the code.

"I'm going down to the gift shop," his mother said. "I ran out of toothpaste."

"You need to stop by the front desk, Kristina. I forgot to tell you. They found your phone."

Willie had closed his eyes, barely registering the exchange between his parents. He raised his hand and waved goodbye.

TWENTY-SEVEN

IT MADE ME NERVOUS to have Agent Falls call Patsy and me out of the crowded hotel room so he could talk to us alone, especially since Patsy and I had kept our little discovery from Barry Pringle's office a secret. We didn't plan to share that information until after our midnight rendezvous with Kelly. I hoped Falls would tell us all about the raids, explaining in the process why the Laughlin office was empty. Instead, he confided something even more interesting. Barry Pringle had finally surfaced that morning and responded to the phone calls from the Mohave County sheriff.

"Pringle's in Miami," Falls told us. "He's been there for the last two weeks."

"Miami?" Patsy seemed flabbergasted. "You checked it out? You know for sure he didn't come here and then return?"

"We're absolutely positive. I can't tell you the details, but my own office knows exactly where Barry Pringle was the whole time."

"Seems like the left hand doesn't know—"

"The agents down there are working on a case totally unrelated to Pringle's, Ms. Thorn. They didn't know who he was until yesterday."

"They didn't know who he was, but they know he was there?" There was no reason for the FBI to tell us where Pringle was or why, unless it somehow impacted our safety. I stared into the distance, over the agent's shoulder, and thought about that for a minute. "The Feds were running surveillance on someone else? And Pringle kept showing up in pictures? Or at meetings?"

"Yes."

"Agent Falls, why are you telling us—"

"Wait." Patsy cut me off as though I were about to dam what little flow of information there was. "If we accept the fact that Barry never left Miami during the time we were here, that doesn't mean he's innocent. He could have hired someone to kill my Vegas PI. And Sandra," she added, almost as an afterthought.

"We're not convinced the murders were directly related to Pringle or his business. He was being filmed when he took the call from the sheriff, but he didn't know that. If he wasn't genuinely upset to find out his wife was dead, then he's one hell of an actor. The Miami agents were convinced."

"I'm not," Patsy said.

I wasn't, either. But maybe I was hoping for an easy answer that would quickly remove any threat to my family and the rest of the Flippers, and Patsy, of course. Not that she couldn't take care of herself.

"Tell him about the accident," Patsy said.

I told the whole story again.

Falls frowned. "You reported this to the Mohave County sheriff's office?"

"Not yet."

"Do it."

"Pringle's fund is invested in the mine. That could tie him to the mine and my accident."

Falls shook his head. "That's a very tenuous connection, Ms. Thorn."

"How can you say that? Barry's wife is killed in the mine, I get thrown out of the mine for looking in the wrong tunnel, and right after that I get rammed from the rear by a truck that was probably driven by a mine employee."

I'd finally caught Agent Falls's interest. "What are you talking about?" he said. "What wrong tunnel?"

I told him that whole story, finishing with, "What do you think? What could be down there?"

He stared at me, but seemed focused on something going on inside his own head. He finally glanced at his watch and said he had to be somewhere in fifteen minutes so he'd talk to us later.

"I'm going up to my room," Patsy said. "Call me when you're ready to meet up."

"Sure." I turned to knock on Dad and Willie's door but stopped when Falls lingered as though waiting for Patsy to walk away.

"Wait up a second," he said.

I glanced toward the elevator. Patsy watched with raised eyebrows as she waited for the doors to slide open.

"I wondered," Falls said, with not one hint of personal interest or flirtatiousness, "if we could meet for a late dinner, or maybe a drink. I'd like to talk to you."

Now what? I had a strong feeling that Damon Falls was about to proposition me again, was never going to give up. I couldn't figure out whether he alone had this nagging desire to put me back to work, or whether some higher up FBI manager had ordered him to recruit me. So far, I'd resisted discussing the matter. Well, I hadn't caved then and I wasn't going to listen to his pitch now, especially since I was already committed to the exploration of the Lone Cactus Mine.

By maintaining deep eye contact and grinning, Falls raised a squiggle of doubt in my mind.

What if he's asking me for a date?

"Sorry, Agent Falls, I can't tonight. I have other plans."

He maintained eye contact too long. I felt uneasy, exposed, as if he could read my mind. I turned away without another word. As Willie pulled the door open, I glanced toward the elevator in time to see Agent Falls follow Patsy inside. He did not look back.

I tried to shrug off the incident as I passed on the news about Barry Pringle to Mom, Dad, and Willie. Mom stayed with the guys while I went to my room to rest.

I set the alarm to wake me up in an hour and stretched out on the bed. It seemed like two minutes later that I was jolted awake by the telephone. I'd only been down fifteen minutes.

"What?" I snapped. As soon as I said it, I realized how rude that sounded. "Sorry, I was asleep. Let me start again. Hello?"

"If you don't want your body looking like your screwed-up car, lady, you better keep your nose out of business that don't concern you." Whoever he was, he sounded like his nose was full of snot.

"Who is this?" Yes, I get the stupid question of the year award. I followed it up with another one. "What do you want?"

"What I want is for you and that private eye broad to get the hell back to Florida where you belong."

I knew I should call Agent Falls and report the threat. Also, the Mohave County sheriff. I still hadn't reported the accident, and I had to do that for my insurance company to pay. I would also call the Laughlin police, since I'd received the threatening call while in the hotel. Maybe the hotel management, too. And I had to tell Patsy that the anonymous caller knew I was hanging out with a private eye. Who would know that?

I had no way to get in touch with Falls except through the two agents. As far as I knew, they were still around. I forced myself up and peeked out the door. No one stood in the hall. Maybe Agent Falls was still in the building, I thought. I slipped my shoes on, grabbed my fanny pack, and walked downstairs.

Marianne was at the blackjack tables and Diane at the nickel slots. No one else I knew was in the casino. No one in the bar.

I hit the jackpot in the coffee shop, however, where I found Falls and both of his cronies.

"I'm letting these guys go," Falls said. "As long as all of you remain in the hotel until your flights tomorrow, I'm sure you'll be fine." He gave his men a nod and before I had a chance to utter more than two words of protest, they were gone.

He wasn't alarmed by the threatening phone call. "That's my point," he said. "If you stay here at the hotel and don't go to Oatman or the mine or Pringle's office, no one's going to bother you."

Again, I had that feeling he was watching me too closely. Then I got the message.

"How did you know we'd gone to Pringle's office?"

"Never mind that."

"Don't you want to know what we found?"

"There wasn't anything there to find."

I wanted to one-up the FBI guy and tell him what Patsy and I had discovered behind the painting, but I was afraid he'd put us under house arrest or something and foil our plan. But then I second-guessed myself on that decision as well. If the gold coins turned out to be significant, they would not be usable in a court of law because of the manner in which Patsy and I obtained them. The FBI's warrant was probably still good. They could go back in and take another look and they'd find something this time, because we'd replaced the coins, though we were unable to retape the tear. So I told him.

He was gone in a flash. I breathed a sigh of relief.

Back in my room, I reset my alarm to a full hour, kicked off my shoes, and collapsed onto the bed. This time I didn't even have a chance to close my eyes before someone pounded on the door and two female voices called my name.

"Sylvia," Marianne said as she rushed into the room, "we can't find Linda."

"We've looked everywhere," Gail said. "Didn't we?" She looked at Marianne, who nodded.

It might have been the first time all weekend the two had seen eye-to-eye.

"Wait. Where was she supposed to be?"

"In the room. Taking a nap."

Lord help her if she'd had the same kind of luck with that as I had. "And you checked everywhere in the room, including the bathroom and the closet?"

"Yes," Marianne said. "Doofus here tried to look under the bed. She didn't know it was on one of those platform thingies."

"Doofus? What do mean by that? You were the one who opened the window and looked out to see if she had jumped."

"Linda's been very upset about Sandra's death," Marianne said. "She still thinks it's her fault that Sandra went to the mine alone. I thought—"

Gail burst out laughing. "Thought? That's an odd way of putting it."

"You're the one who stood to one side when you slid the closet door open, in case she fell out with a knife in her back."

"Why is that so shocking? Just yesterday we found poor Sandra—"

"Okay, ladies, stop. Let me ask more questions. Did you check the casino?"

Gail pointed to Marianne. "She said she did."

"The restaurants and the coffee shop?"

Marianne pointed to Gail.

"The outside deck and the river walk?"

"I checked the deck, but I didn't do the whole walk," Gail said. "Linda knows we're supposed to stay at the hotel. She wouldn't leave."

"What about the bar?"

Marianne and Gail looked at each other. "Linda wouldn't be in the bar," Marianne said. "She'd never go into a bar by herself."

"Have you talked to Diane? Could she and Linda be together?"

They looked at each other again, then at me. "We'll go search some more," Marianne said.

"Sorry we bothered you," said Gail.

They were back on the case, cooperating in the temporary fashion of competing law enforcement agencies. I was sure hostilities would resurface as soon as the case was solved.

I looked longingly at my comfortable bed, debated giving it one more try, then decided it wasn't worth it. I'd join the hunt for Linda and then see who was ready for an early dinner. I wanted all that food I intended to eat to digest a little before I embarked on our voyage to find the treasure in the tunnel.

It took a while for us to track Linda down. Marianne had neglected to check the poker room, knowing that "Linda would never go off to the poker room by herself." But there she was, surrounded by college boys, a gin and tonic at her elbow, taking lessons from a young female dealer.

"I won all the practice hands," she said when I tapped her on the shoulder. She leaned over and whispered in my ear, "I think it's because I'm good at playing a part. I keep fooling them, and they never know when I have the good cards."

Linda didn't have to wear her sunglasses or the big chartreuse hat pulled down over her eyes. She just had to use her recently discovered talent for acting.

"I'm going to play later for real, Sylvia," she said. "Want to come watch?"

"I will if I can. But if I get tied up doing something else, I'll send Mom and Dad to cheer you on."

Linda looked at me suspiciously. "Tied up doing what? Are you going out with the FBI guy?"

"No. Why did you think that?"

"He was around earlier, asking questions. Wanted to know what we were planning to do this evening. Told us we had to stay at the hotel. He asked especially about you and Patsy. I thought maybe he'd ask you for a date."

"Hardly. He's a kid, Linda."

"Oh, honey, he may be younger than you are, but he's no kid. I think he wants you."

I was unable to think of a snappy reply. Instead, I blushed.

Linda nodded knowingly and turned to her cards.

I caught Marianne, Gail, and Diane bustling through the lobby, still looking for Linda. I reported my discovery.

"My gawd," said Gail.

"I want to see this," Marianne said.

Diane nodded her head. "Me, too."

The Flippers were definitely not ready for dinner. I went to tell Willie about the threatening phone call.

TWENTY-EIGHT

AT NINE O'CLOCK, long after dinner, Willie met with Patsy and Sylvia in Patsy's room. Willie wanted to discuss the midnight meeting at the mine, but before he could, Sylvia told Patsy about the threatening phone call she'd received, naming both herself and Patsy as potential victims if they didn't butt out of the mine's business.

Patsy shrugged it off. "I can take care of myself. But are you two still in?"

Willie nodded, as did his sister. Then he heard a sharp rap at the door.

Patsy used the peephole to see who was there, and opened the door without comment. All five Flippers rushed into the room with Willie's father close behind.

"Are we late?" his mom asked. She and her group scattered throughout the room, plopping down on the beds, looking from Patsy to Willie to Sylvia as they waited for an answer.

"Late for what, Mom?" Although he'd addressed the question to his mother, Willie glared at his father, who was leaning against the wall not far from the door.

"Don't look at me." His dad looked pointedly at Willie's mom.

She gave him a dirty look, then turned to address Willie. "I told all the girls what you're up to, and we feel we should be included."

"Mom—"

"Don't 'Mom' me, young man. This is for your own good. If we know everything you're going to do, and when you plan to do it, and if you stay in touch with us, then if something goes wrong, we can call for help."

"How do you propose we stay in touch?" Sylvia asked. "You lost your phone, and Dad's battery is dead."

"No, dear, I have my phone now. We have it all figured out." Willie's mom reached into her bag and pulled out four cell phones. The other Flippers nodded and proudly looked on. "We've programmed all of the numbers into each of these phones. Do you have a cell, dear?" she asked Patsy.

Patsy took her phone from her pocket.

"Good. Let me add these numbers for you. We've used a 'W' for Willie and an 'S' for Sylvia and an 'F' for Flippers, and a 'P' for Peter. What's your number, Patsy? We'll add that to the rest of the phones with, oh, we can't use the 'P' again. Use a 'Y' for Patsy, everyone."

For a few minutes Willie heard nothing but tinny beeps and occasional mutterings as the ladies added the new phone numbers.

"Now, what about the Mohave County sheriff's office and that good-looking FBI agent? Do you have those numbers?"

Patsy reached in her pocket, pulled out two business cards, and handed them over.

Willie made eye contact with his sister. Patsy had a business card for the FBI agent.

"Good," Willie's mom repeated. "This one will be 'A' for Arizona, right at the top of the list since they'll be the closest, and we'll use 'F' for FBI. Oh no, that's for Flippers. How about 'I' for FBI?"

A few minutes later, all of the phones were handed out, with Willie's mother left holding the last one. "Who's taking the first Flipper phone shift?"

Marianne raised her hand. "We drew numbers out of a hat." She looked at her watch, then looked at Willie. "I'll give it to Diane an hour after you leave. Then Gail, Linda, and Kristina get a turn, if you're gone that long."

"What if they're gone even longer?" Willie's dad had flipped his assigned phone open and was beeping his way through the menu.

Willie caught his mom's fierce gaze. "If they're gone more than four hours," she said, "I'm calling the sheriff."

Willie thought about protesting, but if they were gone longer than four hours and not one of them had called in, then there was probably a good reason to be alarmed. He and Sylvia exchanged a look. She nodded. He turned to his mom and said, "Fine."

"Now, what's next?" His mom raised her eyebrows expectantly. "Patsy, dear, you must have a license to carry, and you said yesterday you knew where you could get a gun. Are you armed?"

Patsy hesitated, then reached into the waistband at the back of her slacks and briefly displayed her gun before stuffing it back in her belt.

Willie glanced at Sylvia, noting that she seemed to be as surprised as he was. Where did Patsy get a gun? Was it legal?

"A Glock." Marianne nodded her approval. "That's a cop gun. Is it a twenty-three?"

"How'd you know that? And what the hell is a twenty-three?" Gail's question sounded accusatory.

"Well, there's this guy I know who owns a shooting range and rents guns and gives lessons, and I go there all the time. He let me shoot his Glock." She wrinkled her nose at Gail.

"My gawd." Gail turned to Willie's mom. "What's next? The plan?"

"Yes. Now you need to tell us your plan. Willie? Sylvia? Patsy? When are you supposed to meet that boy at the mine? Who's going to stand watch? How long do you think you'll be down in the tunnel? How will the sentry signal you if someone shows up at the mine?"

Willie squirmed as he felt Patsy and Sylvia turn their gaze in his direction. They clearly thought the only reason his mother knew all the right questions to ask was because Willie had told her everything. Willie shook his head and pointed at his dad.

"Never mind," Patsy said. "This isn't such a bad thing. The

more people who know where we are, the better chance we have of getting rescued if we find ourselves in trouble. What kind of a crook would take three hostages and then go to the hotel and corral six senior citizens and a giant lady biker?"

"A very desperate crook," Linda said in her softest voice.

They were all silent. No doubt, Willie thought, the Flippers were remembering the moment they'd found Sandra's body in the mine.

"Well?" his mom said. "You do have a plan, don't you?"

"Actually, Mom, we were just getting to that when you came in."

Marianne clapped her hands. "Oh, goody. We got here in time for the best part. I have an idea."

Gail sighed.

"You can't use your phones in the mine," Marianne said, "and even if your sentry yells or blows a whistle, you probably won't be able to hear, so we think you should use yarn."

"Yarn." Willie frowned. "You mean, like unrolling a ball of yarn as we go?"

Marianne nodded.

He shook his head as he tried not to laugh. "I'm sure the tunnel goes down too far. Wouldn't reach. And anyway, yarn might break."

"Actually," Diane said. "We thought of that." She picked up the shopping bag she'd set by the bed, then dumped four one-pound skeins of yarn on the bed. "I bought these at a shop in Oatman, enough to crochet an afghan, but I'm willing to donate them to the cause. You pull a strand from each one and tie them together on the end. If you have four strands instead of one, you'll be able to give it a good hard yank and it will hold fine."

"I still don't think it'll be long enough."

"Then do two at a time instead of four, Willie. You'll have to make an awfully good knot when you start the next two, of course, so they don't pull apart."

He wasn't sure what to say, especially since he hadn't yet come up with a better idea. He looked at Sylvia, who seemed to be suppressing a smile as she said, "Could work." Then at Patsy, who merely looked thoughtful and said nothing.

"Okay, thanks," he said. "We'll take the yarn. But we get to decide who the sentry is and we get to make up our own signals."

"What are you going to use for evidence bags?" Gail said.

Linda looked mystified. "What do they need evidence bags for?"

"For evidence, you ninny."

"Evidence of what? They want to peek into the boxes and see what's inside. They can't go stealing stuff."

"But what if they find drugs?"

"They still can't steal stuff." Linda turned to Sylvia. "Can you?"

"No, of course not. As a former officer of the court, I'd definitely have to keep my hands off." Sylvia emphatically shook her head, then exchanged a quick glance with Patsy. "But let's say we found something that we thought we should show the police or the FBI. Technically, that's not stealing, because we'd have every intention of returning it as soon as possible. Do we have anything we can use to bring back a sample?"

"I have it." Gail dug around in her oversized canvas bag. "I had to take first aid classes when I joined the park volunteers, and sometimes we have to pick up dangerous-looking trash, so I always carry latex gloves and plastic bags in my purse." She dangled a quart-size plastic bag that had the gloves and additional plastic bags inside. "Take what you need."

"Excellent." Patsy took the plastic container from Gail, then stuffed two of the gloves and a couple of bags in her pocket.

When Patsy tossed the container to Willie, he said, "I think I'll take sentry duty, so I won't need these." He handed the container to his sister, who stuffed her gloves and bags into her fanny pack.

"I hope you don't expect me to get anything else in this pack," she said as she struggled to close the zipper.

"No, I think we've covered everything." Willie's mom hesitated. "Peter, do you think we need a secret code to use on the phone? In case someone's listening?"

"No, Mom," Willie said. "No secret codes. We have to go."

"You do have sweaters, don't you? It gets cold in the desert at night."

Sylvia pointedly grabbed her sweatshirt and waved it at her mother.

All five of the Flippers jumped up and rushed to the door so that Willie, along with Patsy and Sylvia, had to wade through them, accepting their hugs and warnings and good wishes for a safe return. Willie took one last look at his mom and dad before stepping on the elevator.

WILLIE FOUGHT TO QUELL his anxiety as they traveled Cone Boundary Road from Route 95 to Oatman. The road was lit by the moon and stars, a couple of housing developments, and the occasional cabin or trailer along the way.

"I didn't realize how dark it would be out here," Sylvia said. "Do you think they turn off the big lights at the mine at night?"

"We'll see soon enough," Patsy said.

Willie stared out the window, willing his night vision to improve for at least this one venture.

After a few minutes, Patsy braked sharply and swerved.

"Rattlesnakes." Sylvia uttered the one word and no more.

Willie understood. Rattlesnakes were nocturnal creatures that might lurk around the mine office where small rodents gathered to forage in the trash. They'd have to be careful, especially if the mine yard and the trail up to the mine itself were poorly lit.

As she cruised into Oatman, Patsy slowed the car again, this time to a crawl. The saloon was the only business in town that showed signs of life. One light shone from the window on the second floor of the hotel. The small houses perched above the town, on the bluff and on Nob Hill, were dark. Willie supposed all the night owls were sitting in the bar.

Patsy drove slowly through town, her gaze focused on the road ahead.

Willie studied the storefronts as they rode along. A man sat on a bench in the shadows near the door. He waved as the car passed. Willie did not wave back, but glanced at Sylvia to see if she'd noticed anything. She stared out the window on the same side, apparently looking in the same direction, but she did not raise her hand nor mention the man. One more glance out the back window confirmed nothing. The shadows were so deep; there was nothing to see.

"Oh, shit." Patsy slammed on the brakes and pulled to the side of the street. "Look." She pointed straight ahead. "Parked in that little parking lot by the hill."

"I can't see anything." Willie leaned forward between the bucket seats, stretching as far as he could, and stared out the front window. "What is it?"

"Remember that black truck we saw today, Sylvia? On our way back to Laughlin?"

"Is that it?"

Willie looked at Sylvia. "Do I know about this?"

"I can't remember if I told you. We thought it might be the same black truck that ran me off the road. Nothing bad happened, except we got a little nervous."

"What's it doing here in the middle of the night?" Patsy said.

"Maybe the driver's in the saloon, hanging out with the old-timers. Or maybe it's one of the tourists, spending the night in one of those creepy rooms in the hotel."

Willie suspected his sister wanted to reassure him so he wouldn't balk and refuse to participate in her crazy plan. But the thought of that black truck cruising along behind them to the mine, skulking in the shadows, its occupants watching, gave him the shivers. If he was standing guard, and if a black truck crept into a dark yard with its lights off, would he see it? When he'd imagined sounding an alarm, it was in response to cars or trucks aggressively charging along the road at whatever speed they dared, gravel flying, lights blazing.

"I don't think I'd see that truck if it was trying to sneak up on me." He leaned down again and looked through the windshield. "I still don't see it."

He saw the glance that Patsy and Sylvia exchanged, but he couldn't help it. He had to be honest.

"Would it be better if I played lookout?" Patsy made eye contact with Willie and held it a long time before she grinned and assured him that she didn't mind.

Willie didn't mind, either. As a matter of fact, he would feel a lot more comfortable if he was in the tunnel with his sister, and if Patsy and her gun were topside, ready to yank on that useless yarn he'd agreed to take along.

TWENTY-NINE

We drove slowly past the entrance to the mine's darkened parking lot. Only two small lights were visible anywhere on the grounds. One was from the window in the office. The second was the bare bulb in a fixture over the office door. The rest of the yard, as well as the dirt and gravel track up to the mine entrance, were lit by the stars. It would be a few hours before the moon rose, and if I correctly remembered the night before, we should expect only a quarter-moon, if that. There was little concern, however, since Kelly had promised to give us whatever equipment we needed. I assumed that meant hard hats with headlamps, or heavy-duty flashlights.

"The gate's open." Willie's nose was pressed to the left side window. "Why do you think they left the gate open?"

"Maybe Kelly did it, thinking we'd bring the car inside the yard," I said.

Patsy shook her head. "I don't think that's a good idea." She drove past, just as we'd planned, to park at the pull-off Dad had noticed as they'd passed through the area on Frieda's motorcycle. As he'd told us, it was around a curve, less than an eighth of a mile past our destination. Our car would not be visible to anyone coming from the Oatman side. We wouldn't be so lucky if we had visitors from Kingman, but Willie had suggested we raise the hood on the car to signal engine trouble, and that made good sense to me.

Patsy pulled the release lever. I lifted the hood and moved the support rod into place.

"I hope all the parts are here when we get back," I said. "It's a long walk to Oatman."

The little flashlight from Linda's emergency case was

tucked into a side pocket of my pack. Until we rounded the curve, I used it to mark the edge of the road and to sweep light back and forth in front of us. I still had that rattlesnake on my mind.

Once the dim glow from the mine office was visible, however, so was the road's narrow berm. I carried the flashlight in my hand and flipped it on from time to time to check the way ahead.

"Kelly's here," Patsy whispered. "He flashed a light right after you turned yours off."

"Where? Can you see him? How do you know it's him?" The anxiety in Willie's tone was a concern. He seemed jumpy. Did he sense some greater danger? Had he tuned in to his other world, a place I couldn't go?

I wanted to know before I charged ahead with my usual dumb-ass single-minded approach—pursue the immediate goal and worry about the consequences later. "Willie." Before I could say more, Patsy tapped my shoulder.

"Kelly's on the right side, next to the fence." Patsy's eyes were apparently a lot sharper than either Willie's or mine. Or maybe my night vision was as bad as Willie's. It was a little late in the game to figure that out.

I turned on the flashlight and shined it in the direction of the gate.

Kelly stepped into the light. He handed each one of us a hard hat. "Don't turn the lamps on yet," he cautioned. "We'll wait 'til we're up on the hill." He turned and walked toward the track to the tunnel entrance.

"Wait, Kelly," I called out. "Aren't you going to close the gate?"

"Oh, yeah. Guess I'd better."

"You going to lock it?"

He looked at me as though I was causing him an awful lot of trouble, but he shut and locked the gate while we watched.

"What about the lights? Shouldn't you turn the lights off?" I wondered if this college boy was getting good grades. Or was his only deficiency common sense?

"The one over the door stays lit all the time. I guess I better turn off the one inside…" Kelly wandered toward the office, his words trailing into the darkness as he moved farther away.

There was still enough light that I could see Willie shaking his head. I patted his arm. "Kelly seemed okay when I was talking to him. Give him a break. He might be a little scared."

"Or maybe he's having second thoughts." Patsy stuck her hard hat on her head and strode toward the office. I followed, unsure what she intended to say or do to poor Kelly.

Willie appeared at my elbow and whispered in my ear, "She's having second thoughts, too."

Maybe Willie was reading Patsy's mind now, or else he was putting his own spin on her behavior, hoping I'd rethink tonight's venture.

"Willie, I don't care if you and Patsy chicken out on me. And you can keep Kelly with you, as well. I'm going into the mine to see what's in those boxes. The cops aren't doing it, and the FBI isn't doing it, and that means they don't have sufficient grounds to request a search warrant, because they didn't look at anything except the end of the tunnel and the shaft when they investigated Sandra's death. It was a crime scene, for heaven's sake. How come the mine was open for business in less than twenty-four hours? That's crazy. There's something very wrong here, something that might explain why Sandra died. I want to know what it is."

The office door opened and Kelly sauntered out, followed by Patsy, who was obviously agitated. She kept edging closer to him, talking in a low voice, her hands in constant motion. I had never seen her act this way. Even that moment I'd caught her downing a shot at the bar, right after the Vegas PI was found dead in her hotel room, Patsy didn't look or act particularly distressed.

"What's going on?" I said as the four of us came together a few feet from the office.

"Our buddy here was on the phone when I walked in."

Willie and I looked at Kelly. I could almost hear the wheels turning in Willie's overly cautious brain.

"I told you," Kelly said. "I was supposed to call my girlfriend earlier and I forgot."

"Did you check it out? Hit redial?" Willie's suspicious nature was kicking in big time.

"Hard to believe," Patsy answered, "but they've got an ancient rotary phone in there. No redial."

"Honest," Kelly said. "Who else would I call?"

"I believe him." And I sure as hell hoped I wasn't making a mistake. But this was the only chance I had to figure out what was going on. Our plane was leaving the next morning, and I planned to be on it. "Let's go, Kelly," I said. "You lead the way."

With the help of my tiny flashlight we made it up the rutted dirt and gravel road to the mine entrance without mishap. Kelly had us use the lamps attached to our hard hats toward the end of our climb, but after he turned on the generator that powered the lights inside the mine, we switched the headlamps off to save the batteries.

On the way, Patsy and Willie had their heads together, presumably discussing who was to stand guard and who was to accompany Kelly and me into the tunnel. I had a sneaking suspicion Willie decided I'd need protection, and that a PI with a gun was a better bodyguard than an old guy with no gun. Whatever the reason, Willie stayed aboveground.

"Who has the yarn?" Patsy said.

Willie and I looked at each other and displayed our empty hands. Was Patsy serious? I hadn't thought any of us actually planned to use that silly yarn idea.

Kelly said, "Yarn? What do you need yarn for?"

Patsy explained, chuckling as she described the plans our elderly friends had made for us.

"Not necessary. Just flip the light switch up and down," Kelly told Willie. "Flip it off and leave it ten seconds, then flip it back on to say someone's coming. Flip it off and on two times real fast to signal big trouble."

So simple.

Kelly's expression changed as he realized the significance of the yarn plan from the Flippers. He frowned. "Other people know you're here?"

"Don't worry about it," said Patsy. "Let's get this over with."

"What if the generator quits, Kelly? Runs out of gas or something?" Willie the worrier was still on the job.

"If the lights go off and stay off, we'll assume there's trouble and come out," Kelly assured us.

"Fine. Go. Hurry up." Once again, Willie's tone of voice told me how anxious he was. This time, it raised little prickles of fear between my shoulder blades, but I wasn't going to change my mind now. I pointed toward the entrance and led the way.

We made the trip down the tunnel much faster than had been possible with the tour. The side passage where I'd seen the boxes was unlit as before. Kelly turned on the light and led the way, then hunched in the corner at the end to let Patsy and me look past him into the side room.

The entry was so narrow that the boxes most recently stacked in the space nearly blocked the way in. No more than one of us at a time could squeeze through, and inside there was no space to put boxes on the floor. Pulling them down from the top was not an option, except for those stacked in the entryway. Only those few could be unloaded into the side tunnel itself.

Frustrated by the monumental task before us, I kicked the container at the bottom of the four-box-high stack in the entryway. The contents of the box rattled. I kicked it again, this time realizing that it was a wooden crate, not a cardboard storage box. Sure enough, whatever was inside rattled, or jingled, or something in-between. I had a good idea what was in that crate, and it wasn't paper.

"We can lift these down," I said, thinking Kelly could make himself useful. He ignored me and slouched against the wall, while Patsy reached up to help.

The top box was full of paper. I pulled out a few sheets and examined them. Patsy took a few more.

"Financial stuff," she said. "I'll bet it's from one of Barry Pringle's offices. Look, here's your mom's name."

I peered over her shoulder and then glanced at the papers in my hand. Everything carried the Desert Hedge Investors header. We put the paper back in the box, replaced the lid, and brought the second box down. All papers.

The third box was the same.

The fourth was so heavy, I couldn't slide it forward by myself. It was strong, like a crate for shipping heavy tools. And the lid was nailed down. I unzipped my pack and dug through the contents, placing random items on top of the crate to get them out of the way. The Swiss Army knife had worked its way to the bottom, of course. I wasted additional precious time stuffing most of the assortment back inside my pack before opening the array of tools. I left the super-duper tube of glue right on top, thinking I could refasten the lid that way. No sense in destroying a good Swiss Army knife by using it as a hammer.

Patsy stood so close I could hear her breathe. Kelly abandoned his attempts to hold up the wall and hovered at my side, radiating body heat and the scent of sandalwood.

I pried the nails loose with the screwdriver head and raised the lid. My mouth dropped open.

"Son of a bitch," Patsy muttered.

"Wowee," Kelly said.

The lights went off, then on, in rapid succession. And then the lights went out.

THIRTY

THIS WAS BAD. I hadn't expected it, had charged forward with my usual bull-headed determination to do things my way, and had refused to acknowledge the signs that Willie expected trouble. He knew I wouldn't listen, so he came along anyway, hoping to keep me safe.

Now I was more frightened for Willie than for the rest of us. I switched my headlamp on and jumped up, vaguely registering a sound that could have been gold coins scooped up in someone's hand. I nudged Patsy toward the main tunnel, figuring Kelly could take care of himself.

Patsy reached for her gun, but I shoved her hand away. "You can't shoot that thing down here," I whispered. "Won't it do something bad?"

"You mean, like start an avalanche?"

A smart ass. She was beginning to grow on me.

"Just go," I said.

We made it roughly halfway to the surface, scrambling at near warp speed, before we saw the spots of light dancing along the wall. Someone was around a bend in the tunnel, and there was nowhere for us to hide.

"Go back," Patsy said.

I turned and ran into Kelly, who was standing right behind us, his arms stretched out to the sides.

"Whoa, ladies. You're going the wrong way."

"Kelly," I whispered. "There's somebody coming."

"Yeah, I know," he said, making it sound like an apology. "I wasn't telling the truth when I said I'd called my girlfriend."

"Well, crap!" That pissed me off.

I grabbed Kelly's right arm with both hands, stepped into his embrace and pivoted on my right foot, so I held his body against my back and his right arm forward over my right shoulder. I smashed his fingers together with my left hand, then I pried his thumb back with my right. I brought that little red-headed twerp to his knees, while his left arm was still flailing around trying to get a handful of my hair, which was too short to do him any good.

I bent over Kelly, trying to figure out what to do next, wishing he'd stop hollering and hoping he wouldn't figure out how easily he could pull me off balance.

Patsy solved my problem when she whacked him on the head with her Glock.

I let Kelly go. He toppled over, unconscious.

Patsy stuffed the gun back in her waistband and grabbed Kelly by the back of his collar, trying to drag him toward the side tunnel. It was too late. Two men crept around the corner and stopped short when they saw us. She let go of Kelly's shirt and stood up straight. Kelly's head made a dull thunk as it hit the rock floor.

"What the devil!" said the man whose nose sat slightly askew.

"I told you that kid wasn't worth a plugged nickel," the second guy said. It was my old friend Crash, the tour guide I'd thought so funny and concerned, at least until he'd jerked me around the next day for being too nosy.

They looked from us down to Kelly and then back at us again.

"I guess you broads don't know you're trespassing on private property," said the nose guy.

Crash snickered. "They beat up on Kelly, too. We could get 'em put in jail."

"Jail. That's a good one." The first guy snorted through his ugly nose. He pulled a big dirty handkerchief from his pocket, searched for a clean corner, and blew so hard and so productively, I wondered if his brains were leaking into his sinuses. This had to be the same creep who made the threatening phone call.

I stepped forward as if I planned to walk around the two guys and leave, but Crash stretched his arms out and blocked my path.

"I don't think so, sister. The boss will be along in a minute. He wants to have a chat."

"Step back," Patsy whispered to me. "You need a running start."

Ah. Action time. Sounded like a good idea to me.

"Three-two-one," she said.

We rushed them. Patsy hit the nose guy in the gut with her head, knocking him off balance. He gasped for breath.

I rammed Crash in the chest with my shoulder, but bounced off. He laughed at me.

As Patsy tried to take advantage of her forward momentum and scramble up and over her victim, he grabbed her arm and jerked her off balance.

Crash turned his head to see what his partner was doing. I seized the moment and kicked him in the balls. *Laugh at that, butthead.*

Patsy's charming companion held both her arms and pulled her down onto his body.

I stepped up next to her, pulled up the tail of her shirt, and yanked the Glock from her waistband. The nose guy had an abrupt change of attitude when I pointed the gun at his head.

He let go of Patsy and scooted away, his hands in the air.

"Watch out behind you," Patsy said. "Kelly moved his arm." She patted the nose guy down, then stood up and motioned him to move closer to Kelly.

I hugged the tunnel wall so no one could grab Patsy's gun out of my hand. "Are we going to leave them here like this?"

"Unless you've got a better idea, Sylvia. You didn't put any rope or duct tape in with all the other crap you have in your pack, did you?"

"No. And the glue is back there, on top of the lid to the crate. Wait, there's one thing." I handed the gun to Patsy. Once again, what I needed was on the bottom of my pack. Doing the best I could to keep the rest of the contents inside, I found one end of the bungee cord and eased its length out where Patsy could see it.

"Okay, boys," Patsy said, "take off your belts and buckle them tight around your ankles."

"The kid's out cold," Crash whined. His hands were still cupped over his groin. "How's he going to do that?"

"Prop the little son of a bitch against the wall and do it for him. And while you're at it, pull up your shirt and your pant legs. Kelly's, too. I want to see if you're armed."

I stared at Patsy, the bungee cord dangling from my hand.

She smiled at me as the two men wrestled Kelly free of his belt and secured his ankles, then went to work on their own. Crash had a lot of trouble, groaning every time he moved. He was still struggling to get his belt off, long after the guy with the snotty nose was hobbled.

I waited, still dangling the bungee cord in front of me.

"You can put that away," Patsy said. "It won't work. Too stretchy."

Crash was still fumbling with his belt.

"Wait," Patsy told him. "Before you do that, move over there and sit back to back with your buddy."

Crash grunted in pain with each move until he sat and leaned against the nose guy's back. Crash looked at Patsy and motioned his head toward the man who sat behind him. She stepped closer and whacked the nose guy on the head. He fell over, clunking his head again on the floor.

"Now, git," whispered Crash. He rolled to the side and closed his eyes.

I stared at Crash and Patsy, trying to figure it all out, completely caught off guard. I'm sure my mouth was hanging open. Patsy snapped at me to get my attention.

"Sylvia!" She waved her hand, pointing up the tunnel.

I thought she wanted to leave, but then I saw the tension in her face.

"Somebody's coming," she said. She handed me the gun while she gathered the three hard hats and switched off their lamps. Retrieving her gun, she headed for the mine's entrance with me following close behind. This time there were no dancing lights on the mine walls. I didn't hear any voices. That bothered me. I caught up to Patsy as I reached up and turned off my headlamp.

"Maybe they heard us," I whispered. "Maybe they turned off their lights. If they see ours, they'll know where we are."

Patsy switched off her own lamp. "Did you hear that?"

"No. What did it sound like?" Then I heard it. "Somebody's trying to start the generator. Maybe it's Willie."

The sound was faint but unmistakable. The motor kicked in and coughed a time or two before settling into its rhythmic pattern. Seconds later, the bare bulbs strung along the tunnel ceiling flickered on. Patsy and I took full advantage, breaking into a cautious jog to cover as much distance as possible before something else happened.

There were so many questions I wanted to ask her, but when I gasped her name, she shushed me.

We burst from the tunnel opening onto the gravel area outside. No one was there. The lights were on in the mine office below, as well as the pole lights in the yard and parking area. In addition to Kelly's car, three pickup trucks were parked in the lot. One was black. I figured one truck each for Crash and the guy with the crooked nose, and one truck for the unknown boss who maybe had Willie. I didn't want to think about that. I took the helmets and tossed them into the darkness beyond the mine entrance.

"I wonder where Willie is," Patsy said. She checked every direction, pistol held in a two-handed grip, her stance telegraphing her professional training.

"I wonder who started the generator and turned on the lights," I said.

Patsy didn't answer. She scurried about, checking into the dark corners near the mine entrance.

Questioning my own lapse in common sense, I stepped toward the switch at the entrance to the mine and turned off the lights. Patsy responded by shutting down the generator.

"Patsy, did you used to be a cop?"

"We don't have time to chat," she said, blowing off my question like I'd asked for a carrot cake recipe. "Give me that bungee cord, Sylvia."

I dragged the cord out of my pack and handed it over. I heard the click of metal on metal and switched my headlamp on to see what she was up to.

With one end of the bungee cord hooked to a handle on the generator, Patsy stretched the cord across the mine entrance and hooked its other end to an old rusted wheelbarrow that lay nearby. She dusted her hands together to signal a job well done. "Let's get out of here."

"We have to find Willie."

"I know. He might be in the office."

With one last glance past the lighted area and into the darkness that was the desert, I let out a long slow breath and took a couple of steps forward.

Stop, I told myself. I turned once again toward the desert, trying to make out any shapes at all—scrub grass, a cactus, anything. All I saw was velvety blackness and stars.

Patsy tiptoed to stand beside me, then tugged on my elbow. "We have to go."

Was someone there in the darkness, watching? Was Willie lying unconscious nearby? I couldn't shrug off that peculiar feeling. But neither could I deny the danger we'd face when three angry guys came charging after us, even if one of them was less dangerous than the other two. It was too risky to call Willie on his cell phone. What if he had hidden and the ringing phone gave away his location? Why hadn't we set all the phones on vibrate?

"Patsy," I whispered. "Should we call the cops?"

"Not yet."

"Stop a minute. I need to reset the ringer."

"What, you want it to play a little boogie-woogie?"

"I want to set it on vibrate in case Willie calls."

"We don't have time." She pulled out her phone and checked the display in the lamplight. "Hell, turn it off."

With reluctance I turned off my phone, and we once again headed down the road.

THIRTY-ONE

WILLIE HAD FELT the gun in his ribs and flipped the mine lights off and on before his assailant had time to react. A hand reached around him and shut down the generator. Willie caught his breath. He hadn't heard a thing. He'd seen nothing and no one. He had let Sylvia, Patsy, and Kelly go into the mine, trusting he'd signal them at the first sign of danger. Now they were down there in the dark and it was his fault.

"Turn around," a voice ordered.

Willie did as he was told. A headlamp shone in his eyes, blinding him as effectively as the darkness had before. A second lamp came on. Then a third.

"Who's down there with the kid?"

"Just two women," Willie said. "They don't mean any harm. They wanted to go back to where their friend died, pay their respects. You know women. They do stuff like that."

"Sure," said the man with the gun. He spoke over his shoulder to the others. "See if this guy is armed. Then go down there and get Kelly and them broads. Bring 'em to the office. I'll take this one and meet you there."

"He doesn't have a gun. Just this." The searcher held up Willie's cell phone, then stuffed it into his own pocket.

Willie's captor waved toward the road after the other men had disappeared into the mine. "Get walking."

Willie moved forward and took a side step in the man's direction. The man edged away and raised the gun to point at Willie's chest. Willie nodded, turned toward the road, bent over, thrust his right leg out and back, and hooked his captor's ankle. With one quick jerk, he pulled the guy off his feet.

Arms flailing in an attempt to regain his balance, then

arms down in an effort to break his fall, the man landed on his butt, his gun skittering across the gravel in one direction, his hard hat in another.

Willie couldn't see the gun, so he lunged for the hard hat, grabbed it, then ran into the desert toward the nearest rocky hill, using the hat's lamp as a flashlight. Out of breath, he turned off the light and crouched down to listen. At first he heard nothing but his own heartbeat pounding in his ears. Finally, the sounds of the desert settled around him. A tiny scratching in the sand. A flutter. A rattle.

Holy mackerel. A rattle? But from which direction? He flipped on the headlamp and peered into the darkness in front and to the sides. *Go forward to the open desert,* he told himself. *Away from the rocks.*

He held his breath until he thought he was in the clear. Switching off the light again, he listened, this time more concerned that the man by the mine entrance had seen the light and knew where he was. The night covered him as he crept farther away from the spot where he'd extinguished his lamp. He stopped again and waited. And waited.

And then someone was on him, dragging him down, yanking the hard hat from his grasp and using it as a weapon. Willie fought hard, tried to get a grip on the man's hair, tried to get his arm around the man's neck. Nothing worked. Willie was down, his nose pressing into the sand.

Contradicting every instinct, resisting his body's desire to fight back, he forced himself to go limp. The man waited a moment, then pulled Willie's head up by his hair and let go. At the last second, Willie turned his head just enough so that he'd be able to breathe. His face hit the sand hard. He saw stars and tasted blood.

The attacker clambered off Willie's back and grabbed Willie's foot. He tugged once, again, then gave up. Willie heard shuffling sounds, as though the man circled, searching for the hard hat. Raising one eyelid, peeking through his lashes, Willie saw a headlamp come on, sweep the area, and then move away. In seconds, the desert was silent again.

After four or five minutes had passed, Willie gingerly rolled onto his back and rested there while he flexed his fingers, felt around his face, bent his knees.

A weird sensation settled over him, like a fabric light as air. He opened his eyes and almost fainted. A man squatted next to him, watching him. But this man wasn't wearing a hard hat or carrying a gun. It was the man from the Oatman Hotel—the ghost.

Willie tried to stand up. He almost cried from the pain in the left side of his lower back. Rolling over on his stomach, he gradually got to his hands and knees and struggled to his feet. Once up, he stood at a tilt with his hip thrust forward, his hand pushing his thumb as deeply as possible into the muscle spasm. Each step forward hurt like the devil.

His ghost stood up and nodded.

Encouraged, Willie was determined to get down the hill, one step at a time.

His attacker's light reached the mine entrance. The generator came alive and lights blazed from the tunnel. The headlamp bobbed up and down as its wearer jogged down the incline toward the office.

Still Willie continued his slow, painful progress across the desert, relying totally on the small amount of light radiating from the mine, hoping he wouldn't hear another rattle, hoping he wouldn't trip and fall, hoping Sylvia and Patsy would be okay until he got to the office and rescued them. The ghost that walked beside him seemed a benevolent presence, not a malicious one. It felt good to have him there. Willie reached his hand out to touch him, but the ghost stepped away.

Two lights came out of the mine fast, paused, and turned toward the incline. Willie sucked in his breath. What if the thugs had done something to Sylvia and Patsy, something horrible like tossing them down the shaft where Sandra had been found? But he supposed if that were true, Kelly would be with the thugs. Unless he was wrong about Kelly. Unless the men had killed or captured Kelly. Willie shook his head, sure Sylvia's determination to trust the guide had been a mistake.

Could the two lights be Sylvia and Patsy? Could his sister and Patsy have overpowered three strong men and escaped?

Willie stood still, concentrating on the two lights, repeating his sister's name over and over like a sibilant summons.

The lights moved toward the mine entrance. The tunnel went dark. The silence was sudden and profound when the generator's faint throbbing died. Again the two lights moved down the incline, but then one stopped, came back, and stopped again. It flashed back and forth, back and forth.

With renewed vigor, Willie charged forward as fast as his odd posture and painful gait would allow. But the light didn't wait. The two lights came together and resumed their original trek down the hill. Seconds later, the soft glow of a young moon rose over the desert. Willie pressed his thumb into his sore back with greater energy, visualizing the pain dissolving under the pressure. With a few deep breaths, he mentally set the pain aside.

On his right, his ghostly companion kept pace.

"I'm okay now," Willie said.

The apparition nodded and dissolved into the darkness.

THIRTY-TWO

THE MOON FINALLY MADE an appearance in those dark, dark hours before dawn. I switched off my headlamp and signaled Patsy to do the same, not that it made us less visible as we marched down the dark road toward the lighted yard. We were both so intent on walking carefully, as well as keeping an eye on the office and parking lot, that neither of us thought to toss our shiny white hard hats aside. At the time, we just hoped the boss, as the others had called him, wasn't looking our way, and that he hadn't hurt Willie.

Who had turned the mine lights on, Willie or the unknown boss? Where was that person now? And why had all my senses gone on high alert and tried to lure me into the desert?

I stumbled when I stepped sideways on a stone. It was a mistake to let my mind wander. *Pay attention,* I told myself. *Watch the ground. One foot in front of the other.*

By the time Patsy and I reached the yard and paused in the shelter of the first storage building, it was obvious we could not get to the office without being seen. The men we'd left in the mine might be in hot pursuit at any moment. If Crash was one of the good guys, he could sabotage their efforts. Then again, he might want to keep his little betrayal a secret, let the bad guys think he was one of them.

I wasn't taking any more chances. I pulled my phone out of my pocket, turned it on, and waited while it retrieved all its little signals.

Two missed calls. One from my mom. One from Agent Falls. None from Willie. I didn't listen to the messages. Mom was in Laughlin and there was nothing she could do. Falls was in Laughlin and probably had no jurisdiction in Arizona without a federal warrant. But the Mohave County sheriff was based in Kingman, and for all I knew there was a satellite office in Bullhead City. The sheriff had jurisdiction. He and his deputies had tough vehicles with lights and sirens. And even if we got into trouble for being on mine property, he could get us out safely and help find Willie before anything worse happened. I called the sheriff.

Patsy looked around when she heard me talking, but she didn't say anything, only listened a minute and then turned to watch the office.

"Five minutes," I said after I'd ended the call.

"Five minutes? From Kingman?"

"Dispatcher said they're already on their way."

"No shit," Patsy said. "What a coincidence."

I didn't think she sounded all that surprised.

"Actually, they were looking for us," I said. "Apparently we're wanted for questioning by the FBI. The dispatcher said we better be here when the sheriff shows up, because he's madder than hell about being dragged out of bed to run an errand for the Feds."

"Oh. This might be unpleasant."

And that might be the understatement of the year. I figured we'd stay where we were, hidden in the shadows, until the sheriff showed up. Then we'd surrender without giving the man any trouble. I was totally unprepared when Patsy gave the old move-'em-out signal and took off across the yard.

And even more unprepared to feel a hot sweaty hand clamp down on my shoulder and a voice whisper, "Hush."

I froze.

"It's me."

I did a graceful one-hundred-eighty-degree pivot worthy of a prima ballerina, grabbed Willie around the shoulders, and hugged my crabby old brother as hard as I could.

He groaned. "That really hurts, Syl."

I released him so fast he staggered backward a couple of steps. "What happened?"

"It's a long story. I lost my phone. Have you called anyone?"

"Sheriff. He'll be here in a minute."

"Where's Patsy?"

"She went that way, toward the office."

"I think the guy who beat me up is in there."

"He beat you up? Wait a minute. Where have you been all this time?"

"Up there." Willie pointed toward the mine entrance. "I was out in the desert a ways, walking straight at you, when you stood on the road. If there'd been a moon, you might have seen me."

As I looked up the hill, I thought I saw movement on the road. "The guys who jumped Patsy and me are coming down." I grabbed Willie's hand. "We have to get to the office. Can you run?"

Before he could respond, all hell broke loose. First, I heard the loud roar of a vehicle that had lost its muffler. In the far distance, police sirens. Then someone started the engine on the black 4x4, turned on the lights, and accelerated in reverse while turning the front end toward the gate. The truck moved forward. The driver slammed on his brakes when Willie and I were caught in the glare of his headlights. We froze. I could almost hear the driver's maniacal chuckle as he revved the engine.

I couldn't decide if Willie and I should run to the shelter of the storage building or make a break for the office. Kelly, Crash, and the other guy had to be near the bottom of the hill. The truck was ready to charge us from the parking area. Patsy had disappeared. She and her gun might have been ambushed by the unknown boss. Maybe Willie and I could run straight at the truck and dodge to the side at the last second.

I didn't have to think about it for very long. The distant motor I'd heard grew louder as a vehicle came roaring around the hill from the direction of Oatman. A big motorcycle with a sidecar charged into the parking area and skidded to a stop. The passenger in the sidecar stood up and aimed a shotgun at the front side window of the black truck. The passenger was wearing one of my mom's favorite jackets.

"Over here," Dad yelled as he scrambled off the back of the bike. "Who are those guys? Are they dangerous, Sylvia?"

"Dad, what are you doing here?"

He retrieved the shotgun and handed it to Frieda before helping Mom out of the sidecar.

Two sheriff's cars screamed around the curve from the direction of Kingman, then screeched into the lot.

Frieda quickly stuffed the gun inside the long plastic box attached to the side of the bike, the box I'd assumed held fishing gear or tent poles.

"Frieda!" I lifted my eyebrows and stared pointedly at the gun box.

"Oh," she whispered, after a short confused pause. "It wasn't loaded."

Of course not. What was I thinking?

Dad was suddenly in my face. Mom, bright-eyed with excitement, stood at his elbow. "What are you doing here?" I said again.

But before I could get an answer, Kelly and his buddies had stormed into the lot, yelling that they were legitimate mine employees and the deputies should arrest me and another broad for trespassing and they had been assaulted and, by golly, all three of them would press charges.

While one of the deputies tried to figure out if the other broad they were talking about was my mom or Frieda, another deputy pulled open the driver's side door of the black truck and told the driver to step down. Before I got a look at the driver, the sheriff jumped out of the second car and motioned me to join him, but he did it with a glare and a finger pointed first at me and then at a spot on the ground right in front of him. That gesture said more than if he'd yelled.

"Where's the other one?" he asked. He glanced at the scrap of paper in his hand. "You're the judge, right? The PI, where is she?"

"She went toward the office a few minutes ago. I haven't seen her since."

"Let's go. In my car. Backseat."

I stood my ground. "You better watch those three guys," I said.

"Yeah, I know. One of 'em's mine."

Crash. That explained a lot. But how did Patsy know?

The sheriff was just getting started. "Between the Feds and your little tour group, there've been more slivers in my behind than you'd find on a split rail fence. I've got a simple investigation here—a smuggling ring hiding stuff in a desert mine. I was ready to put 'em out of business, and who shows up?"

Sheriff Yamato was talking at me through clenched teeth, but he kept his voice low, as if he didn't want anyone else to hear.

"The FBI, that's who. And while they're trying to solve their fraud case, you old ladies started finding bodies and then got one of yourselves killed, and next thing I know, I've got Laughlin's homicide detectives over here. Plus, I get a call saying two of you were in the mine doing your own investigating, and my man had to go down there to make sure those other two creeps didn't kill you. How are any of us supposed to solve anything if we keep tripping over civilians everywhere we go?"

"I am not an old lady. Sandra Pringle was murdered and she didn't do it herself. And we checked out the mine because it didn't look like you officers of the law were doing anything about it. And your man is fine. We didn't hurt him hardly at all."

"A judge ought to know better."

"Former judge."

"You still should have known better. Please get in the car."

The office screen door slammed shut, and Patsy marched across the parking lot with a deputy trotting along at her heels. He helped her into the other side of the sheriff's car so that we sat side by side, Patsy alternately rubbing one wrist and then the other. The deputy's mouth moved a mile a minute as he and the sheriff stood a little ways distant from everyone else, heads bent together.

"What happened in there, Patsy?"

"Some jerk got the drop on me. He must have been watching out the window, because he stepped from behind the door and knocked the gun out of my hand before I knew he was there. Deputy found me tied up on the floor. What happened to you?"

I told her everything that had happened, including the chance that she and I had botched the sheriff's case against a gang of smugglers. When I asked her about Crash, she said he'd shown her his shield, pinned inside his pant leg.

Then Patsy shook her head. "There's more going on here than smuggling, Sylvia. That sheriff may think he's looking for drugs or guns, but believe me, no gang of petty smugglers has a crate of gold coins in its possession."

"He's also mad because the FBI woke him in the middle of the night to pick us up."

"How'd the Feds know we were here?" Patsy wore that innocent look I didn't trust one bit.

We leaned over and peered out the window toward Frieda's bike. Mom, Dad, and Frieda were talking to the sheriff, and it looked as if they were all trying to talk at once. Willie stood a few steps behind Mom, his arms folded across his chest. The sheriff rubbed one hand over his face and massaged the back of his neck where he was probably developing a huge pain.

"I'm surprised the rest of the Flippers aren't here." Patsy leaned her head against the seat.

I didn't say anything, but I smiled to myself. The Flippers were probably entertaining Agent Damon Falls with a full account of the emergency supplies they'd provided to cover our self-defense requirements, the phone arrangement, the yarn, latex gloves and evidence bags. He'd have a king-sized headache by the time Patsy and I were delivered to Laughlin.

Which didn't seem as if it was going to happen anytime

soon, since a new set of lights was bearing down on us, coming fast across the desert sky west of the mine from the direction of Bullhead City. I knew it was a helicopter long before I heard it.

With a sigh, I stretched out my legs and waited for the next act, the one where the FBI agent and the county sheriff butt heads for a few rounds until the FBI agent finally whips out his federal warrant and smirks as the sheriff scowls and orders his deputies to stand down. Whereupon, they cluster around their cars and mutter to each other.

It didn't happen quite that way. The sheriff seemed more bewildered than pissed off, and the FBI agents, at least from a distance, appeared to be minding their manners. A couple of minutes after the helicopter landed, two black cars rolled by and parked not far from the copter. Another team of agents jumped out of the cars, unloaded equipment from the trunks, and scattered.

Agent Falls approached the sheriff's car, opened the back door, and motioned Patsy and me out.

"Get FBI vests from the trunk. Then wait here. See if you can stay out of trouble."

Patsy didn't argue. She poked me in the ribs when I opened my mouth to ask why we needed vests. As soon as Falls had walked away, Patsy whispered, "Don't make him any madder than he is. I could lose my license over this."

There wasn't much Agent Falls could do to hurt me, short of sending me to jail. He could take all his anger and frustration out on Patsy and do real damage to her business and maybe her career, but I had a gut feeling Patsy wasn't in as much trouble as she let on.

We retrieved the vests and returned to stand by the sheriff's vehicle. Since his glare was even more hostile than the FBI agent's, we didn't talk to him.

All the action seemed to run down, as if it was moving in slow motion. By the time Agent Falls returned, the eastern sky had lightened from pale black to light purple and I'd heard the faint early morning chatter from a covey of quail.

Mom, Dad, Frieda, and Willie had been escorted to the office not long after the black cars arrived. I hadn't seen them since.

I was so tired that I was halfway asleep, even though I was standing upright with my rump braced against the front left fender of the sheriff's car. When Agent Falls yelled, "Wake up, Ms. Thorn," I jumped so violently I bit my tongue.

"Where's your car?" he asked.

"I came in Patsy's car."

He saw Patsy standing on the opposite side of the sheriff's car and said, "What time does your flight leave?"

Before she could open her mouth, I said, "Dad and Willie are flying out this evening. Frieda's taking them to Vegas on the bike. The rest of us are supposed to be at the Bullhead City airport by ten thirty for the noon flight."

"I want you on that plane." He led the way toward the mine office, where he issued similar orders to the rest of my family. By then Frieda looked as if she'd been chewing nails, but she didn't try to tangle with the FBI.

Patsy, Willie, and I were delivered to our car, which, thankfully, was untouched by vandals or thieves. Frieda, her passengers aboard and the bike idling by the gate, pulled in behind us.

THE NEXT COUPLE of hours were a flurry of activity as Mom and I packed our bags, checked out of the hotel, grabbed coffee and donuts. All the while we fended off the frantic questions of the remaining Flippers, questions for which we had very few answers. At nine o'clock we were seated in the lobby, waiting for the shuttle bus that was due at nine forty-five.

Willie and Dad waited with us. They'd head for Vegas as soon as we were on the bus. Patsy had her keys in her hand, ready to walk out the door so she could beat the rush when she returned her rental car. Instead of leaving, however, she suddenly plunked herself down on the arm of my chair and jammed her keys into her pocket.

Agent Damon Falls had just entered the lobby.

THIRTY-THREE

"IT WAS NICE OF YOU to come see us off." I tried to make it sound sincere, especially since Agent Falls had thrown off his angry, tense, on-the-job identity and was his old relaxed self, the one that gave me warm vibes whenever we made eye contact. This time I looked away before any of the Flippers noticed.

Falls acknowledged my comment with a stern look. "Now that all the excitement's over, I wanted you to know that none of you are in danger, and would never have been in danger if you hadn't taken it upon yourselves to butt in and interfere with police business. Ms. Strump was the only one who had a legitimate reason to be asking questions, although she overstepped her bounds when she searched Barry Pringle's office, then let herself be persuaded to take an after-hours tour of the mine." The stern look returned to me.

I ignored it and asked my first question. "So, is Vinnie Vortinto involved in Barry Pringle's business or not?"

"We can't give you any information about Vortinto. We do know Pringle was laundering cash for someone and some of it was coming from this area."

"But," Patsy said, "what about the coins? You don't find a crate of Eagles, Kangaroos, and Krugerrands just sitting around in a gold mine."

"What you found in the mine was a real mixed bag. The crates on the bottom of the stacks had apparently been there for a while, because most of the stuff was stolen merchandise from jobs done months ago. The sheriff recognized items from private collection inventories, looted lockboxes, an auction house in Vegas. That accounted for most of the truck traffic that implied a smuggling operation."

"What about the papers?" I asked. "The ones we saw either had Barry Pringle's name on the stationery or were financial reports for Desert Hedge Investors."

"All the papers were Pringle's, probably moved from his offices. He suspected something was happening because of the PI on his trail. Buying into the mine was one of his legitimate investments, and he had a warm business relationship with the owners. He hired a packer to clean everything out of the offices, palletize the load, and take it to the mine, claiming he needed quick temporary storage. Pringle hadn't been in the tunnels and knew nothing about the stolen merchandise stored there. He thought his pallets were intact and had no idea his papers weren't secure. The mine owners were overjoyed to have a new investor with deep pockets since they wanted to hire a geologist to run some tests. They didn't know their property was being used by thieves as well as an unscrupulous businessman."

Willie, the only accountant in our group, was more interested in the financial papers than anything else. "What exactly was Barry Pringle doing that was illegal?" he asked.

"Ah, to the heart of the case." Falls glanced approvingly at Willie. "Pringle established his client list with the original investors from Florida—his wife Sandra, many of her friends, including your mother, people he'd met through various business dealings, clubs, and social gatherings. We've since found out he also had a dozen very large investors, all real people with real money."

"And he invested in real things?" I asked. "Property like the gold mine? Companies at risk?"

"Yes."

"So what crime did he commit?" Willie asked.

"Here's where I have to be careful what I say. Pringle is in custody, but the charges are pending until we've been through every piece of paper we found in the mine. From what we know so far, he used stolen identities to create a very large number of fictitious investors. Those accounts funded the dividends to the real investors, as well as distributions to the fictitious accounts that were funneled, eventually, to the real people who supplied the cash in the first place.

"He also created fake ventures that would normally deal with cash customers, and he poured the incoming dollars into their accounts. In turn, that money was funneled to the investors in the form of checks for nonexistent purchases."

"And the cash for the fictitious investors came from where?"

"That's the part I can't tell you."

"Don't tell us that you can't tell us," I said. "Not to stomp too hard on your little secret, but it's obvious. Why would he set up business in Laughlin and Las Vegas if he wasn't getting the money from the casinos? I'd bet the only part you don't know yet is who is doing the skimming and how they're pulling it off, especially since casino security is so tight."

Falls didn't confirm or deny. "By the way," he said, "the Krugerrands you found in Pringle's office?"

Patsy and I nodded.

"Pringle got those from one of his investors. He's holding back names in an effort to negotiate a plea agreement in exchange for testimony. The Krugerrands are the only thing that links Pringle's case to the stolen items in the mine."

"You're forgetting the murders," Gail said. "My gawd, you'd think all this money stuff was more important than Sandra's death."

"I agree," Linda said. "Tell us about the murders."

The Flippers sat up straight and edged forward on their chairs.

"First, the private investigator. Ms. Strump hired him on Mrs. Pringle's behalf to find out if Barry Pringle was having an affair. According to Mr. Pringle, who obviously does not want to get charged with the murders, a couple of weeks ago the PI followed him to a house in Palm Springs, where Pringle was meeting one of his backers. This guy has cameras all over his property, bodyguards, dogs, the whole bit, and his guards caught the detective snooping around inside the walls of the property. Pringle says they extracted the necessary information from the PI before knocking him off. Then the guards made sure the body was left where Ms. Strump and Mrs. Pringle would find it. The intention, of course, was to scare them off so there would be no future accidental discoveries of this investor's part in Pringle's business endeavor. Pringle is reluctant to talk about this investor, so he's also asking for protection in his plea agreement."

With a certain amount of trepidation, I took the small rock I'd found in the tub where the body was found and offered it to Falls. "Here's another link between the Pringle case and the mine," I said. "Maybe the killer wasn't one of the investor's bodyguards after all. Maybe one of the mine employees was involved."

Falls gave me an exasperated look as I explained how and when I'd obtained this piece of evidence and apologized for letting it slip my mind, but he took the rock and put it in his pocket. In my opinion, Barry Pringle would be questioned further before any plea agreement was placed on the table.

"What about poor Sandra?" Linda's voice was so soft and sad that everyone glanced at her to see if she was crying.

Falls replied almost as softly. "We may never know everything that Mrs. Pringle did at the mine that day. We do know that she spoke briefly to a couple of our agents who had spotted her in Oatman and followed her out to the mine. They questioned why she was there, and she said she was meeting the tour group but had come over early. They believed her and left."

Patsy and I looked at each other. "The black car we kept seeing everywhere," she said. "That was the FBI?"

"Yes, ma'am. They had orders to act menacing whenever you were around. I was hoping we'd scare you off." He looked at me. "I should have known better."

I stared right back at him. "Why did you have agents hanging around Oatman if you didn't think there were mine employees involved?"

"Because Pringle had visited the mine office a couple of times. We wanted to know if there was another reason besides his investment in the mine."

"Why did you send FBI agents to Hoover Dam with the Flippers? Wasn't that a waste of resources?"

Falls glanced at Linda. I understood immediately. Linda was a potential witness in the fraud case against Barry Pringle, maybe the only one the FBI had. Ever since she'd made the threatening call to Barry, she'd been under surveillance. Linda apparently had evidence of Pringle's crimes, and the Feds wanted to make sure nothing happened to her. They were still watching her. More than likely, she had no clue of her potential value in the case.

"So what happened to Sandra?" This time Linda's question came out in a wail.

"We think she went into the mine herself because she thought there was a hidden reason why her husband talked up this one investment over all the others. Pringle said his wife was convinced he was about to make a bundle on his gold mine with her investment. He also told us she'd accused him of taking her money and hiding it from her, that she was sure her money was financing his affair with some showgirl he'd picked up on one of his business trips. He said she'd already been to his office in Laughlin and found it unlocked and empty. The PI had reported the same was true of the Vegas office. Maybe she figured out that he could have hidden the stuff in the mine. Two employees who were there the day Sandra died were Kelly, who is an FBI informant, although I think he's also a conniving little two-faced asshole…"

Falls paused and looked around, realizing he'd stepped out of his professional persona in front of a bunch of civilians. Then he went on, as though nothing had happened. "The other employee, the one with the broken nose, was with Crash and Kelly this evening. Both he and Kelly have been implicated in the theft ring."

I wondered which one actually killed Sandra. "Sandra, in an effort to save her own life, could have told them she'd hired a PI. That could explain my anonymous caller's threats." I thought about Kelly, the little creep I'd trusted so easily. "Kelly practically twisted our arms to get us down in the mine," I said, "but, according to you, we wouldn't have been in danger if we'd stayed away. Why'd he do it?"

"He's a talker, so we've gotten more out of him in a few hours than we'll probably get from the others in weeks, although we're not sure how much of what he says is true. Kelly figured the stolen goods were big, but he wasn't allowed to see what was inside the crates, so he didn't know how to cut himself in on the deal. He worked it out when you showed how curious you were, Ms. Thorn. He got you to go with him on a night he was going to be there anyway, he reported your plans to the FBI like a good little snitch, and then he called his boss to tell him you were a prowler and he was going to follow you. He intended to earn points with everyone, hoping for a reward from somebody. It was a big bonus for him when you found the gold. He had his pockets full, by the way."

"The little sneak," Patsy said. "So he's the one who ratted on us. Why didn't you try to stop us?"

It was clear to me that Patsy was baiting the FBI agent, but then I figured it out. Damon Falls and Patsy Strump had been in cahoots the whole time. That was how Patsy obtained a Glock, that was how Falls knew about our plans to visit the mine, and that was how Falls knew Patsy and I had been to Pringle's office. Why hadn't she told him about the coins? Or maybe she had.

"Wait," I said as another question popped into my mind. "Who was the guy in the black truck? The guy you arrested at the mine."

"He's a mine employee. He also happens to be the leader of the theft ring. Kelly said he was the one who tried to secure Sandra Pringle's body and ended up losing her the same day you and the group toured the mine. Kelly blames him for Sandra's murder, says he probably let her body fall on purpose."

I thought of the day we'd discovered Sandra's body, and

the two men who'd sent Kelly off to call the cops while they escorted me back to Crash and the Flippers. It was the in-charge guy who cracked the joke about taking out time to have a beer. "Was he the one who rammed my car?"

"Could be. It was his truck."

So Kelly even lied about that. He'd told me the truck belonged to Crash. FBI informant or not, Kelly was thick with the thieves.

"Well, ladies and gentlemen, your bus is here. With any luck, you'll be on your way to Florida in a couple of hours. Ms. Thorn and Ms. Strump, could I see you a moment before you leave?"

I felt seven pairs of eyes on us as Patsy and I stood up and walked toward the very delicious Damon Falls.

"Ladies, I wanted to let you know that Sheriff Yamato has been persuaded not to pursue any charges the mine personnel wanted to file against you for trespassing or assault. In addition, the deputy who was working undercover has also agreed not to charge you with assault. As a matter of fact, considering the number of crimes you've committed this weekend, you are very fortunate that you're not being charged with anything by Laughlin, Mohave County, or the FBI. However, and let me make this very clear, you are not to interfere in any more police investigations of any kind, anywhere. Do you understand?"

I gave Falls my best innocent, wide-eyed look as I nodded.

He looked satisfied. Motioning to Patsy that she could leave, he stepped in front of me before I could head for the bus. "I want to talk to you when I get back to Florida," he said. "A week from tomorrow. My office. Nine o'clock sharp."

"Business or pleasure?" I regretted my facetious question when I saw his grim expression.

"Business," he said. "Serious business."

When Falls stepped aside, I started for the door where Patsy and Willie stood, Willie listening intently as Patsy talked. He nodded, said a few words, then nodded again. They stepped apart as I approached, Willie moving somewhat gingerly. He was still bruised and sore from the beating.

He gave me a hug and told me to keep an eye on the Flippers, because he thought talking about Sandra's death had upset them again.

As I walked away, I heard Patsy say, "How about meeting in my office on Tuesday morning? We can go over the details then."

"Sounds good. It'll be great to get back to work."

Willie going back to work? He'd only been retired for a few months. And working with Patsy? Doing what? I wanted to turn back and ask what they were talking about, but Gail was screeching at me to get on the bus. The driver was ready to leave.

Why did Agent Falls want to see me? What kind of serious business?

Why do some folks refuse to leave us in peace? Why can't they let us lose ourselves in the latest mystery from our favorite author while savoring a mocha truffle? Or sit in silence and stare into space while sipping an excellent Gewurztraminer? Are they so incapable of attaining a peaceful state of mind that they have to drag others into the cacophony of their lives so they're not alone?

Pretty damned profound, I thought.

One of these days I'd suggest that Damon Falls take up tai chi and learn how to chill.

I checked my bag to make sure I had a book to read, and confirmed that the small bag of yogurt-covered almonds was in the side pocket. No mocha truffles today, but with any luck, I could get a passable chardonnay to accompany my almonds and the sandwich I planned to buy at the airport. As of that moment, I put my curiosity on hold and my anxiety on vacation.

THIRTY-FOUR

ONE WEEK AND ONE DAY LATER, at nine o'clock on a muggy Monday morning, I walked into the West Palm Beach building where the FBI kept an office. I dug out my driver's license for the security guard, and glanced up just in time to see Willie step into the elevator at the end of the hall.

Now what? What new torture would Agent Falls inflict on me, and why was my brother invited to watch? Willie had been so busy all week I hadn't had a chance to talk to him more than a couple of minutes. I had no idea what he was doing.

I'd been busy, too. The day after I got home from the Laughlin and Oatman trip, I had lunch with my friend Tak at our favorite restaurant in Delray Beach, after which she treated me to an acupuncture treatment, a procedure that always felt much better when it was over than it did while it was happening. A couple of days after that, I went to a movie. On Thursday, I visited the library and took home twelve books, six of them mysteries. On Friday, I went to the bookstore and bought four more books, visited my travel agent to talk about the Norway coastal cruise, then went out to dinner alone because Tak had a date, Willie said he was working, and Mom and Dad were attending a dance at the retirement center.

The weekend was much more exciting. On Saturday, I went to Town Center Mall and bought six truffles, a pair of frivolous shoes that were certain to hurt my feet if I wore them continuously for more than ten minutes, a pair of gold hoop earrings, and an instrumental Peter Frampton CD. And two more books. I also stopped at the liquor store and replenished my booze cabinet with gin, vermouth, tonic water, and three bottles of wine.

Sunday had more to offer. I took an early morning hike and found a tai chi group practicing on the beach. I stayed and worked through the forms with them before continuing my walk. After eating a huge breakfast in Highland Beach, I went to another movie. That evening, I'd popped a big bowl of popcorn and mixed a superb martini, selected one of the six truffles, and sat down in my favorite chair to read and indulge myself in sinful treats.

At nine o'clock on Monday morning, however, I strolled into the FBI office reception area, sailed through the second level of security, and was shown to a small conference room where three of the four people present sucked up coffee and chomped on pastries as though they hadn't eaten for days. Willie sipped from his bottled water and ignored the good stuff.

The one woman in the room grinned and waved. I was not surprised to see Patsy there. Falls greeted me and gestured toward a chair across the table from him. The other man in the room had stood up when I walked in the door. He leaned across the table to shake hands.

"Q Santiago," he said.

"Agent Q Santiago," Falls added.

"Q?" What kind of a name was that?

"C-U-E," he said.

I nodded. "Let's get on with this, please. I have a busy day ahead of me." Yeah, books to read and wine to drink.

Willie looked at me curiously, but didn't say anything.

"As you know, Judge, the FBI has a multitude of ways to accomplish the work that needs to be done. Among other things, we use civilian contractors, and we assign agents to front businesses that can perform various services for us."

"And Patsy is one of those civilian contractors?" I felt very clever that I'd figured it out so easily.

"No. Ms. Strump is an FBI agent. We established her office in Boca about a year ago. It's your brother who's been cleared as a civilian contractor. He's going to report to Agent Strump."

"Doing what?"

"It's a kind of auditing," Willie told me. "To look for evidence of fraud and theft by examining records obtained by federal warrant, like all those papers you and Patsy found in the Lone Cactus Mine."

"And this is how you're going to spend your retirement?" I was incredulous. Willie hadn't been retired long enough to be bored.

"Yep. At least part of it."

I looked at Patsy, and then Agent Santiago, and finally Falls. "So, why am I here?"

"Agent Strump needs a research assistant who's already trained in FBI procedures. You, like Mr. Grisseljon, would be a civilian contractor reporting to her. Agent Santiago will install a new computer setup at your condo and train you how to use it. Through Agent Strump's agency, we'll give you access to more database information than you ever knew existed. That, combined with the internet skills you already have, will provide you with the tools to do your job."

"Why me?"

"To keep it in the family," Falls said.

"I don't know. Sitting at my computer all day doesn't sound like much of a life."

"It's not that bad. This is a short-term project, and you and your brother are already familiar with the case. This is about Barry Pringle and tracking down Pringle's associates."

"You mean, this is a one-time deal? We get this job done and we're off the hook?" I glanced at Willie. He nodded his head.

"Maybe I could fit one project into my schedule." I tried to look as though I were mentally rearranging my calendar to accommodate this inconvenience. "Tell me more about the case."

"As it turns out," Falls said, "Barry Pringle is a small cog in a very large wheel, an interstate theft and fraud operation. The investor in Palm Springs that I told you about? He owns an interest in eight different casinos. He has placed his people in several of them, and bribed employees in others. Plus, employees in six banks in four states have been compromised. He has also arranged for at least a dozen sites like the Lone Cactus Mine, where cash, stolen goods, and other contraband can be stashed as members of this ring move it around the country."

"And the only names you have are Barry Pringle's and this Palm Springs guy?" Willie said.

"And a couple of others. You'll get that information from Agent Strump later on. The big task you two face is to track down more of those names. Field agents are still hunting for money and goods, so you'll coordinate with them through Agent Strump as needed.

"In addition, Mr. Grisseljon, you'll hunt for evidence that can be used against any of the investors so they can be charged with income tax evasion."

Falls looked from Willie to me and back to Willie. "So what do you think?" he asked. "Can we count on your help?"

"I'm already in," Willie said.

I didn't want to appear too eager, so I mulled it over for a few seconds. "Do I get paid for this?" I finally asked.

Agents Falls, Strump, and Santiago grinned at each other like they'd hooked a big fish and were reeling her in.

I narrowed my eyes and glared at Falls. "One project. That's all. Just one."

"No problem," he said.

I reached across the table and snagged an almond croissant from the pastry tray and looked around for the coffee. Santiago jumped up and fetched me a cup. I took a closer look at him. About Tak's age, and well trained. Maybe I could arrange for them to meet when he came to install my computer.

Patsy pulled a stack of papers out of her briefcase and placed it on the table in front of me. The little green book slipped to one side.

"While you're at it," Patsy said, "please see if you can make any sense out of this stuff."

I sat there, sipping and munching, and tried to analyze why I felt so damned good. I decided it was the almond croissant.

REQUEST YOUR FREE BOOKS!

2 FREE NOVELS
PLUS 2 FREE GIFTS!

WORLDWIDE LIBRARY®

Your Partner in Crime